ALSO BY BENILDE LITTLE

Good Hair

THE
ITCH

A Novel

BENILDE LITTLE

Simon & Schuster

SIMON & SCHUSTER
Rockefeller Center
1230 Avenue of the Americas
New York, NY 10020

10 9 8 7 6 5 4 3 2 1

Library of Congress Cataloging-in-Publication Data

Little, Benilde.
  The itch : a novel / Benilde Little.
    p.   cm.
  I. Title.
PS3562.I78276I83   1998
813'.54—dc21   98-14836   CIP
ISBN 0-684-83834-6

For
THELMA ELEAZER BRYANT, IDA BROWN,
and CLARA and MATTHEW LITTLE,
those who came and left and the ones who are still here.

Part One

chapter 1

Sometimes it's the easy way that's hard.

Abra Lewis Dixon had carefully sculpted her exterior existence. She paid close attention to her physical environment—the trunk formation of a Japanese maple, the many red shades that came before its brilliant autumnal crimson. She regularly consulted her *Farmer's Almanac* so she could better predict the weather; she liked to be prepared. The interior stuff, however, was too unwieldy, unpredictable, and difficult. She left that unattended, willing herself to believe it insignificant.

She sat at the oak vanity her mother had given her as a housewarming gift, looking at her reflection—so much like her mother's—noticing for the first time that parentheses had formed around her mouth, adding to the diminutive lines under her eyes. Her skin was parched. She twisted open the gold-rimmed top on the heavy smoked-glass jar, scooping out a mound of precious skin cream with her finger, smoothing it over her cheeks, forehead. A different potion, squeezed from a tube, was dabbed under her eyes.

Looking at herself again, waiting to see a change, Abra ran her fingers across the grooves of the antique vanity, the one she'd always loved. She tried to imagine her face covered with wrinkles, her hair the color and texture of cotton, but she couldn't. Childhood was much closer, a blink ago. When she was a child, she'd lose herself at her mother's vanity, playing in all her mother's makeup and perfumed creams and fine talc in cardboard containers; her neck wrapped with her mother's best leopard-print silk-chiffon scarf and her pubescent face made up with lipstick, rouge, and Groucho Marx eyebrows. She'd pulled her eyes back, stretching them toward her ears, and taped them. "Who are you, darling?" she'd say in a loud, dramatic voice. She'd breathe in and pause. She never knew the answer. That was when she learned to stop asking the question.

Slits of light fell across the blue-as-a-robin's-egg carpet; they were the only sources of illumination in the apartment. Her mother kept the windows sealed. Abra would walk across the room, turn on the TV, open the blinds. After she had checked under the beds and in the closets, she'd pile two faux-leather and aluminum kitchen chairs as well as an empty footlocker against the door. There had been a time when her mother would leave a snack—sometimes a tuna sandwich with a pickle and sometimes an ice-cream sundae in the freezer. The phone would ring once, stop, and then ring again. It was safe to answer because it was Mommy calling from work. "Just me. You all right?" Odessa would say every day, and every day Abra would assure her mother that she was, even though she was scared most of the time that someone was waiting for her under the bed or in a closet. There was a number for the building manager right near the phone; that was supposed to make Abra feel safe.

She'd create herself a tent of an umbrella, pillows, and blankets in front of the TV—another fortress she designed to make her feel secure.

Abra looked down at the tray of potions in beautiful bottles, makeup, brushes, hair things, knowing she needed to get ready for dinner. She looked beyond the mirror, through the window that provided a view of the sprawling side yard and more trees than she'd ever seen on private property. She thought about the actual conversation she'd had with Cullen, which was merely one of the dozens of maintenance types married couples have all the time, mundane dialogues with mundane concerns: *Don't forget to go to the cleaners. Do we have any beer? What are we doing this weekend?* This conversation was just to confirm that Cullen would meet her tonight at Sherry and David's at seven. She smiled at the thought of her life.

DINNER PARTIES at the Steptoe-Warrens were a significant part of Abra and Cullen's social life, and, as often happened, the men ended up in one room; the women in another. Abra and Cullen were friends of the Steptoe-Warrens and acquainted with the other regulars. There were friends and there were couple friends, who all got along as long as the evening's subjects remained superficial. Abra sat in an ancillary room, a den off the living room, observing the men who spoke in loud Black American dialects reserved only for each other. She watched Ray through the glassless window in the living room as he talked about the Million Man March, acting out with his hands and arms the emotional impact of the event and what it had meant to him.

"First, I wasn't gonna go. Then I don't know why, but that mornin' I just jumped up, pulled on my jeans, and headed to First Baptist, where I knew I could jump on the van they had goin' down there."

The others, sitting in a semicircle of cane-backed chairs, ottomans, and a love seat, looked at him, nodding, understanding his feelings because they, too, had struggled with the idea of going. All of them, except Cullen, had decided finally to go, to make the emotional pledge with brothers from around the country, to atone, to do better by their families, even though every brother in this room was living America's wet dream. These men were members of America's upper class, the top 2 percent wage earners—going to work in thousand-dollar suits, doing deals in the high-seven and eight figures, living with their intact families in fantasy suburban spreads or enviable co-op apartments. They were all functioning schizophrenics, held master degrees in ruling-class customs, which meant checking anything ethnic at the door. All these men bonded on the duality issue. At their high-paying professions they had to do two jobs: the one they were hired to do and the other unspoken one—to adopt landed White-boy mannerisms. These brothers needed a march to band with other cultural schizophrenics.

"You know, it was like the greatest thing I could've done, man. When the radio alarm went off that mornin', Coltrane was blowin' and y'all know, to me he is what Jesus Christ is to Christians. I took that as a sign," Ray said.

The others were nodding between gulps of Cristal or Coronas with lime, snacking on bean dip, salsa, and blue corn chips, the precursors to the catered buffet dinner. Abra searched Cullen's eyes to see if they revealed sadness for what he'd missed. She didn't detect any. No one asked him if he'd gone, and he didn't volunteer anything.

Cullen graduated Howard, summa, a reformed nerd,

and the most focused person she'd ever met. Abra had recognized him as a swan even before he did, and now she was the envy of most women.

"This White guy at my office asked me why I went. He said he could understand inner-city Blacks marchin' for jobs and education and shit, but he just couldn't get what I'd get outta somethin' like the march," said Ray, a tax lawyer at a Wall Street firm. "I told him, 'Man, you see me here, doin' my thing, tryin' to make partner, but when I walk outta here at night, I say a little prayer of thanks for the car service home. You know why?' I said to him. 'Cause I'm a Black man first, and the moment my feet hit the pavement, the average White person out here is assumin' I'm gonna knock 'em over the head, and I can't get a cab.' The dude kinda looked at me, like he was seein' me for the first time, and he just nodded. I don't know if he got what I was tryin' to say, but I think he thought about it."

Sherry Steptoe and David Warren liked to entertain in their generous pre-war apartment on West End. The two other couples, like the Dixons, had opted for suburbia. Yet David, because of Sherry, held on to their life in the city. David and Cullen had gone to college together. David was a lawyer, but he worked for a record company, on its business side. He was nice but about as interesting as iceberg lettuce. Sherry, on the other hand, had a lively disposition and was a copywriter at the same record company, which is where she and David had met. She was unlike all the women David had gone out with, and she had a kid to boot, a child who was an infant when they first started seeing each other.

David fell hard for Sherry and her son, and they got married at a small affair of about thirty people at a café in Greenwich Village. At the wedding Sherry couldn't stop cry-

ing, and everybody said it was because she was still postpar-
tum, but a few of the couple's inner circle always wondered
if she had married David just to give little Jack a daddy.
Sherry had told Abra that the main reason she didn't want
to leave the city was that moving to suburbia would make
David too central to her life, and she didn't want that. In the
city she still had all of her friends, her work, little Jack's
play groups, and enough distractions. In the suburbs she'd
become Jack's mother, David's wife, and *then* a career person. She ran her fingers through her thick red-brown hair
and wrinkled her nose at the thought, "Eeooh, no thanks."

Abra, on the other hand, had gone peacefully into the
land of leaf blowers because she didn't want to argue with
Cullen, and he *was* central to her life. Where they lived
wouldn't make a difference.

Abra looked around the room at the other couples and
tried to figure which ones were really in love and which ones
had simply settled for the best deal. Ray and Hanna really
loved each other, but they seemed to be like that couple in
the movie *Annie Hall*: Woody Allen stops and asks them
what the secret to a happy relationship is. The woman says,
"I'm very shallow and empty and have no ideas and nothing
interesting to say," and the man says, "And I'm exactly the
same way." Hanna was a dentist, "an orthodontist," she
would say. They were supposed to be waiting until she had
established her practice before having kids, but now that
Ray's partnership looked like a done deal, he was putting
pressure on her to quit and start a family. Bert and Lisa
operated in parallel universes, with neither compromising
courses. She was pregnant and telling everyone that as soon
as she had the baby, they were getting divorced because Bert
was disappointed in her. She had failed to live up to her

resume, which was replete with Ivy League degrees, and she held a job about as well as a sieve holds soup. Bert was pissed and would tell anybody who'd listen that he had thought he'd married a partner, not a siphon. Everyone felt sorry for them.

After dinner, David and Sherry's live-in, Consuelo, put coffee, tea, and assorted fruit tarts on the breakfront in the dining room. Abra was tired and didn't want coffee or tea, but she also never wanted to do anything to upset any custom—people drink coffee or tea after dinner—so she doused her coffee with Sambuca. She chewed a piece of the blueberry tart and watched Lisa and Bert go at it over when Lisa should begin her maternity leave. Abra looked over to give Cullen the "exit" sign, but he was in rapt discussion with David. She couldn't hear what they were talking about, but they both looked serious. She guessed accurately that they were discussing work, complaining about the demands. They were leaning against a built-in mahogany bookcase. Cullen looking fresh out of business school, wearing his English loafers, button-down, oxford-cloth shirt rolled up to the elbows, and blue-and-green rep tie loosened. Abra sighed to herself at how contentedly in love with him and their life together she was and pitied Lisa and Bert for not knowing what marital bliss felt like.

"So how's the dessert?" Sherry asked, sitting down next to Abra and cutting off a piece of strawberry-kiwi tart.

"Great. Did Connie make them?"

"Nah, I picked them up at Pascal's. So how's the business going?" She pulled her chair closer.

"Good, at least the TV part is. We've got a film script in circulation, but so far, no bites."

"Now Natasha does just the film part in L.A.?"

"No, she runs the TV production stuff, too. We both do TV and film. I go out there as often as she needs me to, and she comes here sometimes. Actually she's coming in tomorrow."

"So is she more the creative . . . ?"

"Kind of. I'm in charge of more of the business."

"I just love the name."

"Thanks. Some people think it's stupid," Abra said.

"Anybody in this room?" Sherry smirked and looked in Cullen's direction.

"No, I'd be surprised if he could even tell you the name."

"Hmm, is there trouble in paradise?"

"No, not at all, I just know that my business is not at the top of my husband's agenda. In his mind, he's the breadwinner and my work is like the Junior League," Abra said.

"Puhleeze, these guys," Sherry said, then sipped her tea.

"I'm exaggerating, slightly, but it doesn't bother me."

"Well, you're a better woman than me."

"Look, we're talking about ten years together. We've got this massive house to decorate, we're trying to have a baby, his making partner, me running a business—there's only so much my little sweetie can deal with at once," Abra said, putting the blue-willow patterned china plate on the coffee table.

"You should have a party for your anniversary, I mean ten years—"

"Ten total, together. We've been married almost five."

"Whatever. It's still nothing to sneeze at. I'm not sure we'll make three." She laughed a hollow laugh and Abra smiled sympathetically.

"My wedding day was the happiest day of my life," Abra said.

"You really love Cullen, huh?" Sherry asked, looking at Abra as if she'd just revealed a row of jack-o'-lantern teeth.

"Yeah, I do. He's the most important thing to me."

"You're lucky."

"I know."

"Most married people I know are just, you know, going through the motions. Like look around this room."

"Sherry, you really think that?"

"I know that. The women probably wouldn't have gotten married at all."

Abra looked around Sherry and David's apartment. Spanish jazz echoed through their eclectic home, which they had filled with antiques and African art. The picture of Buppie perfection. How could they not be happy? It was predestined, like DNA—these were the people happiness was meant for.

Cullen tapped Abra on her shoulder, and Sherry got up.

"You ready to go?" he said, sitting down in Sherry's chair.

Abra leaned toward him and kissed him with an open mouth. She held his face in her hands. "Do you know how much I love you?"

"Um, I think so. How much have you had to drink? I saw you hittin' that Sambuca."

"I'm not drunk. I just love you."

Cullen shifted in his seat, hoping no one was watching them. He wasn't one for PDA. "Me too. You ready to go?"

"More than," she said, and smiled a lecherous smile.

Abra ran her hand over his thigh. The weave of his pinstriped trousers so intricate, it was sensuous.

They said good night to Sherry and David at the elevator and walked the few blocks to the garage, holding hands.

"You know we have an anniversary coming up?" Abra said.

"Course."

"So do you want to go away or do something?"

"Well, sweetie, I would, but I don't think I'll be able to get away right now. Things are really busy and—"

"I know not now, but what about in a few weeks? Maybe we can go back to St. Bart's?"

"Ah, that would be great. We'll see, okay?"

The attendant pulled the car around, Cullen tipped him, and Abra got into the driver's seat. She checked her flawless lipstick in the rearview mirror before she drove off.

"Did you have a good time?" Cullen asked, changing the radio to the all-business news station.

"Yeah I did, but I just wish Bert and Lisa would just stop fighting."

"I know. I feel sorry for him."

"What about her?"

"Well, they're both our friends."

"I know. I just want everybody to be happy. Do you think the others are happy?"

"About what?"

"Their lives? Their relationships."

"Why wouldn't they be? They have everything, they're successful. What could be wrong?"

"Well, Sherry's not in love with David, and Hanna and Ray, well they're in love, I suppose."

"Well, there you have it; two out of four are good marriages. We're the cultural norm."

Abra steered the 740 onto the West Side Highway and switched on a Will Downing CD. Cullen had leaned back onto the headrest and would be asleep within seconds. Abra bobbed her head to Will Downing's crooning as it washed over the percussion. She looked over at Cullen sleeping, his mouth open, his glasses half-cocked, and she sighed, reminding herself that she'd structured her life, and it was as close to perfection as possible. Theirs *was* one of the two good marriages. She let that reassure her on the drive home.

chapter 2

WHEN ABRA AND NATASHA were reunited in business school, day one of microeconomics, they hadn't seen each other since they were children, but the memory of their friendship was burned into their minds as though with a brand. Their initial attraction across the elementary-school auditorium, when their gaze locked in recognition, was sensing in each other a restlessness, an itch, a way of viewing the world that was the same. Students were assembled, and the prettiest, most popular girl got up to lead everyone in the Pledge of Allegiance. Natasha and Abra thought her silly.

During lunch, when pockets of children gathered in the playground, a bunch of kids clustered around Natasha. One of the girls pushed her pointer into Natasha's chest and sneered, "You got a problem?" Natasha looked around at all the hostile faces. Before she could respond, the girl said, "I saw you laughing in assembly. That's my cousin." Natasha wanted to shrug her shoulders and say, "So what?" but she sized up that these girls were looking to start a fight, and there was one of her and four of them. Abra showed up out of nowhere and stood between Natasha and the tough girl. "Is there a problem?" Abra said, nose to nose with the tough girl. The growing crowd groaned, and the tough girl's chest deflated a little. "I ain't got no problem with you," she said. Abra turned to look at Natasha, who was trying in vain to keep from looking scared, and said, "You in my friend's face, so that means you in my face, too." A teacher's aide came over just before punches were thrown, and broke up the crowd. Abra and Natasha walked home from school together and from that day, were inseparable—well, until Natasha's family moved away to Chicago when the girls were in high school.

Like most best friends, they were as different as beluga and bologna. Abra grew up a solitary child of a laboring single mom. Natasha was the adored younger daughter of a Huxtable family. Natasha jumped in first and asked questions later. Her father had provided her the luxury of carelessness. Abra checked things out carefully before making a move.

On their first business-school break Abra went home with Natasha. When the taxi pulled in front of the wrought iron–gated, pillared Hyde Park–Kenwood mansion, Abra's jaw literally dropped. Natasha had grown used to that reaction. In Newark, the Colemans had lived in a nice stucco house up the street from the apartment building where Abra and her mom lived. Nice, but not fancy.

"It's just a house. The same Norwood and Marge live in it," Natasha said, as she paid the driver.

"I can't believe you *live* here!" Abra blurted out.

"What'd you expect?" Natasha said.

"I don't know. I guess I didn't realize you guys had gotten rich."

Natasha didn't respond immediately. She closed her wallet and waited as the driver removed their bags. When her grandfather got too sick to run his three rib joints, her dad, Norwood, Jr., had to take over. Her father had taken *his* father's three stores and added twenty-seven more throughout Chicago, becoming the Rib King. Natasha's older sister, Natalie, always happy with the family's juicy income, but ashamed that her dad earned it through ribs, used her passion for science as a passport out of the family business. It was why Natasha went to business school, to take over one day—or at least to be able to watch over the family business once Norwood got too old.

"Well, I'm still the same person, Abra. This is just stuff," Natasha said, reaching over, kissing Abra on the cheek.

Abra felt tears welling up, so thankful to have been reunited with her friend.

The next morning, after having been up all night looking at photo albums and catching up, Abra and Natasha sat drinking coffee, dressed in their pajamas, waiting for Norwood to make his famous breakfast of fried chicken and waffles. It was true that Norwood and Marge held on to their easy Southern ways like Odessa. For Abra, the primary difference between them and her mother wasn't their money, but the fact that they were a unit, a couple who had raised two children and weathered the inevitable waves of life and had stayed together.

"So you're all grown up, Abra Cadabra," Norwood's voice boomed, entering the room before he did. Natasha's dad embraced Abra in a fatherly bear hug, and she returned his hug, savoring his old-man's cologne.

". . . And lately girl I've been thinking, how good it was when you were here." The Dells' classic piped through the speakers that were built into the walls of the house. "Aw, that's my song. Come on, daughter," Norwood said, closing his eyes, holding out his hand for Natasha to join him in an impromptu two-step.

"Oh Daddy," Natasha said, hopping off the stool to whirl around the floor with her father. "You're embarrassing me."

"My thoughts of you don't have an ending," they belted.

"Aw yeah. Now they was some singing fools. Homeboys . . . ," Norwood said to no one in particular. Abra watched with a painted-on smile. Suddenly she was transported back to Newark, back to the Colemans' house on Mecker Avenue, when Norwood would come home from work and come into Natasha's room where the two girls would be playing with Barbies, to greet his beloved child. Abra would grin till her face hurt, watching her best friend who had what she couldn't. She reveled in seeing a real-live daddy up close.

Watching Norwood twirl Natasha around the kitchen, Abra felt a pain with her pleasure. She was no longer a little girl, with her face pressed against the window, living through her best friend's experience of having a daddy. Abra had never known what it felt like to have been doted on: to feel the safety of a daddy's lap; to have his thick fingers fumble through your scalp, trying to braid your hair; to have the reassurance that he was waiting in the airport until your flight left the ground.

It was pain for what she'd missed, but she didn't know that yet.

During that school vacation Natasha introduced Abra to Cullen. Cullen was the only real friend Natasha had made when her family moved. He became the brother she never had. For Cullen, Natasha was the princess on the hill—he from Lake Meadows, the son of one of Norwood's rib-joint managers. They had suffered together through taunts by neighborhood roughs because they wore uniforms to their ritzy high school and endured condescension from their White classmates, who didn't want them there. They grew even closer when they both went to Howard, Norwood's alma mater.

Natasha's intention was not to fix them up, but simply to introduce one friend to another. But from the day Cullen saw Abra, all Fair Isle sweaters and hair bands, with none of the haughty mannerisms of some of the girls in Majors and Minors—the social group for the children of South Side strivers, who had never let Cullen forget that he was a scholarship nerd—he had to have her. She was pretty, but that wasn't the attraction. She had a quiet strength that he didn't have, and he admired her for it. He had thought of Abra as out of his league, so he pursued her the only way he knew how—by becoming her friend. She understood his drive to succeed was fueled in part by seeing how his dad worshiped successful Norwood. Abra fell for Cullen for many reasons —he was focused, ambitious, and reminded her of Norwood. Cullen liked the fact that she had gone to Princeton, and that she looked and acted how he thought the wife of a major corporate player should—restrained but approachable. She knew all his insecurities; he shared them with her, showed her his scars. She didn't do the converse, so he erroneously thought that meant she didn't have either. She couldn't see his faults. Both of them saw in the other what they were brought up to believe they should want. When they decided to marry, right after graduation, no one was surprised, although Natasha tried to convince them that they were too young.

For the first three years of their marriage, they did everything together, never seeing a movie or having a meal with anyone else, other than for business. They were both dressed from the same tedious English clothier, striking a pose of a grown-up Buffy and Jodi in Blackface. Perfectly matched bookends; sex every day—sometimes in the morning, oftentimes in the middle of the night—screaming orgasms that just got more intense. They thought this was how marriage was. Then they started trying to have a baby. After two years of trying the only reason the doctors could come up with for no baby was that amorphous six-letter word *stress*. She quit her Big-Five accounting job and stayed home for a year, decorating the house and trying to get pregnant. While Abra and Cullen were in their cocoon, Natasha was busy building her business, growing from sitcom writer to producer and then creating her own show. After Abra's second year trying but failing to get pregnant, Natasha talked her into becoming her business partner.

"I need help and you're the only person I trust," Natasha told her.

Abra was apprehensive.

"You need something to take your mind off having a baby," Cullen had said.

chapter 3

THE EAST COAST OFFICE of Is My Wig On Straight Productions consisted of a twelve-by-twelve room with a small entryway, near which her assistant, Sandy, sat at a desk and answered the phones. Framed film posters of *Dance with a Stranger, The Postman Always Rings Twice, Goodfellas, The Shawshank Redemption,* and *Eve's Bayou* hung on the dark celery-colored walls. She watched Sandy hold up her MAC compact for the fourth time this morning and apply a shade of burgundy lipstick. Maybe having her lips coated helped her sound better on the phone. Abra had been working at getting their sitcom into syndication and finally had a firm offer. She weighed telling Natasha, who would want to take the first deal offered, to get the money.

Natasha Coleman's life was everything Abra's was not. Natasha was wildly single, and checking out every man in L.A. with a cellular phone and a business card. She wore her hair in brown and blond crinkly extensions down her back and haute couture jackets over skintight pants or jeans, often in the colors of children's toys—citron and periwinkle.

"Looks good with my hair color," she'd say. Abra wore her hair relaxed, uncurled, untrimmed, just straight down, grazing her shoulders and held back from her face with a hair band. Her clothes, while no longer stodgy, were minimalist. She preferred dark pantsuits and splurged on shirts and leather loafers. Natasha had her teeth bleached every few months, so her bright whites looked even more spectacular against her skin. Her most recent indulgence was having a manicure twice a week at her desk; pedicure was every other, also at the office. Abra occasionally got a Korean manicure. Natasha worked with a personal trainer five days a week. Abra sometimes took a two-mile walk through her neighborhood on weekends.

Natasha and Abra had made some bank off *On the Verge,* a show Natasha created about a group of Black actresses living in the same apartment building, but if the syndication deal went through, they'd make enough money to not have to do anything—for a long time. Abra's fear. One of Abra's toughest jobs was to constantly remind Natasha of their yearling status and keep her from spending crazy money. Since all their money was supposed to go back into the business, Natasha justified her expenses as business ones.

"You can't lunch at Mickey-Dee's, darling; it's gotta be Ivy," she'd breathe into the phone whenever Abra would yell at her for her daily three-hundred-dollar lunch tab.

Abra knew that she was the silent, sturdy half of both her partnerships. Cullen and Natasha were excitement junkies, who liked to talk about the deal. Abra was the one who put together all the details and made it go. It wasn't a depressing thought, it was just the way it was.

■

THE SOUL PALACE was the latest entry in the New York Nig-
gerati nightspots. It was the kind of place where actors of all
stripes—soaps, nighttime, and theater—hung out alongside
the requisite large number of models, rap-music moguls, and
a splattering of financial types. Abra understood that the
movie business was to the nineties what investment banking
was to the eighties and that Soul Palace was just the kind of
place Natasha would feel right at home in. Abra arrived,
looked around the packed restaurant, and of course, no Natasha. She quickly surveyed the room. There was a well-
known, middle-aged criminal-defense lawyer dining with
what had to be a starlet, a beautiful thing a third his
age. Abra checked her raincoat, was seated in the sipping
room, and ordered a glass of club soda. Just as she finished
the second section of her *Wall Street Journal,* Natasha blew
into the café. Abra looked at her friend and smiled,
mostly to herself, at the sight. Natasha's multicolored weave
was half piled up and the rest flowing all over her leopard-
print swing coat, which matched the restaurant runner.
She had on wagon-red suede leggings with matching turtleneck and carried a cobalt-blue leather garment bag with
duffel.

"Cadabra!" Natasha shouted, greeting her friend with
part of the nickname she'd coined for her when they were
little.

"Hey there," Abra said, getting up to hug.

They hugged tightly, as they always did. After a drink,
they were led to their table. En route they passed an NBA
player at a table with three women.

"He slept with Sybil, my trainer in L.A.," Natasha
whispered to Abra over her shoulder, "then he dumped
her."

"He's starting a record label," Abra said as they were seated. "They're probably a singing group."

Natasha sipped from her water glass and looked around. "Isn't that that lawyer, what's his name . . . ," she said, snapping her fingers.

Abra supplied the name.

"Who is that he's with? Can't be his daughter with his Yoda-looking ass," Natasha said, disgusted by the sight.

Abra laughed and drank her soda water.

Natasha asked about the syndication deal.

"I just got a verbal from the exec VP of development over at Blax," Abra said. "They're very interested."

"Really? That's great, why didn't you call me?"

"Well, it's not done yet. He's sending the contracts over next week, but I think we need to get somebody else interested . . ."

"Look, we need to be ordering some Cristal, 'cause we got a deal."

"Hold on, Natasha. I'm talking a matter of days. We leak it that Blax is interested and another offer will come."

"Okay, we give it three days."

"I say five."

Natasha let out an oversized sigh.

"You're a pit bull," Natasha said.

"That's what you pay me for," Abra said, and smiled. "We're in play, girlfriend."

Natasha leaned in toward Abra so that they could put their foreheads together.

"We're young, we're fabulous, and we're about to get paid." They held up their glasses and clinked.

"This is gonna be great," Natasha said. "Do you know how much we're gonna get?"

"Not an exact number yet, but let's just say money's not going to be much of a worry."

"So we need to get you to a spa," Natasha said, opening the menu.

"I know. I look pale."

"How about some highlights . . . ? They have all this fried stuff . . . ," Natasha said, frowning at the menu.

"I need to lose some of this weight, it's the Perganol."

"So stop taking that damn medicine."

"I know, I probably should just forget it."

Natasha closed the menu and looked at her. "Are you feeling all right?"

"Oh sure, everything's great."

"I've read that those drugs can really fuck with your head. Why don't you stop taking that stuff? If you and Cullen were meant to have a baby, it'll happen. You don't have time now anyway, which brings me to my next point."

Abra raised her hand to summon the waitress.

"We're having no success at getting some backing on this damn film," Natasha complained.

"We just need to make another list of contacts and start a new round of meetings," Abra said.

"Can you do that?"

"Of course."

"I was thinking, maybe we should just take the syndication money and finance the film ourselves."

"Let's get the money before we start spending it."

"Yeah, yeah, but what do you think of that idea?"

Abra took a bite of her crab cakes. "I think we should look at the syndication money as a last resort. Once word gets around, we become more visible, and I think that's what we need to get the film made."

"Have we talked enough business to write off this dinner?"

"Yep."

"Great, so what else is up? Where's Cullen tonight?"

Abra looked at her watch and said he was still at work.

"So you can come with me. We can hang."

Abra ordered coffee, knowing that wherever they were headed was going to be an adventure.

THEY TOOK A CAB downtown past Canal Street and got out in front of a redone warehouse. They rode a Lilliputian lift that let them off into a sprawling loft lit by blue disco lights. The place belonged to the rap mogul of the moment, and someone had made it up to look like a club. After their eyes adjusted to the dimness of the place, Natasha began seeing people she recognized and Euro-kissing. Abra hung back and looked around. There was a spread of fried chicken, greens, yams on one table; on another, a spread of enchiladas, burritos, rice and beans. A man whose sole job was to mix, shake, and pour martinis stood next to a table loaded down with bowls of shrimp, lobster claws, chopped boiled eggs, crackers and caviar—beluga, bowls of it. Abra took a cracker, shoveled some beluga onto it, and did the math—we're talking $200 for fourteen ounces and here were several almost bucket-sized bowls. She'd heard of the rap producer, even seen a few of his videos, but until she saw the art, the rugs, the layout of the food, she had no idea he was mega-moguling. For Natasha, this was a party; for Abra, an opportunity.

She looked around the room. None of the women had on trousers, and the skirts they wore literally showed their butts. She didn't want to stand out, but there was nothing to be done about the black suit and white T-shirt she was wearing. She also fingered the heavy gold necklace Cullen had given her last year, which she'd thought too much at the time. She located the host, whose head was encircled in a cloud of Monte Cristo smoke. He was jerking his head to a bass beat so strong, she was sure the floor would give in. She walked up to him and introduced herself, although she knew he couldn't hear her. She handed him a business card and he looked down through the smoke, then cocked his head in the direction for her to follow. They went into a soundproof room filled with mixers and an electronic board.

"Nice piece," he said, referring to her necklace.

She instinctively caressed it.

"Oh, thanks. Um, listen, I know you probably don't want to talk business now but . . ."

"Always doin' bitness. Whassup?"

"Well, my partner and I have a production company, we did *On the Verge,* you might've—"

"I know 'bout it."

"Yeah. So we now have a film that we're trying to get produced. We've got Mona Love committed to star, we've got all kinds of directors who are interested, we just need some capital."

"How much?"

"About five . . . five million."

"Short money," he said, looking Abra up and down, trying to figure her out.

She looked back at him, pupil to pupil. He smiled when he realized she wasn't intimidated.

"Send me the script. If I like it, we do it."

"Great, you'll have it on Monday."

"Cool."

With that, he went back to his party and Abra went to collect Natasha.

chapter 4

ODESSA LEWIS had arrived in New York City, wearing a homemade tweed suit and a black velvet hat with a feather in it. She looked as green as corn in May, but thought she was ready. Straight off the farm like millions before her, and, like those before her, she was determined to make a full life for herself in the New World. New York was as different from her native Virginia as honey from hominy grits. Didn't matter. She'd figure out how to use those trains, get her a job, save her money, find a nice Southern gentleman who wanted the same things out of life that she did, and that would be that.

She had completed two years at Virginia State before her folks ran out of money and she had to withdraw. Her daddy had begged her to stay down south, but she wanted excitement and to be around people who didn't have to legally bow to White folks. Her daddy was heartbroken, her mother pretended to be, too, but secretly encouraged her youngest child to see the world, to never settle. "It eats up your soul," her mother would whisper.

Odessa was a sturdy woman with dancer's legs. In her small Virginia hometown, she'd been considered a beauty; in New York, she was merely a pretty woman—nice, but not one to turn heads the way the octoroons who danced at Harlem's restricted clubs did. She was a brownish woman, a mix of a licorice-colored daddy and a peach-hued mama. Her long face had cheekbones that made it interesting, full lips, and a narrow nose with nostrils that flared when she laughed or got pissed.

She had the address of a Miss Bessie who ran a rooming house on Seventh Avenue in Harlem. The day after she'd arrived, she went in search of a job. She figured with two years of college, she'd easily find something: assistant teaching, typing, something, anything but cleaning houses. The reason her parents worked that second farm to send their baby girl off to college was so she wouldn't have to clean up after no White folks. Her true heart's desire was to become a fashion designer, but she stopped telling people that when they kept reminding her that she was a dreamer, that colored people weren't allowed to design or dream.

Weeks passed and Odessa couldn't find a job. Office work in Harlem seemed to be gotten only if you knew somebody. Offices in downtown Manhattan were as segregated as back home. No Blacks, at least no one who was obviously Black, worked as salespeople in the department stores. Teaching required a certificate which could only be gotten if you earned hours teaching in the New York public schools, which you couldn't do without a certificate. She was beginning to get frustrated and nervous, considering her room rent was about due. Then one day, she was on her way to check job postings in the newspaper, when she saw a handmade sign posted on a street lamp. Dressmaker's assistant wanted.

Odessa popped the snap on her clutch bag, fished around for a pencil and some paper, and wrote down the phone number given in the notice.

A woman answered and told her where to go for the job interview. She didn't know the neighborhood. It was way east, near the other river that helped make Manhattan an island. A tiny, round-faced woman with hair as curly as Odessa's opened the door. She had on a bulky sweater and wore eyeglasses on top of her head. Odessa was surprised to see a White woman, but the woman wasn't surprised to see Odessa. Sylvia, who ran the business with her sister Myrna, specifically wanted a colored woman to work in their shop. They needed someone who'd work like a dog for little money and who knew how to make a good seam. When they heard that Odessa was Southern, they hired her that day. The first few years at her job, Odessa felt as if her dream had come true, almost. She got to try on all the latest European knock-offs the store was known for; she loved helping the customers when one of the sisters was on a break; she even liked the alterations work.

As she entered her late twenties, however, she began to worry about becoming a spinster. She didn't meet any Negroes through her work, and by the time she got back to Bessie's rooming house, it was too late to go out. She did manage to go barhopping on Saturday night with some of the other women who boarded at Bessie's, and she met a few men here and there, but they were all good-time Charlies, and she knew that they wouldn't make suitable husbands. Besides, none of them ever moved her. She'd vowed that she would only marry a man who did. She saw her friends just settle for the first thing that came down the pike and a few years later, they'd be saddled with a few too many mouths to feed and no good memories even. That wasn't the life Odessa wanted. Then she met Rayford.

Although he didn't look anything like her daddy, he was everything her daddy was—hardworking, mild-mannered, and ambitious. He was tall and lean, while her daddy had been squat. Rayford was as pallid as her daddy had been ebon. He had a thick head of hair that waved in the front and a smile that went from one end of his face to the other. He was delivering boxes for a parcel service the first time Sylvia saw him. She rushed to get Odessa off the sewing machine so she could get a look at him.

"O, he's just gorgeous. You've got to meet him," Myrna and Sylvia would say. Finally the day came when she could meet him without being so obvious. She was helping a customer try on a suit when Rayford came in with his deliveries.

"Mornin' ma'am," he said to Odessa, nodding his head the way folks did in her hometown.

She liked that about him. He was clearly city, his neatly conked hair let her know that, but he'd held on to the old ways, too. He was everything Sylvia and Myrna had said: a cross between Cab Calloway and Harry Belafonte. After several weeks of planned chance meetings, Rayford asked Odessa out on a date. You would have thought he was taking Myrna and Sylvia.

"You gotta wear something from the shop," Myrna would start.

"How about the emerald-green coat and dress? O, that color is gorgeous on your skin," Sylvia said.

"Oh Sylvia, we have to find out where they're going first? Did he say, O?" Myrna asked.

Odessa said they would go to a supper club in Harlem on Saturday night.

"Perfect. The black-and-gold with the three-quarter sleeves and the knit coat. Yes?" Sylvia said.

Myrna nodded in agreement, and Odessa looked from one to the other as if they were the strangest things she'd seen in New York. They fixed her up with shoes and a bag. She got her hair done and even bought a new hotter shade of red lipstick. When Rayford saw her walking down the narrow stairway of Miss Bessie's Boardinghouse, his eyes widened.

"Evenin', Miss Odessa. You sure lookin' pretty tonight," he said, extending his hand to help her down the last step.

"Thank you, Mr. Rayford, and you look very handsome yourself."

They walked a few blocks to the Baby Grand, where a young Sarah Vaughan was performing. They were escorted to their seats. He ordered a Scotch-and-milk, she had a rum-and-Coke.

They talked about their jobs, their hometowns. As a teenager he had come from Macon, Georgia, to New York with his family. He'd always wanted to become a lawyer and was going to City College at night, but his job was about as good as one at the post office, and folks didn't turn down good benefits and reliable work back then. Odessa found herself being attracted to Rayford, and he was clearly drawn to her. He kept telling her how she was the prettiest thing he ever did see. He made her feel like a showgirl octoroon.

"So, how's it going with Rayford?" Myrna or Sylvia would ask.

Odessa beamed when she told them about their dates—walking in Central Park, going to Ebbets Field just before the Dodgers moved away, riding the Staten Island Ferry. What they really wanted to know was if Odessa and Rayford would marry. Odessa was beginning to wonder that herself but wouldn't dream of being the one to introduce the topic. After almost a year, Odessa invited Rayford up to her room. Miss Bessie had unspoken rules against such meetings, but Odessa figured she'd slip him in, anyway. They kissed up against the door until their lips hurt. Rayford strained to feel Odessa's body through her simple cotton dress, stockings, girdle, heavy cotton bra. Being raised in the south, in the church, Odessa knew sex before marriage was out of the question, but she also knew that Rayford was the one she'd been waiting for. She figured he must want a sample before he could propose marriage, so that night, up against the door, she gave him one. It didn't feel good, at least not the part where he entered her, it hurt, but he seemed to enjoy it. She went along with it. She knew enough to make him stop before he got too excited inside of her. The next day, he picked her up after Sunday service for a walk in the park. He was the same flirtatious way he always was, except he didn't talk as much. After much prodding from Odessa he finally told her.

"I know you been wondering why I haven't asked you to be my wife."

"Yes, Rayford, I have wondered about that," Odessa said, in her usual straightforward way.

"Well, I think you probably the best thing that ever happened to me."

"Rayford, I feel the same way."

"Let me finish this, honey. It's not easy what I'm about to say."

"I'm sorry. Go ahead."

"Odessa, when I first saw you I knew I had to have you. You everything I ever could hope to have."

Odessa ran her hand over his, which had been nervously clawing up and down his pants leg as they sat on a park bench.

"But, I haven't been right by you . . ."

"What are you talkin' about, Rayford?" Odessa said, her voice rising as she sensed her world about to fall apart.

"I haven't been straight . . . honest. All I've thought about was myself and—"

"And what, Rayford? Just say what it is," said Odessa, now getting angry.

"Aw, honey, I want to be with you more than anything, but I can't 'cause I already got a wife."

Odessa's head began to throb; tiny bursts of light flicked against a black sea; she felt as if she'd been hit in the head with a ball gone foul at Ebbets Field. She put her hand on her brow bone, rubbed her forehead a little. She held her head down, looking at her black-and-white Sunday spectators, now dusty from the dirt around the bench. After a moment, the pain in her head subsided and she was able to speak.

"A wife! How? What do you mean? You're married and you had . . . you let me give myself to you, you took me out, you courted me."

Rayford began to cry.

"I know, I'm just a weak man." He rubbed her back. Odessa moved into his chest and began to sob, too. The two of them sat crying on the park bench until night fell.

When they got back to Miss Bessie's, Odessa took one step up the brownstone stoop and turned to look at Rayford.

"I don't know what to do about what you've told me. Everything that I know, that I've been taught, knows that this is wrong and that I should never see you again, but my heart wants you so bad, it hurts."

"Odessa, I feel the same way."

With that, she turned and walked up the stairs, leaving him on the sidewalk looking up at her.

FOR A WHILE, when Abra was a young child, her father made appearances—her birthday, snippets of weekends. At the time, she and Odessa were still living in Harlem, close to Rayford, still hoping that he'd leave his wife. But with each birthday cake she baked for Abra, it became clear that Rayford would never be hers. Abra watched her parents' interaction like children do, unflinchingly. On the nights he stayed over, Abra could barely sleep, she was so excited from her mother's adrenaline. When her father was around, she didn't recognize her mother. Odessa had a different wardrobe for Rayford's tarries: poofy slippers and silky robes that she kept in a satin pouch in her bottom drawer. She used the face powder that otherwise Abra only used during playtime at the vanity. Odessa's lips were deeper red, her curls more fluffed out. When they moved to New Jersey, her father became more of a shadow, and by the time she was in junior high, she didn't see him at all. Her mother had stopped talking about him. He'd just faded from her life, just like the wallpaper in their kitchen. It still hung there, but no one acknowledged the change.

Abra learned about Rayford from fragments of overheard grown-ups' conversations. He'd changed his life, had gone to law school, moved to Long Island, into some neighborhood where Black big shots lived. He'd send checks and Odessa would send them back. Abra watched her mother sit at the kitchen table, smoking, mumbling to herself, pencil in hand, adding up expenses, always coming up short, trying to give Abra the extras so that she wouldn't feel deprived. She'd bring home cashmere sweater sets from the shop, but she stopped leaving snacks. She'd still call Abra every day from the shop, but she would be at the sewing machine, distracted. At twelve, Abra started a baby-sitting business in her building. By the time she was fifteen, she had several girls working for her. By then, when Odessa came home, Abra would have done her homework, cooked dinner, and sometimes had a bath waiting for her mother. They would watch TV together for a few minutes, before Odessa would slump over, breathing like a stuck car engine. Abra would get her mom into her nightgown and tuck her into bed.

As she got older Abra began to wonder about her mother's decision to have her when she did, by a man who already had a wife and family, another piece of information gathered from grown folks' talk. While Rayford swore his love for Odessa, he wouldn't leave his wife and the kids they had together. Not having had a father in the house was a hole in Abra's heart that she'd learned to live with, but it was something that would never heal. Without an everyday image of a mommy and daddy, a close-up view of a grown-up relationship, she was left to mimic what she saw on TV and movies—she was left emulating fantasy. Whenever Abra attempted to talk about it, Odessa would get weepy: "Didn't I do everything for you? Did I not give you the best?" Abra stopped asking, but what she longed for was to be able to yell, "Daddy, Daddy!" and run to him when he came home from work and be scooped up by sturdy, dependable arms and ride through the house on his shoulders and be tucked in at night. What she'd wanted, more than anything, was an everyday dad, like Natasha had.

Odessa still worked in the tiny dress shop, which was wedged between two storefronts on Second Avenue, as she had done for thirty-some years. The store still catered to middle-class women who wanted to appear rich by wearing designer knockoffs and barely-worn seconds. Odessa worked long, backbreaking hours for the sisters, Myrna and Sylvia. They were like aunts to Abra, although Odessa didn't feel sisterly toward them at all. But she would tell everyone that they had been responsible for Abra going to the schools she did and had encouraged her by giving her checks to keep her grades up. Myrna and Sylvia were also supportive of Odessa's early solo parenting efforts, which often meant leaving work whenever Abra got sick or bringing her to work on the days she was off from school. Now the job at the dress shop was something a sixty-something woman did to kill time.

chapter 5

T HE HOUSE that Abra and Cullen lived in was a seven-bedroom, new interior–old exterior, brick Georgian. Their bedroom was two landings away from their huge modern kitchen, which was equipped with stainless-steel refrigerator, stove, and dishwasher, all wedged alternately between blond walnut cabinets. Music from Natasha's exercise video beat in Abra's head. She rolled over and pulled the clock toward her and stretched.

Downstairs, Natasha was in her sweatshirt and leggings with weights gripping her wrists and ankles. She counted out her lunges and didn't stop when Abra appeared in the doorway, wrapped in Cullen's flannel robe. Natasha was sweating and her hair was flying.

"It's Saturday morning, Natasha. Doesn't your body get the weekends off?"

"Nope," she said. "Four, five, six, can't let the bod go, baby. Seven, eight, nine—"

"You want coffee?" Abra asked, turning toward the kitchen.

"Nope, two, three, four. Don't need it."

"I know, you're high on life."

Abra sat at the counter, watching the coffee drip into the carafe. She wondered why Cullen hadn't awakened her before he left for the office.

"I made an appointment for you at Exhilaration. I hear they're the best colorists in the city," Natasha said, joining Abra in the kitchen, wiping off her sweat with a dish towel.

"You got an appointment?" Abra said, snatching the towel.

"I told them you were Halle Berry, so they moved some stuff around."

"Natasha! What are they gonna do when we show up and—"

"Honey, please, they're White folks. You think they'll know the difference?"

"Well, I'm twice her size and look nothing like her. Yes, I think they'll know the difference."

"We all look alike to them. Don't worry, Diva Dear has it all under control. You got any fruit?" Natasha said, looking in the refrigerator.

"You're unbelievable."

"I know, it's what you love about me," she said, biting into a pear. "Now we should get dressed."

Natasha followed Abra upstairs to her bedroom.

Abra dreaded opening her closet to Natasha because she understood her friend didn't get subtlety, and most of Abra's things were either black, beige, or brown. She'd always been reserved, but she had had a little more bump before moving to the suburbs where she'd toned it down because she didn't want to stick out.

"Who are you, your mother! This boring crap has to go," Natasha said, fingering hangers in Abra's closet. "Okay, add Bendel's to our list today. You can wear your black leggings and my pink jacket."

The salon was up-to-the-second chic, the kind of place where all the operators are draped in black and say "fabulous" four thousand times a day. The receptionist, who was trained to detect the authentic, looked at Abra and then Natasha as if to say, "Halle who?" But the receptionist of heavy eyeliner and equally heavy fake-European—country of origin unknown—accent was no match for Natasha, who made the receptionist believe that she had misheard the name Halle Berry. The receptionist knew enough to know that they were *somebody,* dressed in jackets that cost as much as a small Toyota. After a few minutes they were ushered in to the star colorist.

Abra got color, facial, and manicure. Afterward, at Bendel's, Abra caught sight of her post-Exhilaration self in the mirror and smiled.

"Should we call Cullen?" Natasha asked.

"I don't know."

"He should see your new look. Guaranteed to get you laid tonight."

"I didn't need a makeover to get that," Abra said.

"Oh, well excuse me little Miss Siren. I just thought—"

"What? Did Cullen tell you something?" Abra said, picking up a pile of imported cotton T-shirts.

"No, of course not. I would've told you. What's up?"

"Oh, nothing. I'm just hungry. Let's go eat."

It was too late for lunch, too early for dinner, but Natasha wouldn't be caught dead in a corner coffee shop. The Russian Tea Room would do.

After they settled into a corner table and Natasha ordered chilled vodka, Abra asked her how Cullen seemed.

"Like the usual driven dick head that he's always been." They both laughed and clinked their glasses.

"No really, he seems good," Natasha said. "He seems a little more up than usual, actually, which is a good thing. Don't you think?"

"Yeah, he does," Abra said.

"Why do you think that is?"

"Maybe he's been offered another job or he's tasting his partnership. I don't know, but I've been with the man for ten years. I know him pretty well."

"Has it been that long?"

"Together, yeah."

"I can't believe it. What does it feel like? Doesn't it get boring?"

"It feels like a dream. Every day I wake up and I can't believe I'm this lucky to be married to him."

"That's great."

"Do you know there are women who don't even love their husbands?"

"No!" Natasha said sarcastically, and picked up the cloth napkin and playfully tapped Abra.

"No, really, I'm serious. We were at this dinner party the other night at our friends Sherry and David's, you know him, and she's like talking about how she's not sure they're gonna make it to three years together."

"Abra, I think that's more people than you realize. Most people ain't livin' like you guys. You were lucky to find each other when you did, before you got too old and too fucked up."

"You really think that?"

"I do. I mean, look at me. I'm probably not going to find anybody I want who wants me. It's the way of the world after thirty-five. The men you find smart and interesting only want Barbies, and the other ones you don't want."

"God, that's depressing."

"It doesn't depress me anymore. I figure I'm getting paid and about to get even phatter. I don't need an everyday man. When I want to go out, I have certain ones for that, and friends for emotional sustenance. So I'm cool."

"Kinda like the combo platter."

"Absolutely and frankly, I think it's kinda unrealistic to think one person will meet all your needs."

"Is this what L.A. has done to you? I know plenty of really nice, interesting, available men in New York."

"Name three."

"There's, um, Calvin Barker . . ."

"Into Barbies. Saw him in L.A. two months ago, he's dating a Laker cheerleader. It looked serious. Who else?"

"Oh. Um, what about Sam—Sam what's-his-name from school? Sam Bivens."

"Biggest dog on the East Coast. So big in fact, I heard he's moving west 'cause he's fucked everything here."

"Really? He seems so nice."

"He is, especially to you, you're unavailable."

"Okay, what about that Darren guy? The one in real estate who you went out with a few times?"

"Into White girls, and they've also got to be Barbies."

"Mmm. This is depressing. I thought sure—I mean anytime I see one of them at a party or something, I'm always thinking, 'If I weren't with Cullen . . .' "

"Well, sister love, don't be jumping out here. It's dry as a bone."

Abra watched her friend munch a salmon finger sandwich and caught a glimpse of her sadness. Just as quickly, Natasha looked up and shook it off.

"So what are we in for tonight? A video? Hot times in the burbs?"

"We could go out. Or we could have a few friends over," Abra said, cheerfully.

"What? A bunch of married people? No, thanks. I'd rather drink some champagne, catch up with you and Cullen, and watch a movie."

Nighttime in Brookville was tomblike. Abra and Cullen's two acres were enclosed by pines and oaks fifty feet high. Natasha called it "Animal Kingdom" because the raccoons, the possum, and the deer foraged openly for food. The only sounds that occasionally smashed the silence were the screeches from a cat that had wandered into a fight with a raccoon or the almost identical sounds of raccoons in heat. Natasha and Abra lounged in pajamas in the family room, which had a vaulted skylight, a sliding glass door that led onto the deck, and a fireplace the length of a wall, beneath the built-in TV. Nibbling popcorn and sipping champagne, Natasha flipped through fashion magazines, and Abra tried to decide which video to watch first: *The Big Picture* or *The Player.*

"What time did Cullen say he'd be home?" Natasha asked.

"He didn't. He usually gets in around seven on Saturdays. We should just go on and order pizza or whatever you want. He'll be here soon," Abra said, picking through a basket of take-out menus.

THE SUITE at the Peninsula was a sea of beiges. A French decorator would call the color biscuit. The drapes were a floral mix of creams and tans. The bedcover was a broad, subtle stripe with a velvet border and discreet gold trim. The sofa was a peachy beige. Not the sort of place you'd think of when you think of illicit sex.

Cullen sat at the desk and tried to pretend to get some work done. He couldn't focus, though. He was waiting and he knew what he was waiting for was about to change his life in ways he couldn't yet know. A light knock. When she walked in, she was wrapped in a shiny, ivory trench coat. It looked like plastic and Cullen thought he'd never seen plastic look so good. The contrast against her Mississippi–mud cake complexion gave him a rise. The darker the girl in his old Chicago neighborhood, the harder she was—at least that's what his father used to say—but this delicate creature who was standing before him seemed as if she would break if you talked too loud.

He pulled her in by her wrist and wanted to suck her lips, her face, rip off her coat, but he forced himself under control.

"You want something to eat? I could order a salad or something."

"No, I'll have a drink. Vodka, straight," she said.

She took off her coat and Cullen was almost surprised to see that she had clothes on underneath. He'd actually allowed himself to fantasize that she'd show up in a trench coat and nothing else. Her T-shirt looked as if it were two sizes too small and on her tiny frame, that would have meant it came from the children's department. It was a puckered fabric in white cotton that stretched across her tomato-shaped breasts, exposing her dark nipples through the fabric. Her skirt was short, some kind of knit, but not clingy. It hung off her pointy hips, flared out.

They drank their drinks in hungry silence. Cullen sat next to her on the peachy beige sofa. She looked around the room and asked him if he'd been here before. He explained that he traveled a lot for work and knew many hotels well, but none for intimate reasons. She put her head back, draining the highball glass of clear, burning liquid. She held on to the glass and let the nape of her neck rest on the back of the couch. She had an exquisite neck, long and polished, like ebony soapstone.

"Why am I here?" she asked, fracturing the silence.

Cullen, who was rarely at a loss for words, was speechless.

"I mean, do we just fuck, or do you want to have a relationship with me?" she asked. Cullen sat for a moment, leaning forward with his head in his hands, trying to decide whether to answer her honestly, fudge, or lie.

He sat back, looked to his left, at her profile. He leaned into her and placed one of his substantial hands directly on her erect-nippled breast. He wrapped his free arm around her shoulder and whispered into her ear.

"I definitely want to fuck you, but I also haven't been able to think about anything else since last night."

He kissed her neck, while rubbing his hands over her breasts, her chest, and her natural, closely cropped hair, almost as short as his.

"I don't know if I've ever wanted anybody this bad," he said as he began to kiss her.

Cullen pushed up her tiny T-shirt, both hands now cupping her breasts. They felt juicy in his hands. He squeezed them as a shopper of melons would and estimated by their firmness that she was in her twenties. He kissed one, then the other, letting his tongue linger on each nipple long enough to

53

make her moan. He slobbered on down to her navel and pushed up her miniskirt. Her puffy knoll, somewhat covered by a tiny thong, greeted him like an old friend, offering itself to him. He looked up at her and smiled. She was leaning back, face tilted up to the ceiling, and moaning with her mouth closed. He kissed her pile once, then again gently around the lips, he rubbed his nose against her clit. She whimpered. Then he let out the arsenal—his wide tongue that he knew created frenzy. Against her bull's-eye, he fluttered, darted, licked, letting his entire tongue taste it, like a child just learning to lick an ice-cream cone. He swung his tongue like a pendulum, sending her into spasms. He lightly pushed in small circular motions until she let go, moaning, this time loudly.

They lay still: she, still seated on the couch; he, crouched between her legs on the floor. After a while she got up and undressed, revealing a body that was a mix of little-boy boniness and sex goddess. Pointy pelvic bones jutted out from a flat stomach and tiny waist, but her behind and breasts were rounded, almost corpulent. Her long arms were skinny, and her thighs and calves, muscular. Cullen let her undress him. He lay on his back, and she, crouched over him on the floor, tasted him. He wanted to feel her. He pulled her up toward him and kissed her deeply. They got up, rubbing bodies before heading to the bedroom. He was throbbing and knew he wouldn't last long. He cuffed his hands on her waist and gently pushed her onto the bed. He had put some rubbers into the drawer of the nightstand before she arrived. He hadn't worn one in what had happily seemed like a hundred years. She watched him get up to roll on the latex.

"I'm on the pill," she offered.

Those were once sweet words, but he knew that couldn't have any meaning now.

He continued to roll it on.

"It'll help me last longer," he said, not wanting to hurt her feelings.

"Your call."

He pushed her thighs apart with one hand, while using the other to guide himself inside. She grunted and squeezed the skin on his shoulders as he entered her. She was tight, but wet. They began moving slowly, simpatico. Slow at first. He rubbed her thighs, her hips, her breast, her ass. "Mmm," she sighed. "Mmm," she groaned. He began going faster, a little faster, and then pushing harder, then harder still. He was holding her butt, a cheek in each hand, and he was beginning to gallop. She was letting out loud grunts with each of his thrusts. It was a matter of seconds now. He knew that. His sweat was dripping onto her face, his heart was racing, and his face was contorted like someone trying to lift a piano. Another thrust, another grunt, a bigger thrust, then a groan that sounded like a cry mixed with laughter. Finally, he felt something in his larynx, moving up, a scream, a sign that he was about to explode. He could feel her getting tighter, she was digging her fingers into his back, near the base of his spine. Faster, the rubber was moving downward. When he felt himself about to let go, he reached down to hold the rubber on. Instead of collapsing onto her, he pulled out, making sure everything was captured in the little off-white bag.

Cullen walked back into the bedroom, drying off from a quick shower, and found her still naked, lying uncovered on the bed. He'd hoped she was dressed. He needed to get home, continue on with his day, with his life, as if he'd just spent another Saturday at the office.

"You're clean now?" she said disappointedly.

"I gotta get . . ."

"Home?"

"Yeah," he said, slightly annoyed at her for making him say it.

"So when do we see each other again?"

He was surprised, again, by her bluntness.

"I, um . . ."

Cullen was buttoning his shirt, standing in front of the mirror, which hung over a writing desk where his work sat untouched. He felt a pull from her even though she hadn't moved from the bed across the room. He walked over to her and caressed her thigh.

"You don't have to answer now. You know how to find me."

chapter 6

THE CAR pulled into the circular gravel drive. All the lights were on, and Cullen could see the driver's eyebrows raise at the sight of such a baronial-looking place. Cullen wasn't sure if it was because he was Black or because he looked even younger than his thirty-plus years. He wanted to say, "Yeah, it's mine," but he simply thanked the guy and got out. The front door opened into a cathedral foyer; a formal dining room was on the right and the living room to the left. Beyond the dining room was the kitchen and beyond that was a gallery that led to the family room which was surrounded by floor-to-ceiling windows. It was where he and Abra spent most of their time at home. Cullen dropped his keys onto the antique-pine hall table and picked through the mail. Abra had already opened and separated the bills from the magazines, letters. The bill stack was higher. He followed the sound of the TV.

"Hey sweetie," Abra said, jumping to her feet to greet him. She kissed him on the mouth and rubbed his five o'clock shadow. "How's my honey?" she purred in baby talk.

"Good, glad to be home. Hey slice," he said to Natasha, who was sitting on the floor engrossed in an article on the rebirth of a Hollywood player.

"Oh, hey Cull."

"Sorry I'm so late."

"So what tied you up?" Abra asked, trying hard not to sound like she was prying.

"Um, you know, the usual. Do we have any beer?"

"Yeah, inside the refrigerator door."

"I see you got enough videos," Cullen said, picking up two of the three tapes that were propped on the coffee table, hoping to avoid too much talk about his day. "All about Hollywood. Mogul movies this time, not your usual women's stuff." He chuckled alone.

"You hungry?" Abra asked. "We had Indian."

Cullen took off his blue blazer and threw it on the mission oak chair in the corner.

"So how was work?" Natasha asked, seeming to come out of her fog.

"Good. Got a lot done," he added. "I'm gonna go change, I'll be right back." He went upstairs and left Abra staring off after him. Natasha watched her friend and tried to figure out why she seemed upset.

"Look girl, you know he's gotta put in the hours. This is partnership-making time," Natasha said.

Abra nodded.

"What's the matter?"

"You see that he didn't even notice my hair?"

"Yeah, but you know that's just Cullen."

"No, he used to notice."

Natasha sipped her champagne and was silent.

"I know he loves me, I just wish he would notice more,"

Abra said and sipped orange juice. "It's just those stupid drugs, they make me unpredictable, too sensitive. It's such a pain."

Her friend looked at her suspiciously but didn't let on what she was thinking, which was, Maybe the drugs do perform cartwheels with your emotions, but there's something else going on here.

"So stop taking them."

Abra watched Natasha tilt her head back and drain the flute of champagne.

LIFE CHANGES infinitesimally all the time, trillions of tiny, unknowable changes every day, and then, unexpectedly, there comes a colossal change, and you're hit by a thunderbolt, and nothing is ever the same.

Cullen hadn't intended any of it. He saw that kind of thing all the time at his office, but he thought he wasn't the type. Too much stuff to keep track of and he basically thought less of people who couldn't keep it going with their spouse. He understood the temptation and that's all she was —a temptation, a one- or two-night thing, no big deal. It happened in all marriages. Didn't it?

On the days of their assignations, he watched the clock. He was busy, always, and time normally went by much too fast, but on those days, the days that were always too far apart, time dragged. He recognized the symptoms of obsession and it was remarkably like his brother's addiction to crack. All you can think about is getting high and when you do, all you can think about is getting high again. Cullen leaned back in his oversized swivel chair and sighed. He closed his eyes and tried to picture Abra. The Abra he'd met when he was in grad school and full of himself. The one he was so in love with at one time. Even then, it never felt like this. His relationship with Abra was slow and friendly. People had said that was a good sign. "That sweating-palm stuff doesn't last," Natasha had told him and she should know.

What would Natasha say now? Of course he couldn't tell her. It was stupid, he knew. He didn't even know this Cynthia woman. It would put way too much pressure on Natasha to keep her mouth shut. He tried to reassure himself, thinking of all the friends he knew who had had affairs. David? No way. Way too into Sherry. Bert? Too beaten down by Lisa. Ray? Too afraid of losing Hanna. His group was probably the first, no more than the second, generation to look at marriage and have the expectation that love and passion would be a part of it. Their parents, and certainly grandparents, made marriages of purpose. It was about economic survival, not finding one's soulmate and having terrific sex. No role models for how to do this modern marriage. He thought back to his college boys, his frats most of whom he was no longer in contact with. There was one, Jimmy. He ended up leaving his wife for his mistress, the woman he'd loved in college. The panties musta been outstanding for him to have left his wife, Cullen thought, and made a note to call Jimmy the next time he was in Atlanta.

Cullen looked at the mound of messages and folders on his desk. Damn. He had so much fucking work. Always so much work. It never stopped and Abra was talking about taking a vacation. No way. His mind wandered back to the Peninsula. It was like a slow fall, the sex. Well, it was why people had mistresses. He wanted to consume her.

Work on Saturdays was no different than that on any other day for Cullen, except the dress code was relaxed.

Some guys, especially those eager ones like himself who were on the partnership track, wore blue or camel blazers, open necks and a dress pant. There had been meetings and conference calls with Farah, the furniture queen, whose store the firm was going to take national. He'd have to make appointments to see her accountants and lawyers. He had to force himself to concentrate and not slip out to see Cynthia. On the weekends she worked at Barneys. He needed to head home, spend some time with Abra, she'd be waiting for him. Bill, one of the partners, knocked on Cullen's open door.

"Hey Cullen, you got a minute?"

"Sure, sure Bill, come on in," he said, closing the lid on his laptop.

"What's up?" Cullen asked.

"What do you think about the Farah deal? You think it's viable?" Bill asked, taking a seat that faced Cullen's desk.

"Um, yeah, I think her numbers look good, her proposal is solid."

"Yeah, it is. So you wanna run with it?"

"Yeah, of course. I'd—"

"Good. It's settled. Um, expect to be on the road a lot over the next couple of months. I hope that's not a problem."

Cullen glanced at the silver-framed picture of Abra and himself on his desk and looked at Bill.

"Not at all. I'll get right on it."

"Good, good. How is your wife? Arabella, right?"

"Right. She's great. Her company may have a syndication deal."

"Good, very good. Always glad to hear the wife has something to do with her time."

"Oh yes, Abra has a career."

"Business school? The two of you met?"

"Yes, she was at NYU while I was at Columbia."

"How nice. So things are solid?"

"Uh, yes, we're solid."

"Good. Well, my friend, I'm expected in Greenwich in fifteen minutes. Looks like I'm going to be a little late. Have a good rest of the weekend, Cullen, and feel free to come to me with anything on this deal, okay?"

"Yes, I will sir. Thank you."

The sky's light had turned the city amber. Cullen noticed the reflection on his company Town Car as it cut through the buildings on Madison Avenue. He was tempted to have the driver stop at Barneys, maybe take Cynthia out for a quick drink, but his conversation with Bill, a senior partner, had spooked him; reminded him that his career at Croft wasn't just about his resume, it was his entire package. An attractive, intelligent, refined spouse was almost as important as his Ivy League M.B.A. Add on race, or subtract it in his case —he knew his behavior had to be sterling, beyond reproach. He picked up the phone resting neatly on the back of the front passenger seat.

"Hi sweetie. Where are you?"

"I'm in the car, on my way home. I'll be there in a half hour."

"Good, I'm making your favorite."

"Oh great . . ."

Cullen looked out at the Hudson whizzing by and thought about sweet Abra. Her voice was light and clear, like the fragrance she always wore. How could I do this to her?

he thought. Here she is getting sick from all the damn drugs she has to take to try to have a baby for us, for our family, and this is how I pay her back, by fucking some model. He told himself he just had to end it with Cynthia.

chapter 7

NATASHA SWOOPED her convertible through the warm thick air that surrounded LAX and picked up Abra who was waiting at the curb.

"We've got about an hour before the meeting," Natasha announced over the Chaka Khan. "So do you wanna eat or change?"

Abra looked down at the black cashmere top and trousers she was wearing and thought she looked fine, perfectly suitable for a meeting with some independent film execs who'd all be wearing the uniform: jeans, button-down shirts with the sleeves rolled up, and sneakers.

"You don't understand, Abra. It's about a certain kind of jeans and sneakers and shirts. Believe me it ain't just any old thing. You look okay if you don't feel like changing."

"Well, thanks. I won't. Your getup is enough of a statement for both of us."

Natasha laughed and held her hand up for a girlfriend five. She was dressed in a cream-colored top, cropped to slightly expose her navel ring, and matching knit pants.

"I'll wear my jacket," Abra said.

"Got anything that'll show some cleavage?"

"Natasha!"

"What? It won't hurt our chances. This is Hollywood, honey, and it's all image."

"Well, we don't have to play into this madness, do we?"

"Got to play along to get along, darling. When we're Whoopi huge, then we can wear Birkenstocks and not give a fuck."

"But until then—"

"Until then, it's play ball."

The whole time Natasha is talking, she's cruising traffic, checking out any and all the boys who are driving expensive cars. "Eeooh, look at that one," she says at a red light, without turning her head in his direction.

"Is that Wesley?" she asks, referring to the actor.

"I don't think so," Abra said, openly staring.

"Oh yeah, unless he's had a chemical peel. Whoever he is, he's kind of fine."

"You want me to get his attention? Pull over."

"Hell no, Abra, that's not how it's done."

"Oh, okay, so how do you get his attention?"

"I don't."

"Well, if you're interested, shouldn't you let him know that?"

Natasha let out a grunt of impatience. "Abra, you don't. You just let it go."

"I see. So how do you expect to meet someone if you keep letting the ones you like drive away?"

"Well, like I told you, I don't really expect to find anyone. I mean it would be nice, but I've pretty much given up."

"I see."

The hum of the engine grew louder as the silver Porsche pulled closer, as the guy who Natasha thought was Wesley Snipes lightly beeped the horn.

"Excuse me," he said, taking off his sunglasses. "Excuse me."

Abra and Natasha stopped talking and turned to look at the stranger. He explained that he'd gotten turned around trying to find Century City.

"We're headed in that direction. Where are you trying to go?" Natasha asked, all business.

"Um, I'm looking for Dreamtime, a production—"

Natasha cut him off and told him to follow. "We'll get you there."

As they drove, Natasha would occasionally check her rearview and comment to Abra about the brother in the Porsche. "It's rented," Natasha announced.

"How do you know that?" Abra asked, truly perplexed at how her friend would know such a thing.

"The license plate, darling. Wonder where he's from. He doesn't look like he's in the business," Natasha said.

"Why?"

"Mmm, 'cause I would've seen him before, plus he doesn't give off that Hollywood thang. Seems like an East Coast brother."

"He seems pretty flashy to me," Abra said.

"Dick Clark seems flashy to you."

"That was *so* cold."

"I love you anyway, though."

They pulled over and he followed, pulling next to towering waterfalls near the entrance to Century City. He got out and walked to their car. He leaned on the windshield.

"Just turn in there and make a left," Natasha instructed.

"Okay. Listen, thanks for helping me out," he said, handing a heavy-stock ecru-colored business card to Natasha.

Natasha looked down at it and read: *Miles Browning, Managing Director, Soldman Saks.* As a B-School graduate herself, she knew enough to be impressed.

"Thanks, Miles."

"No, thank you . . ." He paused, waiting for her to supply her name.

"Natasha. Natasha Coleman." She reached out to shake his hand.

"Nice meeting you, Natasha."

"And this is my friend and partner, Arabella Lewis Dixon."

"Wow, great names. Arabella, Natasha. You two in the movie business?"

"Yes," they said simultaneously.

"Actors?"

"Producers. We have our own company," Natasha said.

"Oh yeah? That's great. What's it called?"

"The short answer is On Straight. The entire name is Is My Wig On Straight Productions."

Miles let out a loud, uncensored, from-the-gut laugh, which made the two women look at each other and smile. "That's a great name. So listen, I'd better get to my meeting. It was good meeting you and I hope you'll give me a call sometime."

"Yeah, nice meeting you, too," Natasha said, ignoring his other comment.

Miles removed his arm from the windshield and began to walk away, but turned back to ask Natasha for her card.

"Um, sure." She fished around in her backpack for her wallet.

"Here, don't spread it around." With that she backed up and sped around him.

Miles stood next to his car, laughing until their car disappeared.

"Humph, he wasn't that fine close up," Natasha said as she maneuvered the car through a few turns.

"So you're not gonna call him?"

"No."

"Why not?"

"Abra, please. Did you see that suit? His tie cost more than some people make in a week. You know he's got honeys flingin' themselves at him. No, homeboy is too much of a player for me."

"What are you scared of? He was obviously interested," Abra pleaded.

"Of course he's interested. L.A. is full of women in expensive cars, givin' out the digits. It's part of the game."

"Well, they got to pick one and settle down at some point."

"No, they don't."

"I mean, sure there are lots of pretty women here, but how many have their own company, are smart and accomplished, and aren't looking for some man to pay their way?"

"Yeah, but these guys believe that their platinum cards give them all the privileges, and that includes all the women they can handle."

"Oh, would you just call the man? You won't know until you try."

"He lives in New York," Natasha protested.

"And you're in New York all the time. If you don't call him, I will."

"And say what?"

"I don't know. I'll think of something."

They got to the meeting five minutes early and as is tradition at these meetings, they accepted the offer of Diet Coke or Pellegrino.

"You always have to say yes, even if you aren't thirsty," Natasha whispered to Abra.

They giggled like schoolgirls and tried to look relaxed sitting in the reception area.

After their twenty-minute meeting with a vice president of production, they were back in the parking lot. The meeting had gone well enough, but there was still no commitment to their film.

"I should call the office and check the messages, then we can grab dinner."

Abra sat in the car, watching the squat sand-colored buildings pass as they whizzed down Beverly, and listened to Natasha giving the secretary instructions and repeating the numbers of people she needed to get right back to. Natasha thoroughly enjoyed all this wheeling and dealing and Hollywood two cheek–kissing, but she'd only known success as a TV exec. Neither of them was prepared for the butt-kicking they were getting, trying to get their film financed. They had a few more tap dances, more meetings to take, trying to get somebody to back their film, before Abra would be able to go back East and juggle the syndication offers. The rap mogul had passed, too; said the film wouldn't make any money " 'cause Black people don't be actin' like that: goin' to shrinks, eatin' sushi and shit." This kind of thinking was what Abra and Natasha were dealing with all the time, and it was bad enough when it came from White folks and their centuries-old misperceptions of Black people, but it was even worse when it came from other Black folks, who should know better.

Abra dialed Cullen at work to let him know she'd arrived in L.A. but was told by Margo that he hadn't been in all day. Abra did a mental check of Cullen's calendar. She felt a flip in her stomach when she couldn't come up with where he might be. "Okay, well, just tell him he can reach me at Natasha's. Thanks, Margo," she said and flipped the phone closed. "That's weird," she said to no one in particular. Where could he be that Margo doesn't know?

"What?" Natasha asked distractedly.

"Cullen hasn't been in all day and he didn't call Margo."

"Oh, I'm sure it's nothing. You know old dick head gets so wrapped up in all his deals and stuff."

"Yeah, you're right. So you know why we're having a hard time, don't you?" Abra said, shifting back to business.

"They hate the script?" Natasha said.

"No. It's because we're seen as TV people, and film folks look down on TV people."

Natasha paused, thinking about Abra's insight. "You know, you're right. I never even considered that."

"I think we exhaust all the people on our list, and then we seriously think about doing it ourselves."

Natasha wheeled the car into the lot. "I think you're on to something, counselor."

chapter 8

MILES GOT BACK to his hotel room at the Argyle and flopped down on the Art Deco sofa; the fax machine was whirring as was his head. He'd been up since the previous morning, having flown in from Japan, where American investors were taking advantage of Asia's stock market crash and trying to buy everything they saw. He called room service and ordered a sandwich. He needed to check in with his office and then he'd grab a nap before his dinner meeting. He always liked doing business in L.A., especially when it was winter back home. He could see why people lived here, driving a convertible in winter was cool. The women weren't bad, either. They were different from the sisters in New York, not as sharp, but easier. Sometimes you just don't want to work that hard. He thought about Natasha. She had a nice little way about her. She was fly, but obviously not a featherweight. He'd done a little check on her and found out that she'd written and then produced a popular comedy. She could be fun. Fun for Miles was the desired trait, anything more was too much. He didn't ever want to fall in love, although he'd never admit that to anyone, not even himself. He told himself and his close friends that he just hadn't met the right one yet or that the one who could've been the one had married someone else.

The reality of Miles was that he didn't have a clue about what it would take to be married. His parents hadn't been married, and practically everyone in his Memphis neighborhood had been raised by bitter single mothers, who spent all their free time dogging the men who had left them poor and pregnant. Miles vowed he'd never be poor again and never put himself in a position to leave a woman the way his father had left his mother. Fortunately his mother had had the good sense to stop at one child and was able to focus all her energy into seeing to it that her son would have a better life. Every free educational program that was offered in the state of Tennessee, that was within a day's drive of Memphis, his mother enrolled him in it. By the time Miles was ready for junior high, he was plucked out of his local school, near where he lived in the Foote Homes, and sent across town to Christian Brothers Prep.

Miles was fluent in French, could do broken Japanese, and was now teaching himself Chinese. He was a hitter at his firm and that provided his mama and himself a life with superior accouterments. His mother was now ensconced in Whitehaven, a cushy Memphis suburb. After a nap and a bath in the Jacuzzi, Miles picked up Natasha's card and dialed. Sitting on the edge of the sleigh bed, channel surfing, he left a message with Natasha's secretary.

When Abra and Natasha got to Natasha's house, there was a message from Cullen who said he'd try again tomorrow because he was going to bed. There was also the message that Miles had called the office.

"What should I do?" asked Natasha, panicking like this might be her first date with the crush from junior high.

"Uh, how about calling him back?"

"Yeah, yeah. I'll call him back."

"Good."

"What should I say?"

"How about, 'I'm returning your call'?"

"Oh, yeah, yeah, that's good."

"I thought I was outta practice," Abra said.

Natasha picked up the portable and dialed the hotel. Her heart was beating fast when she asked for his room.

"Browning," he said as a greeting.

"Um, hi, it's Natasha, we met—"

"Yes, of course, Natasha. Thanks for calling me back. How are you?"

"Good . . ."

"I was calling to see if you would have dinner with me tomorrow. I'd like to get together before I leave town."

"Um, tomorrow? Uh, hold on a minute." She pushed the hold button on her phone and began searching her backpack and her Wizard. She was jumping up and down while mouthing to Abra that he'd just asked her out. Abra sat looking at her, confused.

Natasha pushed the hold button again.

"I'm free tomorrow night."

"Great. How about eight o'clock at Shutters?"

"Shutters, yeah, that'll be good."

"Great. So I'll meet you there, or do you want me to pick you up?"

"I can meet you there."

"Great. Let me give you my cell-phone number in case something happens or you're running late."

They hung up and Natasha plopped down on the sofa next to Abra. "I can't believe it. A real date. He even offered to pick me up."

"Is that a big deal?"

"In L.A."

"Maybe you need to move. I bet you'd meet someone nice in the Midwest."

SHUTTERS IS A HOTEL with three separate restaurants on the beach in Santa Monica. The rooms are hard to get and expensive even by five-star standards. Natasha and Miles were meeting in Pico, a large, airy restaurant that is so light in the daytime it is appropriate, even necessary, to wear sunglasses. The evening provides a romantic, but not too obvious, charm. Miles was waiting when Natasha arrived L.A. style, forty-five minutes late. He was calmly reading *Institutional Investor* and sipping champagne. Miles looked up from his magazine to check Natasha out as she bustled toward him. She was wearing a copper-colored silk-satin T-shirt, which matched her skin, and snug brown velvet pants. She was carrying a suede blazer and a crocodile Kelly bag. Her cheekbones were covered with a sparkling bronzer, giving her deep tone a hint of sun and making the highlights in her hair even more prominent.

Miles smiled at her.

"I'm so sorry, I . . ."

"Calm down. It's okay. I'm just sitting here enjoying the ocean and the . . . here, have some." He poured her a flute and raised his. "To new friendships."

Natasha clinked his glass and nodded.

"So tell me about yourself," Miles began, sounding sincere.

"Um, you wanna be more specific?" Natasha said, hanging her jacket on the back of her chair.

"Not really."

"Well, let's see, where do you want me to start?"

"Where are you from?"

"We lived in New Jersey until I was fifteen, then we moved to Chicago."

"Oh yeah? I went to U of C."

"Yeah? I grew up in Hyde Park."

"How about that," Miles said.

"So, where'd you go to school?" he asked.

"Um, I went to Howard and then NYU for grad school."

"H.U. How'd you like it?"

"It was probably the greatest time of my life."

"Really? You know I often wished that I'd gone to a Black school."

"Why?"

" 'Cause y'all seem so confident and you know every damn body."

"Yeah, I guess that's true, but I'm sure you're not lacking in confidence or contacts."

"True enough . . . so you went to NYU for film school?"

"The business school."

"The bitness school. I'da never guessed."

"Why? 'Cause I don't wear pinstripes?"

"Basically, but because I know NYU has a big-time film school."

"Well, I'm in show *business*."

"How is business?" Miles asked.

The waiter took their orders. Natasha was relieved that Miles didn't try to order for her. She hated that.

"Well, right now we've got the TV thing going. That's

where I started and I've had a lotta luck in TV, but we've been trying for almost two years to get a film made, and we're not having any luck."

"Success ain't about luck. I'm sure you know that."

"Yeah."

"You're not getting down about it, are you?"

"A little, I mean I know it's hard but we've been at this for a while. It's a hot script but the more time that passes, the cooler it gets," she said.

"Yeah, this is a difficult business because of the unpredictability factor."

"Yeah, it ain't about the work, as my partner wants to believe," Natasha said.

"So you had a hit sitcom and earned your producer stripes, and you may be going into syndication. That's tremendous."

"Yeah, I know. The show was critically successful. Believe me, I'm not complaining. I'm just a little spoiled."

"Well, the film stuff will come," Miles said.

They turned to their food.

"So, what about you? Where're you from?" Natasha asked, after a few bites of pasta.

"Mem phus."

"Really? Oh, yeah, I hear the accent."

"It comes and goes."

"So where'd you go to grad school?"

"Bitness school at Harvard."

"What year?"

"Come on baby, let's not do Negro Geography. You know we probably know at least a hun'ed people in common."

They both laughed and Natasha agreed to leave the small-world conversation alone.

"So you live in Manhattan?"

"Uh-huh. I just moved from the Village to Sutton Place."

"Nice."

"Yeah, it's cool. So how do you like living in L.A.?"

"I like L.A., even though most people living here would never admit they like it. It's fun and it's where I need to be for my business. I don't know if I'll live here my whole life, but it's cool for now."

"Yeah, I could see this being a fun place to live. Do you travel a lot?"

"Just to New York. I don't seem to have a lot of leisure time for holidays and stuff. What about you?"

"Same. I travel a ton for business. I'm doing a lot in Asia now, and this thing with Dreamtime'll keep me coming here for a while."

Natasha had avoided investment bankers like fat, after her disaster with one from school whom she dated for a year and didn't know that they'd broken up until she read about his engagement in the *Times*. Most of the ones she'd known she found either too arrogant or slick, and oftentimes, dull —an intolerable combination. But Miles clearly had way-above-average intelligence and his accent, which became more pronounced as dinner progressed, made him seem trustworthy. She also liked the way his full lips danced as he talked. She figured if he was a dog, he was probably housebroken.

They took a walk on the beach after dinner. She put on her jacket, and they kicked sand as they walked barefoot under a calm, starless night. Miles draped his arm over Natasha's shoulder, his shoes dangling from his fingers, as he told her tales about his Memphis childhood.

ABRA SAT ON the couch, her mug of peppermint tea on the coffee table, going over the amendments of the syndication contract. Natasha came home from her date and went straight to the linen closet.

"I need a wash cloth," Natasha said.

"So, how was it?" Abra yelled to her friend.

Natasha came back into the living room, holding a towel and damp cloth. "It was great," she said, sitting back down to rub sand off her feet. "We went walking on the beach."

"Mmm, sounds romantic."

"It was nice . . . what you doing?"

Abra held up the papers and smiled. "The deal from Blax, FedExed. They've stepped up to the plate."

Natasha looked at her friend and fell back into the over-sized armchair, hand dramatically on her chest.

"You mean we did it?"

Abra nodded. "Done, we got what we wanted."

"Cadabra, this is . . ."

"It's great," Abra said, drinking her tea.

"I can't believe it. So what are we gonna do now?"

Abra looked at Natasha as if to say, "Dummy, what we always do. We keep going, as if nothing has happened."

Natasha looked away, dazedlike, imagining.

Abra interrupted her reverie. "So what's his story, whadcha talk about?"

Natasha didn't respond right away. "Um, he seems like a nice guy . . ."

"Uh-oh, the kiss of death for you, a nice guy?"

"Yeah, he's nice," Natasha said, rubbing her feet clean.

"Translation: You're not attracted to him, right?"

"No. I mean, I didn't want to throw him down in the sand and get busy, but he's cool. I'd see him again."

"Did he ask you out again?"

"Yeah, we're having breakfast tomorrow."

"Breakfast?"

"He's leaving town tomorrow afternoon."

"He must really be interested."

"He seemed interested, but . . . who cares? I'm too busy."

"God, I'm so glad I'm not single. So what else happened?"

"He's a hitter at the firm."

"A hitter? Did he tell you that?"

"No, no. I can just tell. He made managing director in less than five years."

"Oh, okay. He's in investment banking? What year? You know we got to put him on the wire."

"I know. He wouldn't tell me what year, but it had to be early eighties."

"Easy to get his number. Where does he live?"

"He just moved," Natasha said, recalling the conversation.

"Where?" Abra persisted.

"Sutton Place."

"Sutton Place?" Abra asked rhetorically.

"Bonus time," Natasha said.

"And brother got paid," Abra said.

"And you know that," Natasha added.

They laughed and slapped a high five, as much for Natasha's meeting Miles as for a celebration of his success. For this group of post–civil rights achievers, his success created a sense of pride for all of them.

chapter 9

CULLEN SAT at his desk studying the announcement from Jimmy and Delora:

> *On February 14,*
> *fourteen of our closest friends joined us*
> *at the Four Seasons, where we were married.*

These folks are serious, he thought, and chuckled. The panties must be tremendous. While he was laughing at them, he also felt something akin to envy. *Why should they be so damn happy? Probably won't last. How could it? It's a child's way of looking at love. Love is about more than passion and hot sex. It's devotion, it's commitment, it's regularity, reliability. All those things that don't sound sexy and aren't.* It was why he now had Cynthia, and it was why he had to break it off.

He recalled the unromantic way he had proposed to Abra. They were on their way to meet with a realtor who was helping him make the move from studio into grown-up space. They were on the six train, heading uptown. Abra was looking around, hoping the man with the sore that looked like it went through his flesh into the bone wouldn't come to her for money. He was crouched in the center of the train, pleading for change from unconcerned commuters. She always gave panhandlers money, and Cullen always scolded her for it. He finished flipping through *Barron's* and turned his attention to her.

"So how long have we been going out? Three, four years?"

Of course, she knew that it had been four years and 345 days, but casually answered, "Something like that."

"So whaddya think? You think we should get married, or what?"

She looked at the panhandler and at the faces of the other commuters—Caribbean, South American, and yuppie White. She wanted to yell at them, "He just proposed to me!" but Odessa had raised her better than to act a fool in public. "Oh, Cullen. Are you . . . yeah, yes, of course, I want to."

Cullen looked at her, pushed his glasses up the bridge of his nose, and smiled.

"Good. Then let's get married."

Cullen's desk was clear save for a note from Margo, his secretary, that he had E-mail. He turned on his laptop and found one message was from Cynthia. Risky, he thought, while he watched the lines cross his screen. *Hi, please call me.* Innocuous enough, he thought, checking his watch and punching in her number.

One ring. She answered.

"I was just thinking about you," she said.

"Oh, yeah? What were you thinking?"

"I was thinking about what a great fuck you are."

Cullen felt a hot flash and a rise in his flannel slacks.

"I was thinking that I can't wait to see you again," Cynthia continued.

"Well, that's why I'm calling. How about nine, at the same place?"

"I'll be there."

With Abra out of town, Cullen tossed away the idea of ending it now, might as well take advantage of her absence. He'd had Cynthia only a few times, but she was already a habit. He decided that he'd just fuck his way through, that after a while, he'd grow tired of her and go back to his tidy life. In five years of marriage, he'd never actually consummated his cheating. The flirtatious dinners out of town with old girlfriends, the dry-humping in his office with a summer intern here and there seemed like nothing compared to what he was doing now. Truth was, he hadn't met anyone else he ever wanted badly enough to take the risk for, but there was something about Cynthia that he just couldn't pass up. This kind of burning-up passion would fade.

There were three bars in the Peninsula. The third was on the rooftop near the pool, where they'd never been. She'd know to come to the darkest bar. It was also the one that would be hardest to explain if he were seen there. Cynthia didn't look like a client, and it wasn't the kind of place he'd take a client, unless the other bars were full. He could always use that as an excuse if one of his or Abra's friends happened by.

As he waited for Cynthia, sipping a martini, Cullen thought about the wedding announcement from Jimmy. A second marriage. Jimmy's first had been to a proper Durham debutante, and the marriage lasted about as long as their Caribbean-cruise honeymoon. Jimmy had known Delora back at Howard, but she didn't have quite the right profile in his parents' view, and they convinced him that the Durham honey was more appropriate. After a few miserable years, he'd realized he had to live his life his way.

Cynthia was wearing a short camel-colored cashmere coat with a fur collar. The coat was belted at the waist, and she wore a short dark skirt, tights, and dark suede boots to her knees. She was carrying a large tote that she plopped onto the floor before sitting down.

"Hi. A martini?" Cynthia said, eyeing Cullen's drink which was almost gone. "I'll have one, too."

Cullen summoned the waiter and hungrily watched Cynthia untie her coat. She wore a mandarin-collared alabaster silk top through which he could see her dark nipples.

"So how are you?" he asked, not really caring about her answer.

"I'm fine. I had a couple of good go-sees today, cover tries."

"Cover tries?"

"Yes, um, it's like a screen test for a magazine cover."

"Oh, really? That's great. I mean, it sounds good."

Her drink sat untouched, and she reached for a package of cigarettes. "You don't mind, do you?"

"No, go ahead. So what magazine?"

"*View*," she said as she inhaled.

"*View*? Cynthia, that's great."

She picked up her glass and Cullen grabbed his glass to touch hers.

"Here's to the cover try," he said and clinked glasses. He leaned in toward her face. "You know I have to have you."

He reached across the small, round marble stump of a table and rubbed her hand. He wanted her so much at this moment that he felt a thickness, that wasn't quite pain, but a sensation that was close. He would beg if he had to, but she knew when she showed up that she was going to fuck him.

When he came back to the table with a room key, she got up and retied her coat. They entered the room and before they were out of the foyer, they were on the floor with his hand groping at the crotch of her pantyhose. He poked his center finger inside and tore a hole, wriggling his finger around her lips and clit before jamming it. She was kissing him back, hard, biting his lips while trying to remove her coat and unbutton her blouse. Before she had both arms out of her coat, he'd entered her. With a few quick, hard pumps he withdrew from her, letting liquid squirt all over her skirt and hose. He lay on one side of her, both he and she breathing heavily. He was sweating and was still dressed, shoes and all, as he was when he left for work that morning. "Damn," he sighed, thinking that he'd never had sex like this. Leaving her coat on the floor, she unzipped her skirt and stepped out of it. "I've got to dry this."

Cullen lay on the floor, listening to the blow-dryer sounds from the bathroom, his throbbing penis lying on the placket of his Etro pinstripe. He tried to remember if he'd ever made love with his shoes on, although you couldn't call what they'd just done making love. He closed his eyes and imagined having Cynthia again and again. Taking her away on vacation where they could do it three, four times a day, until they were both raw.

"What're you thinking about?" Cynthia asked as she stood over him in boots and torn pantyhose. She went over to the couch and unzipped her boots and put on a hotel-issue terry robe. The white against her black skin was worthy of a Sargent painting. She looked so perfect, so beautiful.

He joined her on the sofa.

He leaned in toward her chest, using his face to open her robe, and began again.

THE FIRST TIME Cullen had seen Cynthia was at the perfume counter at Barneys. He'd gone there to buy a birthday gift for Abra. She'd always hated that her birthday fell between the holidays, and Natasha always had to remind him to get Abra something that she really wanted. This time he had needed help because he couldn't remember the name—only that it was strange, foreign, maybe French—of her perfume. He saw Cynthia's gleaming face and immediately felt at ease. "I'm looking for a perfume for my wife. I can't remember the name, but it sounds something like 'annouck' something."

At first, Cynthia fixed him with a blank smile, then she gave him a focused, more personal one. She liked to see well-dressed Black men in Barneys; she also liked it when they bought presents for their wives. It was wholesome.

"Would you recognize the bottle?" Cynthia asked, placing a tray of various crafted containers on the counter in front of him.

Cullen looked down at the array and tried to envision the surface of his wife's vanity, so many bottles, potions, boxes, old photographs. "I think so."

Cynthia held up a ridge-lined bottle with a gold top. "Did it look like this?"

"Yes, yes, that's it. What's it called?"

"Well, there are quite a few that look like this. Um, do you remember any more of the name?"

"No, but she wears it all the time. I'd recognize the smell, it's like lemons."

"Here," she spritzed a small amount on her wrist and waved it past his nose. "This it?"

"Yeah, that's it. Gimme a large one and some, I don't know, does it have something else?"

"You could get bath oil or body cream."

"The cream. She'll like that."

Cullen reached inside his suit jacket and brought out his wallet. He pulled out a credit card and handed it to Cynthia, who looked at the card and said, "Be right back, Mr. Dixon." She turned to punch in his purchases and bag them. He stood at the counter, unconsciously drumming it with his index fingers. When Cynthia returned and handed him the black bag and his credit-card receipt to sign, he noticed her long, slender fingers. He looked at her fingernails, which were polished a natural looking white. He noticed the contrast of her iridescent pearl earrings against her cocoa skin. He noticed that she was beautiful.

A month later, Cullen ran into Cynthia at a restaurant where she also worked as a hostess. He was having lunch with a young associate. "Hello, Mr. Dixon," she said, greeting him as Cullen and the associate walked up to the podium where she stood checking people's reservations.

"You remember me? I'm impressed," Cullen said.

"Of course. How've you been?"

"Good, and you?"

"Oh fine. Let me show you to your table." She picked up two navy leather-encased menus and led Cullen and the associate to a corner table.

"Enjoy," she said, after putting their menus down in front of them.

"You know her?" asked the associate.

"Not really, she waited on me once at Barneys."

"She's a looker," he said. "Humph, she could wait on me anytime," he said, still looking at Cynthia's trail.

"Yes, I suppose she is quite attractive," Cullen said.

"Cullen, what are you, neutered? You *suppose*?"

"Hey man, I don't even notice these things anymore, I'm married," he lied, and made a mental note to invite her for a drink.

A few weeks after they had become involved, he bought Cynthia the same perfume. He figured he could easily cover his tracks; after spending a day with his mistress, he'd only smell of his wife. He also knew that a jury would convict him for this kind of cunning. He felt like a shit, but not enough to end it with Cynthia. He tried to convince himself that he was still a good guy because, at least, he felt bad for doing wrong.

chapter 10

THE DEAL with Farah, the furniture queen, would require more travel than just trips to North Carolina. That was simply where her factory was. If they were going to invest in her company, they'd need more than one factory, probably in additional states, at least one on the West Coast to keep shipping costs down, and maybe one in the Midwest, depending on how many stores they decided to open there.

Farah was a small, pale White woman with vibrant red hair cut into a blunt pageboy. She wore large, round black glasses and spoke with a quiet, Brahmin tongue. She'd been married a couple of times, but had started her business all on her own, while raising a son who was now a senior at Duke. She and Cullen had met only over the phone; the conversations had flowed, and she was looking forward to meeting this bright young man in person.

Cullen showed up at Farah's shop to take her to lunch at their appointed time. "You look exactly as I pictured," Farah said, arms outstretched to hug Cullen. He stood stiffly for a moment, not knowing the business protocol of what was about to happen. After a few moments, he let go and hugged her back. He could see that Farah made up her own rules. She was dressed in a flowing floral dress, a loud orange cardigan, and granny boots. Her glasses hung from a turquoise-, orange-, and red-beaded chain that she wore around her neck.

He even dismissed his thoughts about her being surprised to see a Black man. She seemed like one of those rare White folks who actually saw Black people as human beings and expected to see them in all variations of life.

"It's great to finally meet you in person," Farah said, moving back from their embrace to look him in the face.

"It's nice to see you, too. You hungry?"

"Starved. And I have just the place."

They got into Cullen's rented Chrysler and headed toward the shoreline. At lunch they chatted about the weather, in the pleasant sixties; Farah's son, the chemistry major; and Cullen's rise at the firm.

"Well, of course you'll become a partner when we're finished," Farah said over a platter of seafood that had been caught just hours before.

"Hope you're right."

"Of course, I'm right. I mean, look at you: You've got all the credentials, you're smart as a whip, and you've got the right style. You're in."

"What do you mean style?"

"You know, that Ivy-League casual superiority thing."

"I come across like that?

"Sure, but nice, not a jerk. You have a nice wife, right?"

"Yeah, who thinks I travel too much."

"Well, of course. Be glad she misses you. See, you've got everything you need. Aunt Farah says so."

They finished their meal and got down to business. Cullen had tax statements from the last ten years, factory-feasibility studies that he needed to go over with Farah. He had a day and a half to complete this part of the project and then it was back to New York.

ABRA HEARD Cullen's cab pull up. She looked outside from their bedroom window, where she was dressed in a chiffon leopard-print robe and a satin silver bustier. Tiny tap pants covered a red, licorice-looking panty. She'd covered both nightstands, the dresser, and a couple of windowsills with votive candles, and Nancy Wilson was blowing on the CD player. Cullen dropped his keys on the hall table and yelled out for Abra. She knew if she didn't answer, he'd come upstairs. He found her stretched out on her stomach across the bed.

"Hey, babe," Cullen said, a little too casually for a week's separation, to Abra.

"You're home. I'm so glad." She rolled over to hug him.

"What's all this?" he asked, seeming genuinely surprised.

"It's my 'welcome home.' I missed you," Abra said, sitting next to him on the bed and loosening his double Windsor knot.

"I missed you, too, babe. I wanna take a shower. Be right back."

With that, he patted her thigh and went to the bathroom. Not until she heard the shower did she finally let herself believe that he had actually left the room. She rolled the down comforter back, snuggled underneath and fought back feeling ridiculous. Cullen came out half wet, with a white towel wrapped at the waist. He crawled on the bed to her and kissed her on the cheek. "I'm sorry, babe. I just felt so grimy."

She wanted to cry but held back. She kissed Cullen, their tongues an impatient duel. Cullen reached into the bustier and grabbed one of her breasts. He cupped it as he flicked her nipple. He slid his other hand up her thigh. His wife's heavy thighs reminded him of Cynthia's athletic ones. He tried to push Cynthia out of his mind and the more he pushed, the more her image came into focus. "Oh Abra," he moaned by rote, hoping if he said her name out loud, that somehow would kill Cynthia's ghost. He continued to run his hands between Abra's thighs while she rubbed his head and back, and moaned. He came upon the tap pants and felt something firm underneath.

"What's this?" he asked, still caressing her.

"Take these off," she instructed, referring to her silk boxers.

He dutifully pulled them down and saw the edible panties. We've resorted to gimmicks now, was his thought. What he said was, "What flavor?"

"Taste it."

Cullen brought his head down, first kissing her thick pile of dark red-brown hair through the panties, and then tonguing her. Abra gasped and squeezed Cullen's back. The panties began to disintegrate as Cullen's tongue touched them. He could taste the artificial strawberry flavor on his tongue. He maintained his erection by thinking of Cynthia and their last time together on the floor, while moaning perfunctorily. He knew exactly what Abra liked. He teased around her center for a while, flicking gently until he sensed she was ready, and then he zeroed in harder with his wide tongue. With that, she let out a high-pitched squeal, and he knew his job was half done. He rolled her over onto her back, removing what was left of the panties. After a few minutes, he was finished.

Just as Cullen knew what Abra liked, so did Abra know her husband. She tried to quiet her doubts, but they came at her like a boxer's speed bag. She didn't want to know, but she knew something wasn't right.

The next morning, Saturday, Cullen got up to dress for work. He made coffee and brought Abra a cup upstairs where she was still asleep. He nudged her slightly and put the cup between votives, on her nightstand. He leaned down to kiss her and whispered that he had to go.

"Wait," she said, sleepily. "What time are you coming home?"

"Uh, the usual time, honey. Six or seven."

"Well, which one Cullen, six or seven?"

Cullen looked at Abra, trying to figure her out.

"What's the matter, babe?"

"I don't know, I guess I thought you'd stay home today, since I've been gone all week."

"Abra, honey, you know I can't. I've got so much work, you won't even believe. I'll be home for dinner, though. We'll open a nice bottle of wine, okay?"

Abra took a sip of coffee—Cullen always made it too strong—and put the mug back on the table, on top of last week's *New Yorker.*

"Okay, okay, go. I'll see you later."

She tried not to pout because she knew Cullen hated it. She searched her mind for things she had to do today, things to keep away the thoughts she'd had last night. She heard him backing the car out of the garage. She let a few small drops fall from her eyes. She wiped them with the back of her hand and looked at the clock. Seven o'clock in L.A. Natasha would be getting ready to go running. She dialed her friend's number.

"Hey, Cadabra," Natasha answered, after checking her caller I D.

"Hey."

"What's the matter?"

"He's fucking around. I think he's fucking around."

"Why're you saying that?"

"Natasha, I know. I can tell. We were having sex last night, and he was so not into it."

"Didn't he just get off a plane?"

"He's always getting off a plane, it's not a big deal."

"So you don't think he was just tired?"

"No. He should've been horny and he wasn't. I could tell."

"Well, did you say something to him?"

"Like what? Tell me who you're fucking?"

"No, I mean, did you ask him if he was feeling all right? Maybe he's sick."

"I know what it is, Natasha, I just know," Abra began crying. "I don't know what to do."

"First, pull yourself together and listen to me. You have no evidence of this, okay? None. Cullen's a good guy and he loves you. It's just not his M.O. to be fuckin' around."

"You really think so?"

"Look, I've known the boy practically all my life. It's not him."

Abra took a deep breath through her nose.

"You okay?" Natasha asked. "Better?"

"Yeah, I'm fine. You're right, I'm overreacting. I'm just tired, all that running around in L.A."

"Yeah, I'm kinda beat, too."

"So you going running?" Abra asked.

"Yeah, later. I was about to call Miles to . . ."

"Miles?"

"Yeah, he sent me a pair of flip-flops."

"Flip-flops? For what?"

"The note said, 'Looking forward to many walks along the beach.' "

"Oh, that's so sweet," Abra said.

"Yeah, I know. This one may be different."

"Okay, you go call him. Call me later."

"Yep. And it'll be okay, Abra. I'm sure it's nothing."

"Yeah, okay. Talk to you later."

CULLEN ALTERNATED his feet between the clutch and the taut German accelerator as he maneuvered up the ramp in the parking garage. He had to get to work, write up the report of Farah's tax stuff, decide on what cities the focus groups would need to be set up in, look at proposals from ad agencies. He'd been out only a few days, but things still piled up. As he worked figures on his laptop, he was annoyed by a ringing telephone.

"Cull man, is that you?"

"Yeah. Who's this?"

"Jimmy."

"Jimmy? Jimmy, what up frat?"

"Yo man, it's you."

"Hey, what you doin'? You in town?" Cullen asked, hitting the Save button on his computer.

"Yup, just for a minute. Had to come up for work. Thought we might grab a brew."

"Uh, yeah, yeah. I gotta shitload of work here but I can take a break. How's six?"

"Cool. I'm stayin' at the Plaza."

"Good. I'll meet you at the bar, in the Oak Room."

"Cool."

Cullen got back to work, forgetting that he was to get together for a quickie with Cynthia later. He continued working, figuring he'd cancel with her before he went to meet Jimmy. Hours evaporated and Cullen forgot to cancel Cynthia. It was a quarter to six and the office was empty. She was calling from in front of his building. He could have her come upstairs, hit it, and then send her on her way. She would go for that, but that was too risky; or he could bring her to the Plaza with him, or he could completely blow her off. Those were his options. He got up from his desk, stretching his arms out in front of him, and thought about his dilemma. Fuck it. He'd meet her in the lobby, give her the lowdown, and pass her off as a colleague. Jimmy wasn't the brightest porch light on the block.

When they arrived at the bar, Jimmy was on his second draft. He got up, all burly six-feet-four-inches of him to hug Cullen, his frat brother from back in the day. After their bear hug, Cullen turned to introduce Jimmy to Cynthia, who fortunately was dressed in a pinstriped pantsuit.

He'd promised her it would only be an hour, but that he had to see his boy. Cynthia excused herself when the conversation seemed stuck on their college days on line, pledging Alpha. While she was gone from the table, Jimmy leaned over to his friend.

"So, how long you been tappin' that?"

Cullen was looking down at his martini. While he was shocked by his friend's inquiry, he fought showing it. He laughed an empty chuckle and blew out, "What you talkin' 'bout, man?"

"You know what I'm talkin' 'bout. Look, Cullen man, I been there, remember?" Jimmy was an earnest guy. A salt-of-the-earth type of Southerner who meant what he said. He and Delora had been fooling around for years before he finally got up the courage to leave his first wife. "Listen man, when I saw the two of you walk through the door I knew somethin' was up. Look, this is me. Your shit will go wit me to the grave."

Cullen took a gulp from his glass and looked around. Cynthia was nowhere in sight. Probably talking on the phone, Cullen decided. "Man, I don't know what I've gotten myself into. I love my wife."

"I know, shit just happens. How long you been married now?"

"Five years. We've been together, I don't know, nine, ten."

"Yeah, you 'bout due."

"What does that mean? This is inevitable?"

"Sometimes. Look, this shit is damn hard; marriage, I'm talkin' 'bout. Nobody tells us this till it's too late and you're already in."

"Yeah, I know."

"Like I say, you gotta marry somebody you're hot for."

"Aw man, come on, it's about more than just the booty."

"Of course it is, but the booty has gots to be stellar. Otherwise, you gonna stray. I think sometimes it takes one marriage to get the second one right.

"You know we just out here, none of us know what

the fuck to look for, talking about spending your life with somebody and all you got to go on is what they like in bed or how they make you feel in bed.

"We get to a point where we decide, humph, it's time to get married, 'cause I'm twenty-five, thirty, whatever. Not do I really love this person, would my life be empty if I didn't have this person in it. No we don't ask questions like that. It's about what my friends think, what my mama want, all that shit that don't mean a damn thing when you wake up and got to look at that mug every morning. So no, I know the shit ain't just about no sex. I knew I loved Delora the second time I went out with her. I was twenty years old, but I knew. It took me almost twenty years to get back to her, but I did. And no she ain't the finest woman I ever been with, she ain't the most successful, but she got everything I ever wanted and that's how I think you should feel about the person you married to." Jimmy reared back and picked up his mug with his catcher's mitt hand. Cullen was quiet for a moment.

"I could never, I'd never leave Abra."

"I ain't sayin' you should, but just know that there's a reason why you out here creepin' and think 'bout it, that's all."

Cynthia walked back toward the table, and Cullen was relieved to see her. He really didn't want to have this talk with Jimmy or himself. He liked to think of this thing with Cynthia as a minor glitch on the screen, separate from his marriage. Abra was his home, his base, his security. She was who he'd grow old with, the person who would get everything if something happened to him. The person he trusted and knew had his back. He couldn't even dream of a life without Abra, even with her flabby thighs. Cynthia was an itch he had to scratch, that was all.

After Cullen's second and Jimmy's third, Cullen and Cynthia got up to leave.

"Man, it's been great seein' you," Jimmy said, opening his linebacker arms to embrace Cullen again.

"Yeah, you, too, frat. Listen, stay in touch, all right?"

Jimmy shook Cynthia's hand, patting the top of it reassuringly. "It was really nice meetin' you."

THEY LEFT and headed down Fifth. Cullen had a hard-on just thinking about how close they were to the Peninsula. He was calculating how long they could have together before he'd have to get home. He was already late, but he knew he couldn't push it too much past nine.

"How're you feeling?" Cullen asked Cynthia, who was walking next to him with her hands in the pockets of her camel-hair coat.

"I'm okay. Your friend is nice."

"Yeah, he's a great guy, big teddy bear. So you wanna go to our spot?"

"Of course. How much time do we have?"

"Not much, couple of hours."

"Fine."

Cynthia waited for Cullen in the dark bar while he made arrangements for a room. He came back, not sitting down, and tapped her on the shoulder. She gathered her coat and bag and followed him out to the elevator. Once they were inside, Cullen ran his hand inside her coat, up her pants leg to her crotch. "Ah, I missed you," he said, as they stood side by side, facing forward.

They got to the room and he took off her coat. "You hungry?" he asked, as he was hanging her coat in the closet. Cynthia came up behind him and wrapped her arms around his waist. She was almost as tall as he, her lips were at his ear.

"Just for you," she whispered.

Cullen turned around, and plunged his tongue into her mouth, frantically moving it, as if he were searching for something. "Slow down. I'm not going anywhere," Cynthia said.

After they made love, Cullen and Cynthia dozed off. When he rolled over, he instinctively reached for the clock radio and saw that it was a quarter to midnight.

"Shit!" he yelled out, waking Cynthia.

"What? What's the matter?" she asked.

"I should've been home by now. Fuck! I've gotta call her. Can you go in . . . never mind."

He got up to use the phone in the bathroom. He paused, thinking about whether it was necessary to ask Cynthia to keep quiet. No, he decided. She would know. He dialed the number while sitting on the toilet. Abra answered on one ring.

"Where are you?" she asked urgently.

"I'm, I'm still at the office. . . ."

"I called you there."

"Yeah. I left and had drinks and then dinner with Jimmy. He was in town for a day and then I went—I mean, I came back here to try to finish up. I'll be home soon." Cullen heard Abra sniffling and felt like a complete shit.

"Don't do that, baby. I'm sorry."

"I know you're lying. I just know it."

"Abra, what are you talking about?"

Cullen asked, but didn't really want to hear the answer. He knew that she was suspicious. How could she not be? She was so tied in to his emotional climate that any change in temperature was always noted and studied.

"Babe, I'll be home in an hour. We can talk then, okay?"

Abra bravely sniffed back her tears and agreed.

When he walked back into the room, he found Cynthia dressed and sitting on the edge of the bed. "She's upset, huh?"

"I've gotta go." Cullen went through the room, gathering his clothes from various floor piles in order to get dressed.

"So, maybe I'll just go," Cynthia said, trying not to notice the heaviness in the room.

"Uh, yeah. You need money for a cab?"

"I have money. Thanks." She picked up her tote and walked to the closet to get her coat. At the door she turned to face him before opening it.

"Cullen, I really respect you, and I don't want to put you in the awful place of lying to your wife."

Cullen heard Cynthia, but was too busy in his head to organize something to address her. He was already in Brookville, trying to explain to Abra why he had missed dinner, why he was coming home so late.

"I just have to figure it out, okay?" he said.

Cynthia decided not to push. She understood that he had already left, which made her want him all the more.

chapter 11

Aʙʀᴀ ᴡᴀs ᴡᴀɪᴛɪɴɢ ᴜᴘ, coffee cup in hand, when Cullen got home. Her eyes were red, but everything else about her seemed calm and normal. Her white cotton pjs with the blue piping and monogram were pressed, and she was wearing her favorite black velvet slippers. She was sitting, feet slightly tucked on the sofa in front of the fire she had going in the family room. Anita Baker's "Lead Me" was playing. Cullen bounced into the room, trying to play it light.

"Hey, babe," he said, kissing Abra on her forehead. "What you drinking?"

"Coffee and amaretto. You want one?"

"Um, no thanks."

Cullen looked on the floor, around the room, hands in his pockets, searching the room for something to talk about, something to distract her.

"Why don't you sit down?"

He looked for the appropriate place to sit. He opted for the tufted window seat, which ran the length of the wall under the palladian windows.

"Cullen, I've never lied to you, and I'd like to think that you've not lied to me either, but I know that's not true. Right now I need for you to tell me the truth, and understand that if you don't, I'll know, because that's how well I know you."

Cullen looked at Abra and saw the serenity of a Tibetan monk. She wasn't playing around and it scared him. At these moments she reminded him of his all-seeing mother, who he was convinced had eyes at the back of her head when he was a child. He thought for the moments he was allowed, trying not to look as if he was thinking.

"Babe."

She held up her hand to silence him. She knew that when he began a sentence with "babe," what followed was surely bullshit. "Cullen, I'm very serious. If you need time to think about this, take it, but don't blow smoke up my ass."

He searched his memory, trying to remember when he had ever seen his wife like this. He knew she had a serious resolve, but he'd only seen this a few times since they'd married. When they began seeing fertility specialists, the way she'd go into meetings with the doctors, the questions she asked them, her demeanor, was so all business that she made the doctors a little uncomfortable.

"If you are having an affair, I'm not going to leave you, but if you lie to me then I have to."

As Cullen's mother would say, he was stuck between a rock and a hard place. His heart was pounding and he was having a hard time thinking clearly, coming up with what to do. He'd punt.

"Abra, you know that I love you more than anything, don't you?"

"Yes, Cullen."

"Do you think I'd do anything to jeopardize us?"

"I'd like to think you wouldn't."

"Well, of course I wouldn't. I've loved you only."

"Cullen, I'm not questioning whether you love me, and you know that. I want to know right now whether you're having an affair. That's what I want to know."

"No, Abra, I'm not."

Abra's shoulders seemed to relax. She looked at Cullen, sipped her coffee, and said, "Good."

That night Cullen slept like a stone. Abra, partly because of the late-night coffee and partly because she was hurting, didn't sleep much. At one point she got out of bed and sat in the chaise next to a window in their bedroom. She sat there until morning, thumbing through the *Hollywood Reporter* and *Variety*. She had glanced at *Buzz* and *Premiere* before hearing the thud of the *Times* dropping onto their lawn. She went downstairs to get the paper. It was seven o'clock. Way too early to call Natasha. She knew Cullen was lying and needed to figure out what to do next.

SUNDAY BRUNCH in Manhattan was a ritual that rarely took place without advance planning but as soon as was reasonable, Abra called Sherry to see if they could meet. Sherry was free, but she'd have to bring little Jack along. Abra was grateful. She got to the rustically decorated restaurant popular among White Upper–West Siders, and sat at a corner table. She wore black sunglasses, and a bandanna under her white mock turtleneck. She sipped hot chocolate and waited for Sherry, who strolled Jack into the restaurant and looked around before she spotted her.

"Hey," Sherry said, pushing the stroller brake on with one Keds-shod foot while holding the handles with both hands.

"Thanks for coming. Sorry for the last minute invitation," Abra said.

"No problem. We weren't doing anything, just going for a walk through the park today, that's about it."

"Isn't it a little cold for the park?"

"Two-year-olds don't care. We just breeze through; it's sunny."

"Where's David?"

"Working. David's always working."

"Yeah, that's what they all seem to do. Does it bother you?"

"Hell, no. I'm glad for the time alone. I mean, Jackie and I have our routine."

"Well, it bothers me," Abra said, reaching for the menu.

"The French toast is awesome," Sherry said, making faces at Jack who was cooing in the stroller.

"Yeah, that's what I'll have. Um, I work hard, too, but it doesn't consume me the way it does Cullen."

"Yeah, well you know they can only do one thing at a time. Oh, before I forget, mark the eighteenth on your calendar. We're having a little party for Ray; he made partner, you know."

"Oh, no, I didn't know. That's great. So, how're you guys doing?" Abra said, taking off her sunglasses.

"Same. Work is fine, Jackie's great, David's the same."

"And how's that?"

"Well you know the story: He's not the love of my life, but he loves me, he loves Jackie, and we get along okay."

"God, Sherry, I have to say, it sounds kinda bleak."

"Bleak, honey, is trying to live that *Wuthering Heights* shit. It doesn't work in real life. The person you're passionately in love with doesn't love you, which is probably why you're passionately in love with him. Don't you know that by now?"

"Absolutely not. I don't agree with that at all."

"Well, you and Cullen may be the exception. I need coffee," Sherry said, running her hands over the top of her head.

Little Jack dropped the cardboard paper-towel roll he'd been occupied with. He yelped, letting his mother know he needed something else to do.

"Here, sweetie," Sherry said, handing him a wooden spoon and a Tupperware bowl.

"Really going all out on the toys, huh, Sherry?" Abra quipped.

"They like all the household stuff." Jack looked at his drum with pure love. Contentment had been achieved, for a moment.

"Can I hold him?"

Sherry looked at Abra as if she'd just belched with her mouth open, and unhooked Jack from his stroller seat. "Sure."

"Auntie Abra wants to hold you," Sherry said to Jack, handing him to Abra. Abra looked down at him; he was grabbing at her nose and smiling. "He's so cute," Abra said.

"Yeah, he is. So, where was I?" Sherry said, pouring cream into her coffee.

"Um, I don't know, we were talking about love and marriage, love in marriage . . ."

"Oh yeah. Look, if you want passion, I say don't get married. That's not what it's for. It's about mortgages, tuition, and building stuff together. Obviously, along the way you become quite attached, maybe love happens, but . . ."

"Sherry, you sound like some character outta Jane Austen or something."

"You weren't an English major, were you?"

"No, why?"

"I never read Jane Austen."

"You get the reference, though."

"Sure," Sherry chuckled, and finished her coffee, "I've seen the movies. Look, it's just that I no longer believe in love, at least not this true perfect love that leads to marriage."

Jack began chanting. He wanted to get down and walk around. Abra ran her hand over his shiny baby curls and kissed the top of his head. "Why not?"

"You learn, you grow up. People disappoint you, that's all," Sherry said.

"Yeah, I guess till now we've pretty much lived the storybook."

"What's the matter, Abra?"

"Oh, nothing. Just, you know, Cullen works all the time, we're trying to have a baby . . ."

"Yeah, I know all that, but what's bothering you now?"

"Nothing. I mean, you know, I just have to figure this stuff out. Like how much I should expect or demand from this . . ."

"From marriage?"

"Yeah."

"Mmm, I don't have the answer, but I think asking for the moon is too much."

They toasted with their mugs. As much as Abra needed someone to talk to about Cullen and her suspicions, her instinct told her Sherry wasn't the one. Their little group had always speculated about Sherry and Jack's father behind Sherry's back, and Sherry knew it. No reason to think Sherry wouldn't return the favor, given the opportunity.

Their breakfasts came, and Sherry reached for Jack so Abra could eat. "Oh no, it's all right," Abra said, holding on to Jack, playing with his tummy. Sherry watched Abra feed Jack strawberries from her plate and smiled. "You're good with him."

"I love kids and he's a good little boy," Abra said, and nuzzled her nose in Jack's cheek.

"So, you're still taking the Perganol?"

"Yeah, but they're going to switch me. It doesn't seem to be working. Plus, I'm gaining all this weight."

"It'll happen," Sherry said, trying to sound encouraging.

Abra's jeans were pinching the skin around her waist. She pushed away half-eaten French toast and looked at her watch. She hoped Cullen was awake and looking for her. "I should head back home."

"Yeah, it's nap time for baby." Sherry reached for Jack and motioned for the check.

"I got this," Abra said, opening her wallet. "Sherry, can I ask you a question?"

"Sure, ask me anything."

"What happened to Jack's father?"

Sherry looked at Abra and put down her water glass. After years of knowing people were gossiping about her and her baby's father, she was amazed that someone had actually said something to her face. "He left me. I mean, we were engaged, he broke it off, and then, a few years later I saw him again. He was seeing someone, we had sex, I got pregnant, and he didn't want to marry me. He married someone else."

Once Abra saw Sherry's pain, she was sorry that she'd asked. Clearly this had been her love, the one she wanted who hadn't wanted her. "Listen, I'm sorry . . ."

Sherry recovered her mask and looked at Abra. "Don't be silly, it's fine really, you can ask me anything. I'd like to think we're friends. Look, I have David now."

"And he's a good guy."

"That's right. He's loyal, he's not unpleasant, and I don't have to worry about him."

Abra found herself envying Sherry for not having to worry, as she put it, about David. Sherry knew he loved her and that he wasn't going anywhere.

Outside the restaurant, Sherry put on her sunglasses and heavy suede gloves, adjusting the Kid Lid on the stroller to keep sun glare out of little Jack's eyes. "So, I hope you're feeling better," Sherry said.

"Thanks for meeting me. I really just needed to get out of the house for a while. We should do this more often."

"Yeah, next time you can go to the park with us."

They hugged lightly and headed in separate directions.

Abra jumped into the Land Cruiser and turned on the radio. Gospel music blared from two of her four preprogrammed stations. Shit, she thought. She wasn't in the mood. She plugged the phone into the cigarette lighter to call Cullen to let him know she was on her way home.

"I was beginning to think you weren't there," Abra said.

"No, I was just getting out of the shower. Where're you?"

"In the car, in Manhattan, I'm on my way home."

"Whatcha go in for?"

"I met Sherry for brunch, I needed to get out."

"Sherry? How's she doing?"

"She's fine, little Jack is so cute. Ray made partner, they're having a little party for him."

"Oh yeah, I heard. That's great."

"Anybody call?"

"Your mom and Natasha."

Abra wanted to call her mother, tell her what she was thinking but resisted. Odessa would panic or tell her daughter that she was overreacting or she'd just sink into her own all-too comfortable blues. Abra punched in Natasha's number.

Natasha answered, clearly panting. "What's wrong with you?" Abra said.

"I'm on the StairMaster. What's up?"

"You called."

"Oh yeah, I'm coming to town this week."

"For what?"

"Um, to see Miles."

"Miles, huh? So this is heating up?"

"No. I'm just flying in for some work party he's gotta go to. It's an industry thing, so he thinks I could make some good contacts."

"Uh-huh, and where are you staying? Sutton Place, by any chance?"

"Oh Abra, damn, what's the big deal?"

"No big deal. I just think you should stay in a hotel or with us."

"Why? 'Cause I just met him?"

"That's right."

"Look, I need you to do some intelligence on Miles. Who do you know at Soldman?"

"Um, let's see, who do we know there?" Abra asked rhetorically. "Jackie Jones. Uh, you remember Jackie, from section F?"

"No. You know I don't remember anybody," Natasha said, sounding bored.

"I'll call her and see what she says. I think Cullen has her number."

"Thanks, honey."

"Call you later."

Natasha hung up and got off the machine. She stood over her four-poster bed covered in a purple velvet duvet. Several outfits were sprawled on the bed, all vying to go to New York. For the party, she wanted to look professional, but not stiff. She was in show business so she always needed to look hip. She'd opt for her black jersey pants and boat-neck top, the pink satin riding jacket, and the cowry shell-and-pearl choker. She thought about what Abra might uncover about Miles. Always had to ask around when you met someone new, just a reference check. He could be some kind of fool and she could end up like one of those women who met guys through the Internet and ended up getting raped.

chapter 12

O<small>N THE STREET, IT'S A MERITOCRACY.</small> The headline hung over a picture of smiling Black Wall Streeters. Miles sneered when he saw the piece, recognizing most of the faces in the photograph. Fools, he thought as he sipped his freshly squeezed orange juice. He looked closely at the photo. Four were fronts for White companies, and three were in public finance, where brothers, and later, sisters, were placed large-scale after riots tore through cities in the sixties and ended with large-scale elections of Black mayors and city councils. Wall Street powers figured they'd get some Black guys to talk that talk to Black mayors and get the municipal bond deals. There was money to be made, but the big dollars were still in corporate finance, where Miles was. The picture in the paper—a coon show, Miles thought. *Glad I turned them muthafuckas down when they asked me to do this shit. Fuck merit. If merit had anything to do with it, I'd be chairman of the goddamn place. Who they kiddin'? It's one thing to hype other folks, but when you start believing the hype, your shit is ovah.*

He sat on his plush green Soho sofa, one of the few new pieces of furniture he and his decorator had picked out for his place. Wearing a silk robe he'd picked up the last time he was in China, he contemplated the week facing him. He pushed the upcoming week into his Wizard to review. Meetings uptown all day Monday; Tuesday, West Coast clients in house, Dreamtime party that night. Natasha coming in. Ah, Natasha, Miles thought. Savoring the image of her. Miles approached women in one of three ways. Routine One was come on hard and heavy right away. Doing his investment banker thing: *Yeah I'm gettin' paid and I got a lotta things, but my life is empty 'cause I don't have a queen. I think you could be the one.* And then by date two, he's spending the big bucks, maybe he buys her something expensive or takes her on a trip. Routine One is only for those he's intrigued by, the ones who don't readily fit into his categories of women. Routine Two is what he's giving Natasha. It's the soft, unassuming sell: *I'm just a po' boy from Memphis who's in the big city, but not really of it.* The flip-flops won big points, he was sure. Routine Three: *Meet 'em, fuck 'em, and send 'em home.* This is commonly referred to as a one-night stand. This routine was only for women he knew were outside his social milieu and wouldn't know anybody in his social network. While he knew he had a reputation, being an out and out yard dog was not it. His was more that of a slightly wayward dog, simply a brother making it in America who hadn't lost his edge—especially with the women—who understood even with all his credentials that the "shit ain't about merit." He knew that settling down would look better on his vitae, and because of that, he'd get to it, one day.

Miles liked Natasha's style. She had gorgeous penny-colored skin, full lips, and a pixie nose. He wondered, though, if the hair was fake. He hated weaves. She was a Black American Princess with funk. She had all the gear he liked—a Bulgari ring worn on her middle finger, the fly, booty-hugging clothes that were a mixture of couture and Gap, and the "It's-my-world" attitude. Yeah, he thought, this is going to be an interesting ride.

ABRA SAT at the kitchen table, staring out of the window that looked out over the backyard: There was the eyesore, the greenhouse, with its three large glass panels missing and an old, rusty, oxidized radiator inside, along with overgrown plants and several large Styrofoam coolers that were way past useful. The greenhouse that belonged to the previous owners. She'd have to have it cleaned out at some point. The leaves had fallen from the Japanese maple. A thermometer sat next to her elbow on a napkin. She was ovulating and they should be having sex, but Cullen was upstairs, probably avoiding her, she decided. She was beginning to feel lost. What would she do without him? How could she even entertain the thought? If he is fucking around, so what? Why should she give him up?

Cullen lay in bed, reading the *Times,* folders from work spread out around him, waiting for his attention. Wrapped in his heavily piled terry robe, he thought about last night. Not about his confrontation with Abra, but about Cynthia. Her ripe breasts, her pudendum. It was like nothing he'd ever felt. She was like some kind of greedy plant, a sunflower. She devoured him and he loved it. Of all the other things they did, which were enjoyable, indeed, he only wanted to be inside her and stay that way. The scary thing was that it wasn't just the booty. She read him poetry and talked about things he didn't know about, like the world. She had gone to boarding school in Switzerland, worked in Italy, Tanzania, and South Africa. Her combination of European and African cultural sophistication made her impossible to resist. She wasn't Afrocentric but Afrochic. He knew he couldn't give her up, certainly not yet. Abra would just have to hold on.

Abra was trying to explain to herself why Cullen was acting so strange. Maybe it was all the pressure of sex for procreation's sake. Maybe he was just completely immersed in the Farah business. Making partner was crucial to Cullen, and this was the year. If he didn't make it, it would be a slap in the face and a vote of no confidence, and he'd have to go someplace else. The someplace else would also look askance at him: *Why didn't you make partner?* So it was "crunch time," as he would say.

She found Jackie Jones' card, turned it over to find the home number. Before dialing, she thought about what story she could tell Jackie. She could say her company was doing business with Miles, but it would be unnecessary for her to check him out through her. Or she could tell the truth, which would surely yield more information. Their network, this group of mid-, late-thirties Black professionals, was one at which AT&T would marvel. One, two phone calls would connect you with all the information you needed on someone in their milieu. Jackie answered, and she and Abra spent the first few moments exchanging small pleasantries and work gossip. Who was up for partner, who didn't make it, who from their class had started their own thing. A short pause was a cue to both of them that Abra needed to speak to why she was calling.

"So Jackie, you're at Soldman, right?"

"Yeah, still in the salt mines."

"So, do you know Miles Browning?"

Jackie let out a slight humph. "Yeah, I know him."

"What's up with him?"

"That's a good one. He's a piece of work," Jackie said in a tone that was a mixture of awe and disgust. They both chuckled and Jackie paused. Abra understood that that meant she had to tell why she wanted to know.

"Yeah, one of my friends is dating him."

"Ol' Miles, yeah, he's somethin' else. Let's see, he's University of Chicago and Harvard. Um, a golden boy, made managing director in less than five years. He's single, but you probably know that."

"Yeah, at least that's what my friend's assuming."

"Um, he's down, you know, although he enjoys the good life. He lives very well. I think he lives on Beekman Place or someplace like that. He's on a couple of boards, one uptown —the Boys Club, Harlem Boys Choir—something like that. Um, what else . . . ?"

"What about women, old girlfriends?"

"Oh, that stuff. Well, you know, there're plenty of 'em out there. Miles is definitely a player, but I think he's pretty up front. Other than this one girlfriend he had for a year or two, I don't think he dates one person for too long."

"So he sees a lot of people?" Abra asked.

"Yeah, that's pretty much what I've heard. He's one that you could easily fall for, but I would tell your friend not to."

"Oh really?"

"Yeah, I think it's better to keep it light with Miles. He's pretty much into himself."

"Mmm. Not the marrying kind, huh?"

"Don't think so. You wanna have a good time, he's your man. You want a Tiffany setting and registered china, I'd look somewhere else."

"Hey listen, Jackie, thanks so much."

"No problem. Single sistahs gotta stick together. It's rough out here . . . but you wouldn't know about that."

Abra felt Jackie's sting and let it go. Don't take your shit out on me, she said to herself.

"Okay, Jackie, thanks again."

chapter 13

ABRA SAT at the table, doodling around the information Jackie had just provided. How much of this would Natasha want to know? The important thing was that he wasn't the marrying kind. For all the hipster stance Natasha put forth, she was really quite traditional and wanted the husband and kids.

The phone rang and Abra jumped. She picked up the cordless phone after two rings and heard Cullen and a woman's voice on the extension. How could he be so damn bold? she thought, trying to hold her breath and quiet her pounding heart as she listened.

Her: "I'm sorry to bother you at home."

Cullen: "Oh, that's all right. Is something wrong?"

Her: "Yes, and I didn't know who else to call."

This bitch! Abra thought. You *bedda* find somebody! At the point where she was ready to lose it, she heard the woman say something about the '92 financials being tied up in her ex-husband's business and figured the voice belonged to that Farah woman. She continued listening and heard

118

nothing but talk about the business, nothing flirtatious that could be misconstrued. She held on, because she didn't want him to hear her hang up. A few minutes after he was off the phone, she went upstairs.

"We need to talk," she said upon entering the room.

"Speak," he said, not looking up from his papers.

"I'd like to have your attention."

He rubbed his eyes under his glasses, pushing them to his forehead before setting them back in place.

"What's the matter, Abra?"

"I'm having some problems, we're, I don't know, I think you're having an affair, and I feel like I'm gonna lose it."

"I thought we had this conversation already. I don't know what I can do to convince you."

Abra sat down at the foot of the bed and sighed. "I don't know either. I just know I'm feeling distant from you, and I know that you're consumed with this project right now, but you've been consumed before, and I haven't felt abandoned like I do now."

"Honey, I don't know what I can do right now. I'd say let's go away for a weekend or something, but I really can't afford the time. I mean, right now I should be at the office. That's why Farah just called here. This thing is gonna be twenty-four/seven for the next few months."

"I understand all that, Cullen, it's just, I don't know, I can feel that something's changed."

He stretched out his arm to rub her back reassuringly. "It'll be all right. It'll be over soon, okay? I promise." Abra got up and looked at him. She saw the ream of figures spread across the bed like a runner, the piles of folders, and she felt sorry for him. "Okay," she sighed, and left Cullen alone with his work.

She went into the family room and clicked on the TV. She flicked the movie channels, settling on a ludicrous romantic comedy. After a few minutes Abra realized it was one of those movies that Hollywood executives often mentioned as great, which meant that it was to be emulated. It had grossed $50 million. She tried to focus on the dialogue: *How long are the scenes? What's appealing about the main characters?* Just when she'd successfully distracted herself, she heard Cullen bounding down the stairs.

Cullen stood in the doorway for a moment, watching Abra wrapped in the chenille throw they kept on the sofa in the family room. She was studying the television. He knew his wife was in trouble and that it was his job to help her, but he couldn't. He felt as if he were paralyzed at the shoreline, watching her drown, but unable to jump in and save her. He was in deep waters himself, not quite drowning, but in too deep. His situation was just more pleasant, but equally helpless. He had temporarily given up on what to do about the missing '92 tax statements Farah was going to need. Monday was looming like a root-canal appointment. He'd decided he needed a distraction.

"Babe," he began.

She turned to focus on him.

"I left some papers at the office. I need to go pick them up . . . you all right?"

She looked at him with a mixture of loathing and something quite opposite. Her expression looked slightly crazed, eyes focused and hard, but her mouth was smiling. "It's Sunday, Cullen."

"I'll try to be back for dinner. I'm not getting a whole lot done here. Are you all right?"

"Why do you keep asking me that?"

"Okay, well, I'll see you later." Cullen turned to walk away, but reflexively turned back to peck her on the forehead. "This will be behind us soon, I promise," Cullen said, and rubbed her back.

He got into his car and before the garage door had opened, he was on his car phone, hastily punching in Cynthia's number. He knew Abra was on to him, but he felt himself becoming powerless. He just wanted the fix that was Cynthia. His voice sounded desperate on her machine as he left his car-phone number. Just as he entered midtown, his phone rang. He thanked God when he heard her voice.

"I'm in town, I wanna come over," he said urgently.

"I just got home."

"Can I come over?"

"Now?"

"In about ten minutes."

"Sure," Cynthia said, looking around her studio, which had several small piles of clothes on the floor. Hanging up the phone, she looked at herself in the dressing-room mirror. She unzipped her jeans and hurled them onto one of the clothes piles, pushing all of the mounds into her walk-in closet. She looked through a rack of clothes and pulled out a long cream-colored cotton-knit dress. It had a scoop neckline and cap sleeves. She put on makeup that made her look as though she didn't have any on, and she took off her underwear.

When she opened the door a few minutes later, Cullen was standing there with a bushel of daisies.

"I didn't know what kind of flowers you liked," he said, handing them to her.

"I love them. Come in."

Cullen walked into the tiny apartment and was reminded that Cynthia was in her early twenties. She had a few original pieces by unknown avant-garde artists, hung on the walls; a huge gold chair with wooden legs and armrests. Her sofa was covered with an off-white, seemingly homemade slipcover, and her windows were covered with an iridescent bronze fabric that funked up what was still, to him, a dump.

She laid the flowers on the long coffee table that was painted pistachio green and covered with French fashion magazines, *The Economist,* and poetry softcovers.

"You want something to drink?"

"No. I want nothing except you."

Cullen was sitting on the sofa, and Cynthia walked over to him and straddled herself over his thighs. Her long, skinny arms rested on his shoulders.

"Baby, I missed you so much," Cullen said, and began nibbling her neck.

Cynthia threw her head back, and Cullen moved down her chest, into her cleavage.

"I'm in love with you," Cullen said, between kisses and licks.

"I love you," Cynthia said.

"I have to have you, baby. I can't think, I can't concentrate."

He rubbed his hand up her thigh, going under her dress to find moistness waiting for him. He inhaled, breathing in her lemon-smelling skin, rubbing her head, neck, holding her face as he dug his tongue into her mouth, the hollows of her cheeks. He fondled her vulva, her lips, her clit till she was bucking him and begging him to stop.

"I don't want to yet," Cynthia sighed.

He continued a few more seconds, until she couldn't stand it anymore. He laid her on the sofa. She had gathered her dress up around her crotch. On his knees, on the floor, he turned her so that her back faced him, kissing her neck as he unzipped her dress. Perfect ebony skin, she had. There wasn't a blemish anywhere in sight. He looked at her back, marveling at the spine as he traced it with his finger, winding down to her perfectly African ass. He pulled off her dress. She lay still. He rubbed her feet and kissed the bottoms, he licked her arch. He put his nose between her toes and wiggled it. She laughed and reached down to rub his head. He stood up to undress and squeezed onto the couch in a spoon position with her, his hardness resting on her sculpted behind. He wrapped his arms around her waist and wished he could stay there forever. Cynthia drifted into a light sleep.

"What do you want?" Cullen asked, puncturing the silence.

"Why are you asking me that?"

"Because I want to give you everything."

She thought for a moment before she answered him. She wanted so many things. She wanted her career to blow up. She wanted a cosmetics contract, a restaurant. She wanted to have houses in Tuscany and Paris and Capetown.

"Cullen, you have a wife."

"I'll figure it out. Why don't you come with me to North Carolina next week? Stay in a nice place on the water," he said.

"I'd love that, but how . . ."

"I'll manage it. You don't worry about it."

He squeezed her breasts and moved his hands down to her behind and cupped each cheek. "You ready for me?" he whispered.

"Always," she responded.

They maneuvered on the sofa until she was kneeling,

palms down. They locked slowly, moved rhythmically. He began a humming groan which quickly became a grunting one; when he couldn't stand the pleasure anymore he stifled a yell in his throat, with his jaw clenched. He raised one arm and made a fist in the air; the other arm was sealed around her waist. After their summit, she collapsed onto the sofa; he rolled off onto the floor. They were both covered with sweat. He lay on his back, looking up at her as she rested on her stomach and faced him, tracing his wet forehead with her finger.

"You're incredible," she sighed.

"You're the one," he said.

"I'm hungry," Cullen said, putting her finger in his mouth.

"You want to order Vietnamese?"

"No. Let's go out to dinner."

Cynthia was surprised at his suggestion, but figured he was responsible for his situation. So, she named a few places, and they settled on a pretentiously unpretentious bistro that was tucked away in her Chelsea neighborhood. They walked in, holding hands, and were seated at a corner table reserved for lovers. They ordered a Bordeaux and between sips, fingered each other's hands.

After entrées and dessert, Cynthia looked down at the tiny marcasite watch she wore.

"Ooo, what time is it?" he said.

"Eight-thirty."

"I should make a phone call. Be right back."

Cullen went downstairs to the bistro's pay phone near the rest rooms; he dreaded talking to Abra. She would've called the office, and he knew his excuses had become lame. To his surprise, the service answered. He was concerned, but more relieved. He'd deal with it later.

Back at the top of the stairs, before joining her at the table, he watched Cynthia sip her espresso, the tiny cup seeming just right for her slim fingers. She was dressed in jeans, black suede boots, and a silver silk shirt. He knew every man in the place wanted her as badly as he. She sipped, and looked like an angel. When he first decided he had to have her, he told himself it was just about sex. They were hot for each other, and they would just fuck through it. Just fuck until they were sick of each other and then he'd return to his nice, neat life. But now, looking at her, he thought about what Jimmy had said. He knew he wanted to spend the rest of his life looking at her and everything before Cynthia seemed like a protracted lie: His safe life, his perfect house in the ideal suburb, his appropriate M.B.A. wife. He'd just bought the whole fake package. He'd done it all wrong. Somehow he hadn't been paying attention to the texture of his life, to what was really important. Cynthia was what he'd always wanted. She was the one.

chapter 14

THE HUGE LOFT was packed with types—Hollywood types, Wall Street types, model wannabe-actress types. White-jacketed White boys hoisting silver trays covered with flutes of champagne made their way through the throng. Natasha casually searched the room for Miles. Although the place was packed and integrated by Manhattan standards— thirty Whites for every one Black—it wouldn't be difficult to spot a bean in this sea of vanilla. No sooner did she lift a flute from a serving tray than she felt warm breath on her neck.

"So glad you could make it, Miz Coleman."

She felt a big, goofy smile cross her face. She lessened it some before turning around.

"Hey Miles," she said, trying to sound casual.

He reached for her hand and pulled her toward him, kissing her cheek. "You look great. How are you?" he said.

"Back at you," Natasha said, eyeing his subtle check suit, French-blue shirt, and orange- and blue-striped tie. "I'm fine."

"I know you fine, baby. You don't think this tie is too loud?" Miles said in a moment of fake insecurity.

"It's great. You look fabulous."

They stood making small talk a few minutes before Miles took her by the hand and headed toward the back of the room. They reached a walnut-paneled door and Miles knocked. Another white-jacketed White boy answered, nodded at Miles, and let them in. Inside was a living room with Persian rugs, weathered leather armchairs, and Moroccan tapestry sofas. A Monk classic tinkled quietly in the background. A full buffet was set up as was a bar. Guys and women smoked fat Cubans and couples and triples clustered off, seriously locked in conversation. Most of the women were dressed in black and wore deceptively simple, expensive jewelry and hairstyles. The guys wore sport jackets with jeans, or European-cut suits.

"My man Miles," a sandy-haired Griffin Smith said as he made his way toward Miles and Natasha.

Miles turned toward him. Natasha recognized Smith from a magazine article. He was a veteran Hollywood player, who was now a studio head, known as a champion of the small film.

Miles shook his hand and introduced Natasha, who shook his hand, and for a moment, couldn't think of one thing, intelligent or otherwise, to say.

"So Natasha, Miles tells me you're in the business," he said.

"Um, yeah."

"And you wrote that sitcom," he said, snapping his fingers for the name.

"Yes, *On the Verge*," she said, slowly feeling herself return.

"Yeah, yeah. It was good, very good."

"Thanks, I appreciate that."

"So, what are you up to now?" He seemed to genuinely want to know. Miles stood by nodding, encouraging Natasha to speak up.

"Um, we just got a syndication deal, and we've got a hot script circulating."

"How hot?"

"We've got Mona Love committed. A Sundance writer wrote it."

"That does sound hot. You haven't placed it?"

"No, lots of interest but no one has given us anything firm."

"Why don't you send it over, let me have a look at it? Thursday?"

"Uh, sure. Thursday, it is."

"Cool. Listen, nice meeting you. Miles, gimme a call tomorrow?" Griffin said, shaking Miles' hand before backing away.

"Sure thing," Miles said, his diction tight. Miles looked around the room and quickly surmised that they'd just talked with the most important person in it.

"Let's blow this stand," Miles said.

Natasha's head was spinning as she replayed the conversation in her mind.

"You hungry?" he asked.

"A little."

He grabbed her hand and headed back through the crowd, greeting every third or fourth person they passed. The handful of Black folks in the room greeted him as if he were Michael Jordan. They shook his hand, tapped him on the back, or just stood back and whispered. Some of the

White folks called him by name, but most of them just nodded or stared, thinking he must be someone they should know. Miles prided himself on seeming oblivious to the attention. Outside, he and Natasha got into a dark sedan, which had been waiting. "Company car," he said to her as they were driven to the restaurant. Miles said nothing to the driver, who just knew to drive to Canastel's. She figured it to be one of Miles' spots.

Other than the dark wood trim around the doors and at the base of the windows, the restaurant was encircled with glass. Heavy in weight, but light in appearance, drapes gently accented the windows, and pillars lined the way into the dining area. The place had the air of a private club. There were no commercial traces visible. No cash register, no signs telling people which kinds of credit cards were accepted. There wasn't even a pay phone. If you needed to use a phone, a portable one was brought to you. They assumed if you were there, you had good upbringing not to make long-distance calls on their dime. It was the kind of place where only the host—regardless of gender—had the menu with the prices. The owner greeted Miles like an old friend and treated Natasha as if she were one of the delicacies in which the restaurant specialized.

"I hope you like it," Miles said, once they were seated.

"It's fabulous. Thank you."

"I wanted to do something special . . . for you."

"Miles, you've already done that. I mean, introducing me to Griffin Smith like that."

"Oh, well, I hope something comes of it. You can give me an associate-producer credit or something."

"Well, we're running out of contacts, that's for sure, and I'm getting sick of the big blow-off."

"If he's interested, he can certainly make it happen."

After dinner, the dark sedan took them to Miles' apartment.

"Welcome to my 'umble abode," Miles said. Natasha walked in and was drawn to the window that opened out onto a sparkling view of the East River; to the high molded ceilings, the pillars, the marble floors. Natasha deemed it exquisite.

"You like it, baby," he said more as a comment than a question. "Take your shoes off, relax."

"Can I look around?" Natasha asked, already in motion.

"Of course. I'll give you the two-cent tour," he said, while draping his jacket over the sofa. "Let's see, where should we start?" He walked toward the kitchen, which was reached through a gallery hall, but set off on its own. It was a full kitchen, complete with a large marble-top island and a seating area big enough for six. Off the kitchen was a small bedroom that was empty except for a twin-size bed.

"They call that the maid's quarters," Miles said sardonically. "I figure I'll leave it empty, in honor of the ancestors." Natasha laughed but wasn't sure he was making a joke.

They walked through the dining room, which had an intense Persian Serapi on the floor and a funky blown-glass chandelier, that led to a hall off which three bedrooms sprouted. One of two spare bedrooms had an iron canopy bed, a pine chest at the foot, where he set her duffel bag, a dresser, a nightstand, and a radio alarm/CD player. Miles' room had a king-size sleigh bed made of cherry wood, with an armoire, dresser, chest of drawers to match, and a treadmill set in front of a large-screen television. The linens were forest green, as were the towels in his master bath. The only furniture in the living room was his green velvet sofa, a cognac-colored leather armchair and ottoman, and a coffee table; a compact stereo set anchored a corner of the rug. Natasha didn't resist showing Miles how impressed she was.

"So, you want anything? Wine? Soda?"

"Um, a little tea would be nice."

"Tea, it is," Miles said, leaving her standing in his bedroom, the last of the tour. Natasha stood there alone for a moment, examining the Elizabeth Catlett sculpture that sat on a nightstand, before deciding to go into the living room. She went to the stack of CDs—Awadagin Pratt, James Brown, Wynton Marsalis, and Aretha—stashed in a corner. He came back from the kitchen in his stocking feet, carrying a tray that held a glass of wine, a mug, an assortment of teas, grapes, cookies, and a bowl of barbecue potato chips.

He was already crunching on a chip. He held out the bowl. "You want some? I love these things."

"Me too."

They both laughed as they stuffed chips into their mouths.

"What kinna music you like?" he asked.

"Oh all kinds. Um, Kenny Lattimore, Erykah Badu . . ."

"The new R and B with a jazzy tinge," Miles said in a mock DJ voice.

"Whatever. I see you like a wide range."

"Yup, that pretty much sums me up . . . likes a wide range," he said, and took a gulp of wine. "A toast," Miles announced, holding up his glass. "To Natasha, the next great Hollywood mogul."

He clinked his Baccarat gingerly against her mug. Natasha was flattered by the toast and looked him in the eye, saying, "Hear, hear."

Miles grabbed a bunch of grapes, putting one into Natasha's mouth and then one in his. "You know I think you're fly as hell," Miles said, while popping more grapes into his mouth.

Natasha looked at his face, and for just a moment, he looked like a little boy. He reached over and put his hand on the side of her face and lightly rubbed it. "You've got beautiful skin," he said, and kissed her, first on the cheek and then on the mouth. Their tongues danced a nice waltz before breaking into a frenzied tango. He leaned toward her, she leaned back into the sofa. He reached for her breast and she pushed his hand down to around her diaphragm. He moved it away and stopped kissing her.

"You don't have to worry. I ain't gonna try for the panties . . . not tonight."

Natasha didn't know how to respond to his bluntness, but she suddenly felt foolish as though she'd overreacted to his overture.

"You did notice that I put your bag in the guest room?" he said.

"Yeah, I did."

"I really like you, Natasha, but I'd prefer to wait awhile for that."

"Really?" she said, eyebrows raised to let him know she doubted what he was saying.

"Honest," he said, holding up his right hand. "I ain't got to be fightin' for no panties, baby."

Natasha laughed. "I'm sure they're throwing them at you, Miles."

He laughed out loud, showing his slightly gapped front teeth. "Well, I 'on't know 'bout throwin' 'em."

Miles' cockiness unnerved Natasha. On the one hand,

she was turned on by someone so clearly confident, on the other, she was put off. They listened to Aretha while Natasha finished her tea. "I'm beat, I'm going to go to bed," she said.

Miles sat for a minute, reviewing his strategy. "Yeah, that's a good idea, tomorrow is a school day."

"I've got to be on that eight o'clock flight back."

"I wish you could stay another day."

"Me too, but I really gotta get back."

"Okay, I'll call a car to take you to the airport."

"That would be great, you're a sweetheart," Natasha said, and kissed him lightly on the lips.

"You need anything? Toothbrush? Towels are on the shelf in the bathroom. If you get cold, there's another comforter in that chest at the foot of the bed."

Natasha got up and so did Miles. They stood facing each other. Miles kissed her forehead. "Night, baby." He walked off, leaving her standing there expecting more.

Natasha had snuggled under the cream-colored flannel sheets and down comforter and happily drifted off. She was in deep drool slumber when she heard a loud tap on the door. She felt like she'd just gone to sleep. Miles opened the door, fully power-suited in his work gear. It was still dark out.

"What time is it?" Natasha whispered.

"It's almost six, the car will be here in a half hour." Miles looked too good, his super-starched white shirt setting off his midnight blue pinstripe.

"I'm gonna be in L.A. next week. I'll call you. Maybe we can have dinner or something."

"Sure, sure," Natasha said, rubbing her eyes, trying to wake up, hoping she didn't have too much crud around her mouth and eyes.

"Do you always go to work so early?" she asked.

"Yup. I like to be there for some of the foreign trading. Plus, you know what they say about the early bird."

"Yeah," Natasha sighed and yawned, "but who wants a damn worm?"

Miles chuckled, and told her it was great seeing her again. He walked to the side of the bed and kissed the top of Natasha's head. Natasha heard the door close and sat up in bed. What just happened? she thought. Was it a good sign that they didn't screw, or was it that he wasn't turned on enough to really go for it? Shit, she thought, this dating stuff is a pain in the butt.

She got up to check herself in the mirror to see what he'd seen. Yes, there was some dried saliva around her mouth, but it wasn't too bad. Something as mundane as dried saliva probably went unnoticed by him. Miles was unlike anyone Natasha had ever met. She dialed Abra, but there was no answer. She went into the kitchen, hoping to find some high-test tea. He'd left a mug out for her, and there was some coffee left in the carafe. A stainless steel kettle sat on the stove, and she filled it with water and put it back on the burner. She went through his cabinets and found some Earl Grey, put a tea bag in her cup, and went off to take a quick shower.

chapter 15

WINTER WAS GENTEEL in North Carolina. The air was
heavier, warmer. The sky, brighter. On the coast, people wore
jackets and sweatsuits as they walked along to the beach.
Cynthia had overpacked. She wasn't sure what the place
would be like and wanted to be prepared. Cullen was just
the opposite. The business suit he'd worn, plus one pair of
khakis, a blue blazer, a cotton dress shirt, and a cotton polo
shirt was it. They checked into a turn-of-century white Victo-
rian hotel that faced the Atlantic. Their room had an enormous marble bathroom with an armchair and Jacuzzi tub, a
chintz-covered king-size bed, and a small wooden terrace
where two wicker rockers sat facing the water.

"This is perfect," Cynthia said after she'd looked
around.

"Only the best for you," Cullen said as he dialed his
office number. He'd have to work through their rendezvous,
but it would be better than nothing. He thought about Abra,
knowing that he should call her, tell her where she could
reach him, but knowing right now he wouldn't. He wanted

to get too busy to feel guilty, but guilt was always rumbling around his insides. He'd have to meet with Farah.

"You know I have to go out for a while?" Cullen said, after hanging up the phone.

"Sure. It's fine."

"You gonna be all right?"

Cynthia got up and walked over to where Cullen was standing as he packed papers into his briefcase. She slipped her arms under his and hugged his back. "I'll be fine. I'll lounge around until you come back."

Cullen turned around. He looked into her face and couldn't believe that he was with this perfectly chiseled creature and that she would be spending the day just waiting for him to come back. They would have two days and two nights together. He'd actually be able to hold her all night, have breakfast with her. Two whole days of not having to leave her, of listening to her read him poetry, of having the most incredible sex ever. How could this be bad?

Before Cynthia went into the bathroom to run a tub of water, Cullen kissed her deeply. He felt a rise, and Cynthia tried to get him to stay, but he resisted.

"I really have to get to this meeting."

"Oh, just a quick one."

"Can't, baby," Cullen said, unwrapping her hands from the nape of his neck. Cynthia pretended to pout and Cullen tapped her on the butt. "I'll be back in a few hours, I promise."

With that, he left, rise and all. He deserved this, he said to himself all the time. Rules, like fidelity, didn't apply to people like him. He lorded over his own world and destiny. Rules were for lesser minds, for people who needed structure, people who couldn't figure things out for themselves. People like him deserved everything they wanted and could have. If you could figure out how to eat the cake and have it, then do.

The drive to his meeting helped Cullen temporarily clear his head of Cynthia and focus on the purpose of this trip. He arrived at the meeting held at Farah's lawyer's office and found an array of middle-aged White male accountants and attorneys chatting amiably around the boardroom table. The talk stopped when he walked in. They all knew one another, went to church, belonged to the same country clubs, did business together. Not only was he an outsider, a Yankee, he was a decade younger *and* Black. He read what their eyes said, a boy in a Brooks Brothers suit, but he'd had years, a lifetime's worth of training that had taught him how to deal with being underestimated and outnumbered. Not only did he know about them, as much as they didn't about him, he knew about himself, his history, his family's history. About ancestors who'd literally slaved this soil for nothing resembling pay for more hours than any of them would've been able to withstand. Who's the outsider? Who's the boy? The dismissive glare hardly fazed him anymore. It was the reality of being Black in a White land. Farah watched Cullen as he went around the table, introducing himself, looking them in the eye, shaking their hands, slapping some backs, talking to them, using their colloquialisms as if he had been using them his entire life. It was what he always did in these situations, what all cultural schizophrenics do, he became the safe Negro. It was exhausting, but it worked every time.

The meeting went on for hours. "Well, see, last year our numbers weren't as good as the year before," her accountant began, "but you see, some of that was on account of the storm. You know, that one we had last year was bad, but the

one three years ago, now that was a storm. Folks said they
ain't never seen nothing like that, before or since. Just a
shame what happened to folks' property. Some folks still
ain't recovered . . ."

"Um, sir, I'd like to hear about the storm, but our time
is short here today," Cullen said. On more than one occasion,
he'd had to remind someone to stay on track and was met
with a look from Farah and a "sorry" from whoever it was
doing the talking.

Cullen looked at his watch every quarter hour. Finally,
after hours of too many stories, he let his mind drift to Cynthia, waiting, moist, bathed, and creamed in fragrant herbs.
He wrapped things up. Farah took off her glasses and looked
at him with her eyebrows raised.

"We've covered a lot of ground today and . . . ," he said.

"I don't think we're ready to end the meeting just yet,"
Farah said.

"I have all I need right now," Cullen said, not meeting
her stare.

"Well, when will we meet again? We didn't even look at
1990."

"I will go over it myself and get back to you tomorrow.
I'm here for two days, remember?"

"Okay, but don't you think we should talk again?
Maybe have a dinner meeting tonight?" Cullen heard Farah
and knew he probably should make the time to meet with
her again, but his carnal mind was winning out over his good
sense. "I'll call you later," he said, breaking into his killer
charm smile.

When he got back to the room, Cynthia wasn't there.
For a moment he felt panicked. He looked for a note,
checked the bathroom, looked in the closet to make sure her

clothes were there. He went to the terrace door and looked out and saw her in her canvas hat, a thick white sweater, and white jeans. She was facing the ocean and holding a book up to her face. He picked up the phone to call Abra, who'd already left for the day. He called her in the car.

"Hi," he said, trying to sound normal.

"Hey," she said, sounding down.

"Why'd you leave work so early?"

"Doctor's appointment, the usual. How's North Carolina?"

"The same. Weather's nice, people talk too damn much. Abra, are you okay?"

"Fine. Things at work couldn't be better. Natasha sent our script over to the head of Dreamtime Pictures. He called her after he read the first fifty pages and said it looked great, so we may be in play."

"That's great. Tasha's probably already celebrating."

"Probably."

"I miss you, babe."

Abra closed her eyes for a second, stuck in traffic, wanting to believe what he'd just said. "I miss you too."

"I have to go, but I'll see you in a couple of days. Chin up, things are going to be fine." With that, they disconnected, and Cullen slipped off his suit, put on his khakis, and headed outside to Cynthia.

"Boo," he said as he sneaked up on her.

"You scared me." Cynthia laughed, even though she didn't seem startled.

Cullen sat down on the sand next to her and put an arm around her shoulders. He ran his hand into the sand, each time scooping a handful, then letting the granules fall.

"So, you wanna go upstairs?"

"Sure."

He put his face to hers and kissed her deeply. "Let's go," he whispered.

After sex, she slept while he sat propped up in bed and read through focus-group reports. He looked down at her back. He looked down at their skins touching. It was hard to see where hers ended and his began. Their complexions were that close; they practically matched, which was close to impossible, given the enormous range of tones among Black people. He considered that some sign that they were each other's destiny, from the same ancient tribe. He imagined that if they'd been born centuries ago in Africa, that even then they would've been together—an arranged marriage that would have worked because they were two matched souls.

EVERY MONTH Abra had to go to her OB-GYN. Her urine was taken and tested, as was her blood. Her Perganol was monitored and she had a vaginal exam. It was something she'd learned to just roll with. There were no big barriers to her getting pregnant. Her doctor was frankly stumped at why she hadn't become pregnant in the years she and Cullen had been trying. After this routine visit, however, she got a call back. They called only if there was something wrong with one of her tests. She was sitting at her desk, having just gotten off the phone with Natasha, who, although she had no firm deal, was already talking about the contract with Dreamtime Pictures.

The nurse sounded the same, but she told Abra to hold a second for the doctor. Abra's heart sank; she was terrified at what they'd found and was already imagining the worst when the doctor got on the line.

"It's nothing terrible." Her doctor's voice came through the phone.

"Well, that's a relief. So?"

"Um, you have chlamydia. It's a . . ."

Chlamydia? Abra played the word around her head a few times. It swirled like words from a bad pop song.

"I know what it is. I mean, I know it's something transmitted through sex, right?"

"Um yeah. It's easily treatable; I'm writing you a prescription for tetracycline. You're lucky we caught it so soon."

Abra was silent. She heard the words, *lucky* and *soon,* but they didn't register. She sat at her desk and looked down at her thighs lumped together, looking like one mass on her seat. She looked at the framed mirror that sat on her desk and old and tired and fat and ugly stared back at her. All she could do was thank the doctor and write out *tetracycline.*

Untreated chlamydia could cause sterility; she remembered reading that during the early phase of her infertility. Abra tried to figure out how she could have possibly contracted it. She couldn't let herself believe that Cullen had given it to her, even though she knew that the only way it was transmitted was sex. She felt ashamed.

From the day they married, she'd constantly pushed away the feeling that one day Cullen would kick her guts out, that he would leave her, disappoint her, just as her father had. She always knew that she would pay for her Labrador-like compliance, the deep belief that he was more than she, that she merely provided the blank background for his sparkle, piquancy, vigor. All the things that she wasn't. The mundane would never make Cullen happy, at least not for long. She knew he could justify her, the safe route, for a little while, but eventually he'd grow bored and have to find bigger mountains to climb. That's who he was, who he is. It was why she loved him and why she knew that one day, he'd find someone who was more like himself and that one day, he'd leave her.

No. *There had to be another way. Or a mistake. How many times had they tested it? Must have been someone else's urine. Cullen would never do this, not to me. Cullen was kind. He loved me. He'd pursued me. Who would he have time for? He really didn't have the time. Poor thing was exhausted from working fifteen-, sixteen-hour days; starting the day in New York, flying to Chicago, and ending the day in North Carolina.*

Cullen had sought Abra, had told her she was everything he had ever wanted. He needed a wife who had the right air and Abra was that. Of course the air that appeared around her wasn't really how she felt about herself, but that didn't matter to Cullen, at least not in their courtship phase. Her lack of sparkle was also a plus for him; he didn't want anyone to outshine him. It was only later, when they were married, that he began to see all the cracks in Abra's psyche, to feel the choke hold around his neck. He began paying the price for her father, the father who didn't marry her mother; for the mother who lost herself to sorrow and couldn't mother; for Abra's scars that had been ignored and never healed.

Abra got her coat, gloves, and sunglasses. She left the office while Sandy, her assistant, was on the phone. She wouldn't have to tell her where she was going or talk to her. She just wanted out of the office. She walked to Columbus, deciding to get the prescription filled at a different pharmacy, one where she wasn't known. She got the antibiotics, a bottle of water, and some Fig Newtons. She needed lunch. She needed to see her husband. She needed to process. She walked to Riverside Park, sat down on a bench that, at night, became someone's bed. She took a swig of water, then opened the cookies, shoving one in, then quickly a second. Chewing the mushy mound she pulled the pills out of her coat pocket and looked at them. Three a day, for fourteen days. She took one out, finished chewing, and swallowed some water and a pill. She wanted anger to come, but she felt nothing. She just zoned out, watching the river.

chapter 16

CONFIRMATION OF WHAT SHE KNEW all along. As much as she had wanted proof, she also knew she didn't want to know that her husband was fucking around. Abra sat on the flowered-chintz chaise and stared out of her bedroom window. The phone rang, and she wouldn't answer. She didn't have the energy to face anybody. She couldn't talk to Cullen. She didn't want to talk to Natasha. She sat at the window for hours, not getting up even to go to the bathroom. She wanted to feel frozen, as if somehow, if she remained still, she could keep her emotions immobile as well.

By the time late afternoon came, she was still in her pajamas, still hadn't brushed her teeth or returned any of Natasha's calls. At dusk, she'd managed to move to the bed where she drifted in and out of dreams. In one, she was walking through a jungle thick with leaves and branches that attempted to block her path, and she fought through— elbows out, arms getting scratched and cut, her blood creating rivers around her as she moved. In another, she saw her mother and father having sex on the sofa, both drunk with passion, sweating, and watching her as a little girl watch them. They were laughing at her. Abra woke up and tried to remember if that had ever really happened. If she'd ever seen her parents having sex. She closed her eyes and began to sob. It was the first time she'd cried since she found out about the chlamydia. First they were silent, deep sobs, then she began to groan and got louder and louder until she was screaming and thrashing and looking around the bedroom for something to break.

A silver-framed picture of Cullen and her on their honeymoon in France, propped on his nightstand, was the first thing she spotted. She hurled it across the room where it shattered and nicked the television screen. She got up on the bed and grabbed a lamp and threw that against the wall, creating a huge gaping hole in the plaster. She got down off the bed and went into Cullen's office. His degrees and awards were framed and in a box. She took them out, one by one, and jumped on them until they were smashed sparkles in the carpet. She opened the drawers, saw his perfectly filed folders and took them out, handfuls at a time, and emptied them onto the floor. She grabbed a brass desk lamp and banged on his computer terminal and keyboard until it was a pile of plastic and glass.

Looking like a primate in search of food, breathing hard puffs through her nose, she went searching for something that meant something to him. A devious smile crossed her face when she remembered his beloved collection. He'd accumulated two thousand bottles in his wine cellar. She threw open the door, raced downstairs into the basement, entering the perfectly climate-controlled 55 degrees–70 percent humidity of the vault crammed with shelves of burgundies, Bordeaux, chardonnays, champagnes, cabernet sauvignons,

Graves, ports. She grabbed a couple of bottles and flung them to the Spanish-tile floor. Heady, fragrant grape immediately filled her nostrils. She stopped for a moment, thinking about which were his most prized bottles. She didn't want to waste energy breaking the unimportant, easily replaceable ones. Which ones, which ones, she thought, commanding her memory to kick in. Yes.

She climbed up the stepladder. She wanted to hurt his ass. She recalled the Australian phase and quickly trashed several $200 bottles of Penfold Grange. Then, like a gift, she remembered the most coveted in his collection, a Domaine de la Romanée-Conti, a $650 burgundy that they'd picked up in Provence. She cradled the precious bottle, remembering their honeymoon, how happy he was to find this vintage, and how thrilled she was just to be with him. As her tears dropped onto the label she softened at the memory of them, as a young couple. So excited to be in love and in Europe for the first time. The sense of freedom and fear all mixed together, creating a new feeling that they wanted to hold on to forever. Sure they would always be this happy. Then she remembered his betrayal. She threw the bottle to the floor with the force of a major-league pitcher. As she watched the glass, liquid, and paper slowly meld together on the cellar floor, Abra began to feel a smile cross her lips, then a laugh. First it was a small chuckle, then a giggle, then a wave of uncontrollable gut tickles so strong that she had to sit down on the stepladder to keep from falling.

Abra's outburst had been a release valve. Laughing in the face of what she had been dealt scared her, made her feel as if she might be losing touch, losing her mind. She threw some

T-shirts and a pair of jeans into a nylon overnight bag. Got herself dressed and in the truck.

Odessa still lived in the two-bedroom, two-bath apartment in a complex of high-rises that had been a part of Lyndon Johnson's Great Society. When Abra was a baby, and it had become clear to Odessa that her life would be lived without Rayford, she looked around for the best place for her money and her child. Myrna and Sylvia had become New Jersey suburbanites and were close enough to help out with Abra in an emergency. Back when she and Abra moved in, the apartments were luxury cooperatives in Newark, right on the bus line into Manhattan. The units were built to sell as cooperative housing, creating a class of owners, instead of just tenants, who would take care of what they owned. While it looked like early public housing in terms of brick and size, there were no graffiti or fetid smells that later overran the projects. To many it was a haven, but once Abra was in high school, the place began its descent and now it was surrounded by overgrown weeds and covered in spray-painted names like Shakim and Boo and LaQwanda.

As Abra drove the luxury truck around the neighborhood, she realized that she didn't care if it was stolen or vandalized. She parked near a bus stop, didn't put on the Club, and grabbed her bag. Crossing the wide street, the used-to-be maple-lined boulevard, she realized that while her house was less than an hour away, it might as well be in Utah. All the residential property in Brookville was zoned for a minimum of two acres. Odessa's entire complex was crammed onto less. During the day the courtyard was filled with adolescent mothers pushing expensive carriages. Occasionally gunshots would keep Odessa awake. In Brookville the only sounds to prevent sleep were the sometimes unbearable nothingness, punctuated by the sporadic noises of animals foraging for food. Abra's stomach knotted as she waited for the elevator and thought about the many arguments she'd had with Odessa about moving her out. Her mother simply refused. This is my home, she'd say, marking the end of the discussion. Abra had traveled so far between worlds, a different person would have been paralyzed by the whiplash. Right now she was grateful she had someplace to go, and this place, with all its vicissitudes, would always be the place where she felt safe.

The apartment was empty when she entered and for a moment her reflex was to look for a snack and bolt the door. She remembered that it was Friday, and that was the day her mother got her hair done. She went into her old bedroom and sat on the twin-size bed that she'd slept in throughout her youth. Her mom had changed the daisy-print spread for a more contemporary blue horizontal-print bed-in-a-bag number. Her posters—a faded picture of a scorpion and one of the Jackson 5 and their *ABC* album—were still on the pale-blue walls held by aged, topaz-colored, tape. There was a Princeton flag hung over her headboard. A picture with her freshman housemates featuring Abra's lone, sad, brown face sat atop the chest of drawers. The same multicolored rug covered the middle of the floor, and even her component set hadn't been moved. She sat down on the rug and leafed through her albums stacked in a red plastic crate. There was Marvin Gaye in the rain, Chaka Khan in a rabbit-fur bra, and Michael Henderson dressed in a white suit, standing in front of a Rolls Royce. She had kept her ABBA, Carpenters, and Bee Gees in a separate pile so that she could easily hide them whenever a few of her neighborhood friends came over.

The smell of bergamot mixed with pressing comb snaked into Abra's nose. "Hi, Ma!" she yelled from the back to keep from scaring her mother into a heart attack.

"Arabella? That you, baby?"

"Yeah."

"What you doin' here?" Odessa said, removing her coat and going into Abra's old room. She found her daughter sitting on the floor, legs crossed, with albums spread out around her. "Baby, is everything all right?" Odessa asked, sitting down on the bed.

"I'm okay, I just came to stay for a while . . ."

"Stay? With me? What? Where's Cullen? You scared to stay in that house by yourself?"

"No . . ."

"So, what're you doin' here?"

"Oh, Ma," Abra leaned against her mother's knees and began to cry.

Odessa patted her daughter's hair. "Just get it out, just let it go," she said.

"Cullen's seeing someone . . . he gave me chlamydia . . ."

"What? Chlamydia? What the hell is that?" Odessa asked, now holding her daughter by the shoulders.

"It's a sexual disease . . . he got it from screwing somebody."

"Lawd ha' mercy. What the hell . . . baby, you sure?"

"I'm sure. The doctor had the lab rerun the test."

"My Lawd . . . are you all right?"

"Yes, I'm taking antibiotics."

Odessa, who was usually quick with the tongue, was stunned into silence. Her baby, was all she could think about; how she hurt for her child, knowing intimately the pain Abra was feeling. Nothing was like the hurt that a man whom you truly loved could put on you. She wanted to pick Abra up the way she used to whenever Abra tripped in her street skates; to kiss the pain of the boo-boo away, make it all better. But her girl was a woman now, and there was nothing she could do to ease her pain. Knowing that caused Odessa's heart to ache.

Abra was sobbing loudly now, pleading with her mother to make this thing make sense.

"Oh, baby, I know, I know," Odessa said, tears now streaming down her face, holding Abra's head tight to her chest.

"How could he do this to me, Mommy? Why?"

"Baby, I don't know, but the Lawd does. All things happen for a reason . . ."

Abra let out a noise that sounded so rough and raw, as if she were being tortured. She pushed away from her mother and began rocking herself with her arms wrapped around her knees. "Ma, I don't know what to do. How am I going to go on without Cullen? He was my whole life."

Odessa felt a flash of anger run through her. While she felt her daughter's pain, years of struggling to raise her daughter right had created a steeliness in her. *I'll be damn. How could you think he's your life after all that you have, all I've sacrificed to give you? An education, good skills, manners, you could do anything you want to do. The hell with some man! How have I missed teachin' my girl to be independent and strong? How did she get to be such a mess, so damn crippled? You stay or you leave, but you don't let him crush you like I let Rayford do me.*

"Baby," Odessa said, carefully measuring her tone, "Cullen is just a man. He don't walk on water or turn it into wine."

Abra looked at her mother and tilted her head to one side, like a German shepherd.

"Every man is gonna slip and fall. You just settle yourself down some, I'm gonna get you some tea." Odessa pulled Abra up from the floor and put her on the bed. She arranged the stiff polyester comforter over her.

In the kitchen, she searched her cabinet for some peppermint tea as she tried to find an answer to where she went wrong in raising her child. *Didn't she see me make a way for her? Didn't she listen when I lectured her on the importance of an education?* "Nobody can take it from you, once you have it," *I would say over and over to her.* "Always stand on your own two feet." What she hadn't figured, though, was what her daughter *didn't* have. It was so simple that it escaped Odessa. Not having had a father every day was a hole in Abra that never healed, and it pushed her to Cullen, made her create an illusion of Cullen instead of realizing who he actually was. In Abra's mind he *could* turn water to wine, if he'd wanted. Sure, she went to good schools, got good grades, got a graduate degree, but that had nothing to do with filling up her hole. Cullen became her entire life, her reason for living. It was something Odessa would never be able to understand. She'd had her daddy and that daddy loved her, something she was incapable of passing on to her fatherless child.

After she drank her tea, Abra took a nap. Odessa sat in her kitchen, staring out of the window that faced a courtyard, and retraced her mothering steps. Maybe the fact that she and Rayford never married had scared Abra. Maybe the way she was absorbed with her own blues had harmed Abra. Who knew what kind of message she was sending to her child, being with a man, sleeping with him without being married to him? In her mind, Odessa figured she'd just raise Abra to be an independent, free-thinking woman, who wouldn't need a man. Odessa picked up the cigarette that had burned almost to the tip and drew a long drag. She blew out curly smoke and rubbed her face, now puffy with age. She looked around her kitchen at the faded orange-and-yellow floral wallpaper and thought about how different Abra's life was from hers. She wanted her daughter to be happy, but how was that achieved? People in Odessa's generation didn't put a lot of stock in happiness—what was that anyway? Her outlook was different, she knew, from Abra's. Odessa believed that you got up every day, thanked the Lord for waking you up, and put one foot in front of the other. She had let go of her great expectations of life. Maybe that was her mistake.

chapter 17

CULLEN READ the same line in the accountant's report three times before he realized he wasn't concentrating. He felt warm and asked the flight attendant for water. He would take a taxi right to Sherry and David's, even though he was in no mood for a party. He had too much work, but he knew Abra would be there waiting for him. He glanced at his watch.

Cullen was one for careful decisions. He thought that he'd done the calculations, all the math, before marrying Abra, and he had. The one thing he hadn't factored, however, was the variable—that piece that couples who have the real thing own. He didn't know about that thing, couldn't think about it before he met Cynthia. How little he knew made him cringe. The affair had simply highlighted to him how unfulfilled he'd been with Abra. He could continue doing it, keep his marriage intact; plenty of people survived that way, but mere survival wasn't good enough for him. Having Cynthia once a week wasn't going to be enough. The more he had, the more he had to have. He knew what he was going to have to do, but the thought of telling Abra, the woman who loved him as much as his own mother did, caused agony. The very thought of it made him feel hollow, like his insides might have cannibalized themselves. He knew that if he left her, she would be destroyed, and it would be his fault. How could he live with that? He was her world and everybody knew it. But, if he stayed, he would destroy himself. It wouldn't be fair to either of them.

When he arrived at the party, the usual crew was there. Bert and Lisa, new parents, now too tired to fight with each other, were showing pictures to Ray and Hanna, who'd just come back from Nevis, tanned and blissful. Sherry and David sat with Abra, who looked as if she'd started drinking before she had left home. She'd put on too much eye makeup, her dirty hair was slicked back into a bun, her blue silk pants were wrinkled, her black suede pumps were scuffed. Everyone noticed, but no one said anything about her appearance. She greeted Cullen with a chill that everyone felt, barely looking at him with her wan eyes. Cullen sat next to his wife and tried to talk to her.

He whispered, fearing her answer, "Everything okay?"

"Okay? Okay, Cullen?" She raised her voice. "Course, dear," she said even louder. "Everything is okay. Why wouldn't everything be fucking okay?"

"Abra, why don't you give me that?" he said softly, reaching for her goblet.

She jerked her glass from his reach, red wine bleeding onto her pants. "Fuck!" she yelled, standing up. Now everyone was fully tuned in, watching unabashedly what was clearly a woman coming apart.

"Abra, lower your voice," Cullen demanded.

Sherry brought a towel and rubbed Abra's shoulder.

"Why don't you come into the bedroom? You can—" she said.

"No, Sherry, I do not want to go and gather myself," she said, again loudly. "I'm rather enjoying falling apart in front of all my dear friends, and especially my wonderful faithless husband, you muthafucka."

Cullen looked down, dying of embarrassment.

"Abra," he said, sounding in control, "let's get your coat."

"Fuck you, Cullen. I'm not going anywhere with you!"

Cullen sat, closed his eyes, and tried to think of what to do next.

Abra looked at Cullen for the first time. "I trusted you and I loved you and you repay me by fucking around. I thought you were better than that, Cullen." He looked at her and saw her tired, black-rimmed eyes were filled with hate.

"I hope you and your disease-filled whore find happiness, you piece of shit."

At this point, folks began gathering coats and purses and hurriedly saying good night.

"You don't have to break up your party, I'm leaving," Abra said, and grabbed her coat from the mirrored rack and ran out of the door.

Cullen sat looking like he'd seen a revenant. Sherry went after Abra.

At the elevator, Abra stood shivering, her black cashmere coat hanging off her shoulders, face stained with mascara and smeared lipstick. Sherry grabbed her, holding her tight, getting into the elevator with her. Abra cried into Sherry's shoulder and continued crying as they walked down Riverside Drive, December puffs of air crowding around her face. After walking several blocks, Abra sniffed back her tears and looked at Sherry, who was wearing only a tunic and leggings.

"Sherry, you must be freezing."

"I'm okay. Do you wanna go somewhere where we can sit down?"

Abra didn't answer but let Sherry lead her to a coffee house.

Sherry steered Abra to a back table and went to order hot chocolates. She grabbed some napkins for Abra's face.

"I can't believe I did that," Abra said, when Sherry rejoined the table.

Sherry took a sip. "We don't have to talk if you don't want to. And don't even think about what you did. Sounds like Cullen's the one to be embarrassed," she said.

Abra nodded, grateful to have an ally.

WHEN ABRA WENT HOME the next morning, she entered through the always-unlocked back door and found Cullen sitting on a kitchen stool, sipping coffee. They looked at each other: one looking like a bruised animal; the other, like a defiant but broken master.

"I was worried about you," he said.

She looked at him and said nothing.

"Did you stay at Sherry and David's?"

Why is he talking about them? she thought. Shouldn't he be apologizing, trying to explain, attempting to console me?

"You want some coffee?" he asked, not knowing what to say.

She went to the cupboard where hand-painted mugs were kept and poured a small amount.

"So I guess we need to talk . . . ," he said.

Again, she said nothing.

"Abra, I don't know what to say."

She looked at him and noticed for the first time that he seemed to be in pain also.

"I didn't plan for it, I never meant to hurt you, you have to know that."

"So what were you planning, Cullen? Maybe a secret little thing that I'd never have to know about?"

He looked at her and then into his coffee cup. Searching for how much to reveal, how much to try to salvage. Trying unsuccessfully to remember what he had been thinking before he fell in love with Cynthia. Everything before that was a blur, he wanted to tell her that, but he knew that would be cruel.

"I can't bear what I've done to you . . . I know for you to act that way . . ."

"I don't care anymore about what people think," Abra said. "I've lived my whole life worrying about what other people think, how I appeared, always trying to be perfect, always trying to front, and look at what all that perfection got me."

He sat and listened and tried to figure out what to say next.

"So who is this person you've been seeing?"

"This is not about her."

"Oh, so what's it about?"

He was silent.

"Our marriage was falling apart anyway, Cullen? Is that what you're saying?" She was crying now.

Cullen couldn't look at her. "Abra, I'm so sorry . . ."

She blew her nose and looked at him pleadingly. "Why didn't you say something? Why'd you lie when I asked you about it?"

"I'm so sorry."

"About what, exactly? The affair? The disease? What?"

He picked up his coffee cup and put it down, realizing the liquid was cold.

"All of it, the lying, the way I've hurt you. For not being able to live up to what you thought I was."

"So are you in love with this person?"

He paused, looked toward his cold coffee, then looked at her. "I think so."

Abra sucked in air, holding on to the edge of the counter, as if she'd just been punched with a labor pain. "What about all this, all that we've been together?" She continued, not waiting for him to respond. "What was this? Was it all my fucking imagination?!" She slammed her hand onto the marble countertop, knocking over her cup, sending chunks of ceramic flying.

Neither of them moved.

"Did I imagine that we were in love with each other, that we had a life together?"

Cullen couldn't look at her. "What do you want, Abra?"

She bit her lip in a vain attempt to stop her tears. "I want you to love me."

Cullen rose from the stool and went to his wife who was holding herself, attempting to keep from collapsing into tears. He put his arms around her arms, patting her back, pleading with her to stop.

"I don't feel it anymore," he whispered. "Abra, I'm sorry."

Part Two

chapter 18

EVERY IDEA in Hollywood is derivative and Natasha and Abra's script was no exception. It was about three women who attend their tenth college reunion and reflect on their lives through flashbacks of their mothers' lives. It's a story about denial and self-acceptance—a Black *Joy Luck Club*. Griffin Smith was interested in backing their project, and Natasha needed help in pushing him from flirting to marriage. She had learned to straddle Black and White Hollywood, and while she knew everybody, she trusted none of them. It was one of the reasons why Abra moved to L.A., to have Natasha's back.

There were the people like Griffin, who had the power to make a film happen, and many others who were simply scramblers. There were the Black folks who made up Black Hollywood, which consisted of a thimbleful of stars who crossed over and an even smaller number who could get a film green-lighted; those directors who churned out predictable fare about violence and poverty and the few earnest ones who fought constantly to make lapidary movies showing Black people's humanity.

Hollywood is built on three Ds: development, deals, and derivatives. Lots of people walk around boasting about having three picture deals, which really means you're part of a group of people who go to lunch, try to sign writers and actors for their deals—90 percent of which never get made. Plenty of people still managed to make a commodious living without ever making a picture. Natasha, coming from hardworking Black Midwestern stock, was fighting like a mother lion to get her project to the coveted green-light stage. She simply couldn't swallow the notion of being in the movie business and not making movies.

Abra had moved to L.A. with one suitcase and a garment bag. She'd looked in her closet and decided to leave everything that was boring or reminded her of Cullen. That didn't leave much. In the months that she'd stopped taking the Perganol, she hadn't had much of an appetite, so most of her clothes were too big anyway.

By the time Abra got to the production office, On Straight was in full swing. Word had spread through the tiny community that Griffin was interested in their movie—with a few *minor* changes—and that was enough to get Natasha on the list of the Most Wanted. Phones rang nonstop with calls from reps of directors, actors, and screenwriters. Invitations were constant to power breakfasts, lunches, and cocktail parties, but instead of giving Natasha pleasure, this attention just created an annoying distraction, because she had to respond.

Abra joined Natasha, who sat waiting for her assistant to send in her next appointment, a director.

"You know, you can't let him know that you think he's a lawn jockey," Abra reminded Natasha.

Natasha looked at her, dramatically closed and opened her eyes. "Did you see his last movie? What a piece of shit!" The director's most recent picture, a creative and financial disaster, was a spoof so horrendous that Natasha considered spearheading a campaign to have him run out of the race. She checked her expression in the wall mirror near her desk.

"Do I look neutral?" Natasha asked.

"Um, let me talk first," Abra said

"I just wanna blow him off."

The director had a thing for hats and white suits, Tom Wolfe style. He often wore a fedora, which made his small frame seem even tinier, and brown-and-white shoes. Very un-Hollywood, thought Natasha, who was dressed down in black bootleg pants, cowboy boots, tight cotton sweater, and a vintage vest. Abra wore leggings and a riding jacket. The rule in Hollywood is to never look as if you're trying. You must have expensive accouterments—the four-thousand-dollar Breitling watch, the handmade loafers you picked up in Italy, but you must sport them with pieces from the Gap and Banana Republic. The more powerful, the more costly casual. Agents and studio heads were about the only people who appropriately wore suits. So the director was already many notches down in Natasha's eyes, for not getting the culture code right. He was there to do his pitch.

"Hey Natasha, great seeing you," he said, removing his hat.

"You, too. Meet my partner, Abra Lewis."

"Hey, hey, Abra. Cool name."

"Thanks. Great suit," Abra said.

Natasha rolled her eyes.

"Oh yeah, little something I had made in New York."

"So how're the kids?" Natasha said.

"Oh, great, they're great. Gotta have some kids, Natasha. You have kids, Abra?"

"No."

"It's changed Jenna, motherhood. She's just so . . . what's the word? . . . fulfilled."

"Yeah, I'm sure. So, what can I do for you?" Natasha said, satisfied that they'd spent enough time on small talk and that her earlier assumption about him was correct.

"Well, first let me say, 'You go, girl,' gettin' Mona Love signed on, and I heard about Griffin Smith."

Natasha looked at Abra, nodded, and moved some papers around her desk.

"So, hear me out. I'll be fast. This is how I see it. One of the girls' mother is really a transvestite, and when the girl finds out, she realizes she must be adopted. That sends her on the road to find her real mother. It becomes a kinda *Joy Luck Club, Thelma and Louise* meets *The Crying Game.*"

Natasha sat listening, a pained smile across her lips, and slowly shook her head. He was even worse than she'd imagined. They listened a few more minutes before cutting him off.

"You know, that's a really interesting interpretation of the script," Abra said.

"Yeah, but as you know we don't have a deal yet—we'll be in touch," Natasha added with less diplomacy.

"Aw, Natasha, that sounds like you tryin' to play me."

"Oh." Natasha put her fist over her heart. "You hurt me when you say things like that. Really, you'll be hearing from us," she said.

Abra stood up and extended her hand. "It was an honor to meet you."

"Well, thank you. You obviously know class."

He paused before opening the door to leave. "You know where to find *moi.*"

When he'd closed the door the friends looked at each other. "I thought you were exaggerating. He was worse than I thought," Abra said.

NATASHA TOOK a deep breath and took in the redolent orchids that filled the space. Ah, Natasha said, hitting her forehead with the heel of her hand. She'd forgotten that she was supposed to meet Miles for lunch. She checked her watch and called him on his cellular phone. Miles, always Max Julian cool, told her not to sweat it. He'd be waiting. She hung up the phone and smiled. Abra was on the phone at her makeshift desk. Natasha mouthed to her that she was going out for a bite.

In the car she thought about Miles and smiled at the thought of the flowers he'd sent. He reminded her of the boys she'd grown up with in Hyde Park, the ones who'd managed to keep their edge. She liked that about him. One of the reasons she'd given up dating was she'd stopped meeting guys like that. The brothers she did meet, the ones in her sphere, either wanted only White women or anything that looked *other* than Black. Many of them acted like suburban White guys. They'd lost their walk, their laugh, or they became jokes, like the director who'd just left her office. Miles had held on to his street stuff, figured out how to use it to his advantage in the corporate orb. It took a special brother to master that trick, and Miles was nothing if not special.

Humph, Natasha thought to herself, snap out of it girl. If I see all that, know that every other sister on the East Coast and here sees it and wants it, too. It was true. Women liked Miles and Miles liked women, preferably smart and accomplished. He was casually seeing a few investment bankers, an M.D., and a Ph.D. who was working in D.C. on a national study on race. And they were all lovely.

Natasha burst into the café and saw Miles calmly sipping a Pellegrino and wearing a black pinstripe, white shirt, and a raspberry polka-dot tie. He looked better than the cappuccino cheesecake this place was famous for.

"Catch your breath," he said.

"Whew, I know. The traffic alone in this town will wear you out."

"Not in a Porsche," Miles said, and they both laughed.

"So what you got there?" Natasha said, looking at Miles' glass.

"Expensive water."

Miles raised a finger for the waiter and they ordered lunch.

"So what you been up to, slim?" Miles said.

"Oh God, it's been a killer time, but at least Abra's finally out here."

"How's she doing?"

"With the work, she's brilliant. She cuts through all the L.A. crap just like an East Coast accountant. The work is just what she needs."

"What about her head?"

"Well, she's hurt, but she's tougher than I even knew."

"So how's everything else?"

"We're close to a deal with Griffin, I can taste it, and everybody in town wants to take a damn meeting. We just don't have time, but you've gotta make time or people get pissed."

"Life in the fast lane, but you're handling it. You look good."

Natasha had looked down at herself; it was the first time he'd seen her when she wasn't done done.

"You always do," Natasha said, fingering Miles' tie.

"So, you miss me?"

"Of course," Natasha said.

"Liar, you ain't got time, baby."

"I know, but I think about you between appointments."

"I'm touched."

Miles took a bite of his sandwich. "You know, I've been thinking, maybe we should get away for a few days. Go up to Hawaii. You ever been to Kauai?"

Natasha's stomach flipped at the thought of their going away. In the months that they'd been dating, they hadn't slept together. She pushed away her salad and took her Wizard out of her backpack.

"I could do a long weekend," she said.

"Cool. Have you been to Kauai?"

"Nope, just Maui."

"I think you'll like it. It's a lot more laid back than Maui, and God knows, we both need the rest."

Her cellular phone that sat on the table rang two quick rings. She looked at Miles apologetically and then picked it up.

"This is Natasha," she answered. She heard her assistant, who always sounded frantic, reminding her that she had a three o'clock. Natasha thanked her and hung up.

"I gotta go soon. When are you going back?" she said.

"Tomorrow. I gotta head up to San Fran now. I'll call

you later about Kauai." He reached for her hand and squeezed.

They smiled at each other, and Natasha leaned over to kiss him.

"You really are fabulous, Miles."

"Thanks," he said. "You better get going."

Natasha drove back to the office with the top down, thinking about the prospect of being with Miles for a couple of days. In the months that they'd been dating they'd fooled around on his sofa, necked in the back of a taxi, felt each other up at corner tables but no contact more intimate. She wondered what it would be like, what would happen to their relationship afterward. *Relationships always change A.S., after sex. He's sucking me in, but he's wonderful. Shit, look at how Cullen, Mr. Perfect Husband, turned out. Who would've ever predicted that shit? So, who knows? Miles could just seem like a dog and really be a loyal, decent guy underneath.*

Natasha walked into her office and found Abra eating sushi, sitting on the floor with actors' head shots spread out around her. "I ordered enough for you," she said, not looking up.

"Thanks, but I ate with Miles," Natasha said, and plopped down on the floor.

"So what's up with him?" Abra asked, still not looking up.

Natasha had resisted talking about Miles to Abra, figuring she didn't want to hear about any guy stuff, considering what she was going through with Cullen. "I'm crazy about him," Natasha blurted out.

Abra looked up from the piles of photos. "Really?"

"I know, he's probably a dog, but I can't help it."

"What are you talking about?"

"I mean, he's probably got all kinds of other women. Remember what that woman said?"

"Jackie Jones? Yeah, but he likes you, that's clear."

"You really think so?"

"Of course."

"Why?"

"Duh," Abra nodded toward the flowers. "He calls from Japan like it's Rancho Cucamonga. Always makes time to get together with you. He sends you thoughtful gifts, come on. Plus, he likes that you're a mini-mogul," she said, turning her concentration back to her lunch.

"So, you think he's into my career?"

"I'm saying that he likes you for you, and he also likes the flash of what you do."

Natasha looked confused. She stabbed a California roll with chopsticks and stuffed it into her mouth.

"So, that's a good thing?"

"Sure, but I would still be cautious."

chapter 19

W HEN CYNTHIA'S *View* cover ran, a stream of work began to flow so heavily that she needed a tourniquet to stop it. All her years of struggling, working two and three jobs, were over for the moment. She was doing the bigger shows in Europe and shoots for everything from *Shape* to *Shoe News*. A model's life doesn't readily match a venture capitalist's. He has to be up early every morning, on planes—usually domestic—and he always has to be available to clients.

The alarm sounded at six and Cynthia didn't move. Her face was deep in goose down. Cullen looked over at her and wondered how she could breathe. Clad, as always, in one of his white T-shirts and her white bikinis, she was sprawled on top of the white down comforter, her legs looking like a huge chocolate-covered V. Cullen sat up and lost himself for a moment looking at her. Their apartment with the good light made him hopeful, even though Cynthia didn't even wake up to say good-bye. Abra used to get up when he did, grind beans for them to have coffee together. Oh well. Cullen dismissed the thought, although a part of him missed being so taken care of.

On his way to work, Cullen thought about Farah's case. It was all but over and there hadn't been any more talk of his making partner. He'd made sure that only Margo knew his new address and phone number. Even though she'd surmised that he and Abra were separated, he never came out and told her. He knew he had to keep that a secret from the firm, or he'd never make partner. Being separated was bad, but being with a model was manslaughter. Anyway, he couldn't worry about that. It was almost over and they'd have to give him the partnership. He'd busted his ass for several years, had all the credentials, of course he'd get it.

The funny thing about leaving Abra was how unfunny he'd felt. He and Cynthia had established a new routine. They ate dinner together one night a week at home, went out several, and made love pretty much every day. He knew she wasn't warm and buttery, but there was a frostiness to her that he'd missed when they were just screwing. Living with her presented him with a side he hadn't seen. On the rare occasions, however, when he was honest with himself, he sometimes wondered if he'd made the right decision. He questioned whether she had any motherly instincts, and he knew that she would never, ever move to the suburbs. She was urban. She knew every new restaurant that opened below 14th Street; knew who was shown at what downtown gallery; was on a first-name basis with all the bartenders at hip places, as well as with the salespeople at the haute couture boutiques that sold clothes that looked like thriftshop giveaways but cost a striver's monthly salary. Living in the city was negotiable, but for Cullen having kids was not. And being on the forty side of thirty, he wanted progeny, bad.

He was sitting at his desk, trying to decide which fire to put out first, when Bill, one of the senior partners, summoned him through Margo. Cullen stood in Bill's doorway as he finished up a call and waved Cullen in. Cullen half listened in on the conversation. It was personal, maybe his wife, something about theater plans.

"Sorry about that, Cullen. So how's it going?"

"Good, we're just crossing the Ts on the Farah stuff."

"Good, good, glad to hear it. That was a bear, huh?"

"It got a little complicated, but it's over now."

"That's my boy. So what I wanted to talk to you about, I'm sure you've been wondering about the partnership . . ."

"Well sir, I have . . ."

"Understandable. We just got preoccupied with BCC shutting down and bringing in some of their folks and . . . anyway you don't want to hear about all that. I just wanted to let you know that you're still high on our list. We're very pleased with your work, Cullen, particularly on the furniture deal."

"Um, thank you, sir."

"I'll have Edith call Margo to set up a lunch date for us."

"Okay, sir, looking forward to it."

Lunch with one or several senior partners at the Century Club meant one thing: partnership. It was a formal welcoming into the fold, and Cullen was dancing in the sun. He thought about how his life was working out as he headed back to his office. He couldn't have planned it more perfectly. In deep love with a young, beautiful woman, a stake in a major venture firm. Cynthia was making big bucks, too. They should start looking for a summer place; he'd call a realtor as soon as he got back to his office. He figured right after the partnership was announced, he'd begin the divorce so that he could marry Cynthia. Life couldn't be sweeter. This was the reward for taking life by the reins and going after what you really want. All good things, all good things, Cullen chanted to himself.

chapter 20

KAUAI IS THE OLDEST in the string of islands that make up Hawaii and has the most naturally beautiful beaches. The most spectacular of them, so remote that only a boat or plane will get you there. Miles rented a Cessna to take them to the tiny, exquisite Peach Beach Club on the Na Pali coast.

Their room was a sprawling berth with a cherry-wood canopy bed draped with white gauze, creating a tropical womb. Bouquets of birds of paradise and African cactus squatted in corners and on the wicker coffee table next to a bottle of champagne in a silver bucket.

"They think we're on a honeymoon," Miles drawled as he pulled the bottle from the ice and examined the orange label.

Natasha put her blue leather luggage on the rack at the base of the bed. She looked around the all-white room, at the glimmering Pacific a few feet from their elevated patio, where two green- and white-striped lounge chairs sat under a matching awning, and took a deep breath.

"This place is gorgeous, Miles. How'd you find it?"

"I've got my ways and I just know what you like."

Natasha unzipped her bag and began fishing around for her bikini. "I want to just sit in the sun and bake," she said.

Miles noticed the tiny pieces of orange fabric she lifted out of her bag. He took off his shirt and shoes and went out to the patio, champagne bottle in hand.

When Natasha joined him, she was wearing an orange thong bikini. Even Miles was shocked by the exposure of so much, and everything was just so. If he didn't know better, he would think that all she did was work out. Natasha had beauty-queen measurements—full on top, small in the center, and no hips. She did, however, have a perfect Black-girl's booty. Damn, Miles thought. He smiled at her and took off his sunglasses.

"Lookin' good, slim," he said, and handed her a flute of champagne.

Natasha checked out Miles' chest, which was ample and covered with peasy curls of chest hair. His white linen pants hung down from an unbuckled crocodile belt.

"Here," she said, handing him a tube of sun block, "rub some of this on my back, please."

She turned over on the chaise and Miles felt a rise. He'd wanted to wait a little while before jumping her, but seeing her perfect onion facing him was more than even he, with his tremendous self-control, could resist. He stood there for longer than he probably should have, just watching her. Other than a few stretch marks, her skin was unmarred. She turned sideways and looked at him.

"Is there something wrong?"

"No, I'm sorry. I was just lost in thought."

He sat down near her calf and squeezed the white cream

from its tube. He began rubbing it on her legs, slowly, then moved up to her back, avoiding her behind. He massaged her back and shoulders. Natasha groaned. He put more cream on his hands, rubbing them together, looking down at them as if he were about to do something he wouldn't be able to control. He rubbed the cream on her buttocks in round, rhythmic motions. After a while he began to feel woozy from the sun and champagne, as was Natasha. She was moaning, and Miles slid up onto the chaise, still rubbing her back and buttocks. He moved his hands under the tie of her bikini top and around to her voluptuous breasts. He squeezed them both first gently, then harder. She moaned. Then he cupped his hands around her nipples and flicked them with his fingers. Miles knew he'd hit her spot and continued to work on her breasts, kneading and squeezing until she got louder and louder.

"Let's go inside," Natasha mumbled.

Miles leaned down and kissed the back of her neck and licked her ear. He reached for her hand and pulled her from the chaise. They stumbled into the small table that sat between the two chaise lounges before making it through the French doors. They kissed as they walked to the bed. Miles went to his bag, took out a box of rubbers, and dropped his pants. Natasha bit the inside of her mouth to keep from laughing at the display of so many. She took an envelope from Miles' hand, put her hand inside his briefs. She peeled open the condom and kissed him as she slid it on.

"You're wonderful," Miles whispered to her and kissed her neck, ear, and cheek.

"So are you," Natasha said as she let him lead her to the bed.

"This bathing suit is too much. You know that, don't you?" Miles said, crawling toward her. He rolled her over so that he could look at her behind again. He held on to the side strings and pulled off the thong as he straddled her. He massaged her behind and her back and untied her top. He kissed her up and down her back, while massaging her breasts, her nipples, until she begged him to enter her. He turned her over, looking deeply into her eyes, with one hand on the bed, above her shoulder, and the other guiding himself into her. She was dripping, and the feel of that alone made him want to come. Could she really be that turned on? He wanted to make it last, so he didn't move at all at first, her hips doing the work. He watched her, her eyes closed, mouth open. She was so hot, maybe the hottest, not counting the one-night stands who weren't in the serious contender category. He smiled and let himself go. Just as he was reaching the end of his climax, she began hers.

After they'd cooled down, Miles rolled over and ordered room service, and Natasha pulled a revised script from her bag, put on her glasses, and began reading in bed. Miles smiled as he looked at her with reading glasses perched to ward the end of her nose. He liked that Natasha was as driven as he. He was zapped and was only able to watch her and wait for dinner. They fed each other greens with pineapple, shrimp scampi, and lobster, in bed.

"You know I could get used to you," Miles said, cracking open a lobster tail.

Natasha was nibbling her greens. "Oh yeah? What does that mean?"

"It means, I digs you, baby," Miles said, kissing her with his mouth full of rice.

"This food is so good," Natasha said, eating too fast, trying not to consider what he was saying.

"I know," Miles said, practically inhaling his, "but not nearly as good as you."

Natasha was naked except for the reading glasses now resting on her head. She sat cross-legged on the bed, her tray balanced on her knees. "You aren't half bad your-self."

"Better than you thought?"

"Oh yeah," Natasha said, and reached over to rub his chest hair. "I was beginning to wonder . . ."

"Never fear, my dear," Miles said.

Natasha took a gulp of champagne and shoved another forkful of scampi into her mouth. Miles enjoyed Natasha. With her he didn't have to be on, all the time, and when he was, she seemed unimpressed. He liked that he couldn't quite figure her out.

"You know as much as we talk, I know very little about you," Miles said.

"What don't you know? I work all the time, I'm from Chicago. I love my family, even my perfect older sister. What else do you want to know?"

"How come you're not hooked up?"

Natasha stopped chewing vigorously and thought about what Miles was getting at. "We've had this conversation, haven't we?" she said, reminding him of her disaster with the other investment banker, the one who dumped her.

"That one really messed you up, huh?" Miles pressed.

"Yeah, 'cause I violated one of my rules. I didn't listen to my dad."

"Daddy's always right?"

"Yup, he saw through the guy like cellophane."

Miles' laughter was covered with a sneer. "I can't believe your dad is Norwood of Norwood's Barbecue! I lived on that stuff when I was in college."

"Actually the Norwood is my grandfather, he started the business. Daddy's a junior."

"Yeah, but he's the man."

"Yeah, he grew the business."

"And you're daddy's little girl."

"We're very close."

"What would he think of me?"

"You remind me of my dad. I think he'd like you."

Miles tried to picture Norwood Coleman, Jr. The self-made millionaire he'd studied in business school. "I don't know about that."

"I think he'd have an appreciation for you. He'd respect that you're self made."

Miles thought about what Natasha was saying, and wanted to tell her that her assessment of him was wrong. The thought of meeting Norwood made him uneasy. But he felt himself falling for her and knew that meeting Dad was inevitable. He knew Natasha brought out different feelings in him, and it made him uncomfortable. Sure, she was fine, but they were all fine. Fine was simply an admission ticket. Smart and successful was something else that they all were, but what he liked about Natasha was that she was someone who had made it, but didn't buy the hype. She liked fly shit, like he did, but it didn't define her. She still saw herself as the daughter of Chicago's South Side, who had to constantly prove herself to White and Black people. Someone who didn't feel totally comfortable around bourgie Black folks—because they were too busy either kissing up or trying to initiate her into the tribe or hanging around monied Whites, who looked down on her because her family money had grease on it. Rank-and-file Whites basically viewed her as just another flashy sister with a 'tude. Her way, the way she dressed and carried herself, would stand out in his corporate environment like brown shoes with a blue suit, and he didn't know how he'd deal with that. But he was looking at forty and knew he had to do something.

"I want you to meet my mama," Miles announced. Natasha had a sense that to Miles, her meeting his mother was a big deal, but she didn't know that only two women had actually met Earlene, the true love in Miles' life, to whom he felt forever indebted because it was she, not he, who'd *made* him.

After their respite spent in bed, the lounge chairs on the patio, and in the water, sans bathing suits, they felt less sleep-deprived, even revived.

"All my new bathing suits went to waste," Natasha said as she packed.

Miles grinned and put his arms around her waist. "We'll use 'em next time."

Natasha leaned her head to one side so Miles could better kiss her neck. "I had a great time," she said. She was trying her best to hold back, to keep from falling for him. She kept remembering what Abra had found out from Jackie Jones. "He's good for fun."

"Me too, baby. So, you wanna try for Memphis next weekend?"

"I don't know if I can, let me check."

He squeezed her and kissed her neck and said, "I adore you."

She let herself feel warm and goofy all over. She debated with herself, don't do it, don't say it, one mind said; the other had lapped up the weekend, the romantic view, his dazzling mind, the great sex and told her to let go. Fall for him, it's okay. She took a deep breath and heard herself say, "I adore you back."

chapter 21

ABRA SAT at her desk, digging at her cuticles, trying to resist biting. The denim overalls she wore hung off her like a sheet on a scarecrow. She'd worn the same ones to work all week, her hair color needed to be touched up, but she looked better than she had in years. The first thing she did when she moved to L.A. was cut off her fried hair. The natural made her bones prominent and she looked fresh, although her mother hated it. Never did a conversation with Odessa not end with, "When you gon' straighten that head?" It was Abra's first act of insurgence. The second was moving to L.A. She was finally learning to hear her voice, and she was getting to sleep at night. Her dreams about Cullen were fewer, and during the night, she reached out for him less and less. The last time he'd called was to tell her he was putting the house up for sale. She'd cried all night, but that had been months ago.

Now she was learning to dance with her demons.

Natasha had seen the author of a book about fatherless daughters on a talk show and had called the show to get information about her therapy group. The author cited a study that said twenty years after a divorce or abandonment, the now adult woman will still feel abandoned, lonely, and afraid that all relationships will fail. They fantasize about men because they've not seen a real day-to-day relationship. When Natasha heard this, she thought about Abra.

"That has nothing to do with me. How can you miss what you never had?" Abra had said. But after Natasha's insistence and promise that she'd go with her, Abra finally went to a group.

The meeting was held at the therapist's house in San Pedro, about a half hour from L.A. Her narrow house sat perched on a hill and overlooked much of the former fishing village and the L.A. Bay. It had a working sense about it, the town. A million miles away from L.A. in terms of its spirit. It was both real and fantasylike. Natasha yanked the emergency brake, the crank had a finality to it, and looked at Abra.

"You want me to go in or wait out here?"

Abra sat for a minute, looking at the house, and said she wanted to go in alone.

" 'Kay, I'll be right here."

They kissed each other, and Abra walked in and found a door opened to a room with several women sitting in a semicircle on pillows. The host, the author/therapist, greeted Abra and put her arm around Abra's shoulders, ushering her in. She offered her tea. Her face was thin, kind of pinched; her dark eyes were set deep, and her short hair had bangs that framed an alert face. The group was a mixture of Black, White, and Latina; heavy, thin, gay, straight, mothers and not. After a small time passed and a few more women came, a thin blond actress began.

"I had to first learn that I had a problem. I kept doing the same thing in relationships with men, making the same mistakes, choosing the same guy." The other women nodded solemnly. She added, "I even married the same one twice." Everyone chuckled.

"My problem was I wouldn't go past one or two dates before I began making up excuses for why I couldn't become involved. I'd go out, feel myself liking the guy, and I'd start to feel nauseous. Then I'd begin coming up with excuses for why I couldn't continue to see him. Then I would eat everything in sight," a heavy caramel-colored woman with a pretty face said.

After a few more confessionals, the therapist told the group that their reactions were all perfectly human responses to what they'd been through. "Abandonment makes us feel we can't trust, so we do as Jolene does, pushing away possible intimacy, filling up our holes with food; or like Nancy, we get strung out on relationships with men who we know are no good, who we know will leave us or try to control us or abuse us in some other way."

Abra shifted on her pillow. It was her turn.

"Almost a year ago my husband left me. We were married for five years, together for almost ten, and he said he realized that he never really loved me. He's now with the woman he was having an affair with . . . it's why I'm here . . . I never thought much about not having a father . . . but now I think there may be a connection, maybe why Cullen, um, my husband, left and my father . . . I put Cullen on a pedestal, made him a man no one could live up to. He was perfect in my eyes, and I did everything he wanted. I just wanted to please him so he wouldn't leave, like my father did, but I think now that deep down I knew he would, that I needed to play out something that was bigger than me. I don't know, this may be all . . . I really don't have anything else I want to say." Abra wiped her nose and sipped her tea. A woman next to her patted her back.

After more women talked, Abra listened, cried with some, laughed, and recognized some of her behavior with Cullen in others. The time went by fast, and Abra was warmed at the thought of her best friend sitting in the car outside. The therapist walked her to the door and handed her some Xeroxed articles. Abra looked down at a highlighted paragraph.

> *The early relationship between father and daughter is a powerful sexual conditioning, . . . For the daughter, it's an essential stage in developing a sense of self-worth and confidence in relation to other people. Without a father's protectiveness and reassurance when you're becoming aware of yourself as a sexual being, you're likely to devalue yourself. As a result, you base your sexual relationships on what other people think of you, without daring to rely on your own opinions. However caring the mother, this is one area in which she can't substitute. (Boston, Anne. "Growing Up Fatherless." In Fathers Reflections by Daughters.)*

"It's difficult the first time," the woman said.

As Natasha drove, Abra cried all the way back. The prospect of home being a rented apartment with rented furniture didn't help.

"So what happened?" Natasha asked, and reached out to hold her friend's hand.

Abra pulled her hand away and covered her face. Her

shoulders shook as she tried to tell Natasha what had happened.

"I just had no idea . . . it's so deep . . . it's primal."

"What?"

"This feeling of wanting both your parents to be together."

"I know, I know," Natasha said, patting Abra's thigh.

The idea that she was playing out unfinished business with her father, that she'd chosen Cullen because somehow she knew he'd turn out to disappoint her or that she'd been so ill-prepared to select a mate because of the absence of her father, spun around in her head. She leaned her head against the window, looking out at forever freeways, trying unsuccessfully to push away the hopelessness that she felt. Her mouth filled with saliva, and warm tears ran down her face.

"So how was that woman, the therapist?"

"She was kind, she seemed wise, but I just felt uncomfortable talking about all this stuff to strangers. A lot of it I don't even understand."

"So did you get anything out of it? Do you think there's anything to this father-hunger thing?"

Abra considered for a moment. "I do. I just can't really talk about it though. I don't know how I feel, I'm just kind of numb. I know that when we were little, I was so envious that you had a father and even now, when he sends you flowers or calls, I just feel so deeply for what I didn't have."

Natasha looked out at the road before her. She didn't know what to say. She'd had no idea. "I always thought you couldn't stand Norwood."

Abra chuckled and her friend joined her.

"You know it's going to be okay, don't you?" Natasha

touched Abra's damp face. "I'm always here and we're going to get through this."

"I know you are," Abra said. "I love you."

"I'm always here. We have each other."

chapter 22

ARLENE BROWNING'S house in Whitehaven, Tennessee, was a high-ranch vision. The living room was all white, except for the lamp bases—heads that were carved from plaster and painted ebony, wearing large gold hoop earrings. The ivory sectional was covered in plastic protection, the white carpet had just been vacuumed and had the marks to prove it. The place was immaculate and was clearly, other than Miles, Earlene's bliss.

Earlene was an attractive, full-bodied woman. Her face was youthful and dimpled, and she wore her thick dark hair in a relaxed bob. She had large breasts that pointed high and wide from her chest. She looked like so many invisible Black women who worked hard, raised their children —many times, solo—but who always made time to bake a cake for Miss Mary down the street, who was under the weather.

There was a large white-framed picture over the white faux-marble fireplace of Earlene and Miles, taken when he was a teen. Earlene had on burgundy lipstick and wore her hair in a Jherri-Curl. Miles was wearing a powder-blue blazer and shirt, with a white tie. It was taken right after Miles had been accepted, with a full academic scholarship, to Christian Brothers prep. Their future looked happy.

Earlene fluttered around the house, getting ready for Miles and Natasha's visit. She'd laid out a platter of Ritz crackers and cheddar cheese, deviled eggs, cheese curls, plain chips and a little of her onion dip, along with Miles' favorite barbecue potato chips. For lunch she'd prepared potato salad, fried fish, and tossed salad. She baked Miles' favorite coconut cake for dessert. *If my baby is bringin' a girl home, this one must be special. He had so many girls, I 'bout given up tryin' to remember their names. Hardly never did mention one more than once, other than one a few years ago, who I never did meet. He made reference to that one several times, but she got married to a doctor, Miles said, 'cause she got tired of waitin' for him. Now this one, Natasha, what a pretty name, now she must be somethin'. Got some big job in Hollywood, but I never could figure out why Miles always went for these career gals. Who's gonna raise the babies if he ever did decide to settle down and get married? But I guess he'll figure it out and, Lord knows, he could, 'cause he's as smart as they come. I ain't just sayin' that 'cause he mine, but everybody was always sayin' it. Could fix anything, fixed our old Comet when he was just 'bout eight years old. Said, "Mama, I thank you gotta just take these things out." Talkin' 'bout the spark plugs and clean 'em off. Sure 'nuff, that was it. Car started right up. He was always askin' questions, askin' me stuff I ain't never even thought about, much less knowed the answer. Afterwhile, I'd just leave him at the library, and he was happy as a clam, in them books all day long. The colored, I mean, Black, librarians, Miss Marion and Miss Jessie Mae, loved him to death, they still ask 'bout him all the time.*

The doorbell played "She'll Be Comin' Round the Mountain," and Earlene took off her pink-and-black lace apron and hung it in the hall closet. When she opened the door she saw a brown, round-faced girl with a lot of brown and blond frizzy kind of hair. She wasn't that much shorter than Miles and they stood there, both wearing sunglasses and suit jackets.

"Hey Mama," Miles said, and reached out to hug Earlene.

Natasha stood back, took off her sunglasses, and smiled.

"Come on in, baby," Earlene said.

Natasha stuck out her hand and told Earlene what a pleasure it was to meet her.

"You, too, baby. Y'all come on in, take a load off."

Natasha looked around and took it all in. "Your home is lovely," Natasha said.

Miles looked at her and gave her a nod for her astute appraisal. The way to Earlene's heart was to compliment her gothic decor. "Let me show you around. Miles, hang up Natasha's jacket."

Natasha followed Earlene downstairs to see the family room, entertainment center, and laundry area. The entertainment center had a 120-inch screen, a turquoise leather sectional, and leopard-print rug. The walls were pine and covered with Ernie Barnes paintings.

"The family room's really the livin' room," Earlene said, flicking on the light. The room was furnished in burgundy leather and pink curtains and throw pillows. A chrome-and-glass coffee table with copies of *Ebony, Essence,* and *Black*

Enterprise—one with Miles on the cover—sat between the leather sofa and love seat. A marble-stump end table sat next to the leather armchair. Not one speck was out of place in Earlene's house and Natasha knew that this was not the work of a paid housekeeper, but that Earlene lovingly dusted, fluffed, and scrubbed every inch herself.

"You hungry? Let's go upstairs and get you somethin' to munch on. You can see the rest later." Natasha followed Earlene up the stairs to the kitchen, where Miles was on the portable phone with someone at his office. Earlene playfully shooed him out of their way, and he took his call out onto the deck, which could be reached through sliding glass doors off the kitchen.

Her kitchen was a cabbage-rose bonanza. There were cabbage-rose poufs over the windows with matching seat cushions, place mats, napkins and dishcloths and towels. The food platters were laid out on the glass kitchen table, which was always set with plates, glasses, and silverware.

"You didn't have to go to all this trouble, Mrs. Browning," Natasha said, trying to decide what to eat.

"Earlene, please, call me Earlene, honey. This ain't no trouble, just a little cheese and crackers."

"Well, thank you. It looks great."

"Thank you. I took a entertainin' course at the adult learnin' center over at the high school. Uh-huh, they teach you how to lay all the stuff out real prettylike."

Miles, done with his call, joined them. He hugged his mother again. "So how you doin', Mama?"

"Oh fine, son, just fine. Just talkin' with Natasha here."

Miles picked up a deviled egg and stuffed it into his mouth. "Oh boy, has she started grilling you yet?" he asked Natasha.

"Oh stop that, boy," Earlene said, playfully hitting his elbow.

"No, we were just talking about her course at the adult school," Natasha said.

"That's right. You see my platters?"

"Very nice. Your garden looks good," Miles said.

"Yeah, this looks like it's gonna be a good season. Y'all hungry? I fixed lunch."

"Whatcha got?" Miles said, peeling back plastic wrap off a platter.

"I know you always hungry," Earlene said. "We can eat in the dinin' room."

"You don't have to get fancy for Natasha," Miles said. "We can eat in the kitchen."

"Miles, mind your manners now," Earlene said, "Natasha's company."

"Really, Mrs., I mean Earlene, you don't have to—"

"Save it. We're gonna eat in there."

The dining-room table was also preset, this one with black patent-leather place mats with gold-lamé trim and black napkins in gold napkin rings. In the middle was a centerpiece made of black, white, and gold silk flowers.

"Can I help with something?" Natasha said, watching Earlene bustling back and forth.

"Nope, everything's here. We can eat. Say the grace, Miles."

They bowed their heads, held hands, and Miles said a brief grace. It was the same one Natasha's family said: "Gracious Lord, we're thankful for the food we're about to receive, Christ, our redeemer. Amen."

"So, is this your first time in Memphis?" Earlene asked.

"Um, yes," Natasha said, savoring a mouthful of potato salad. "Miles talks about it all the time. Your neighborhood is very nice."

"Miles didn't grow up here," Earlene said quickly.

"Mama, she knows that. I showed her Foote Homes before we came here."

"You did?" Earlene said incredulously. "Did you see anybody down there?"

"Naw, I rang Miss Mary's bell but nobody answered," Miles said.

"So where you from, Natasha?" Earlene asked.

"Um, Chicago and New Jersey."

"Where your folks from? They from Chicago or New Jersey?"

"Um, my mother is from New Jersey, Newark, and my father grew up in Chicago, but was born in Mississippi."

"Mm-mm, where 'bouts in Mississippi?"

"Um, it's a little town, Moss Point, not far from Biloxi."

"Did y'all go back there for visits?"

"Not much, because my grandparents moved to Chicago. We went a few times to see my great-grandmother, when she was still alive."

"I see. And you live in California now?"

"Yes, in Los Angeles."

"Natasha's a big-time movie producer," Miles interjected.

"Really? Which ones?"

"Well, nothing you would have seen yet . . ."

"Natasha wrote that TV show you used to watch, *On the Verge*."

"Really? I liked that show. Why they take that off?"

Natasha blushed at Miles' boasting and looked down at her plate. "Uh, I don't know. Bad time slot. They said there wasn't enough of an audience for it."

"Humph, they always say that about the Black shows where ain't nobody carryin' on like a buffoon. Everybody I know watched that show, and liked it, too."

"Yeah, I know. We got a lot of letters after people heard about the cancellation, but it was too late, then."

Natasha's cellular phone rang and she excused herself from the table to answer it.

"You can take that in one of the bedrooms," Earlene called out.

"Thanks," Natasha said, and took the call in the all-pink bedroom.

"Oh, Miles, I like her," Earlene said in a whisper. "She's just as smart and down to earth."

"Yeah, she cool, huh?"

"And she pretty, too. Is all that her hair?"

Miles laughed out loud at his mother who was dead serious. "I don't know, Mama. I don't think so."

"Well, that's all right. They all wearin' that weave style now. So, how long you stayin' for?"

"Just overnight, we both have to get back to work."

"Work, work, work. That's all you do, boy. I hope you puttin' some away for your retirement."

"Yes, Mama, I am."

Natasha came back to the table. "Sorry about that. It was my partner."

"Everything okay?" Earlene asked.

"I think it will be. Thanks," Natasha answered.

"Abra's going out to dinner with Griffin," Natasha said to Miles.

Miles smirked and reached for more fish. "Mmm, you worried?"

"Nope. She can handle him. Can you pass the potato salad, please? You're going to have to give me the recipe, Earlene. It's delicious."

Earlene beamed as she held the bottom of the bowl and passed it to Natasha.

GRIFFIN DROVE his '67 Austin-Healy convertible around the Pacific Coast Highway curves like Willy T. Ribbs. Abra nervously watched him expertly shift between fourth and third gears as they climbed the mountain. The top was down, so conversation meant screaming, and neither was up for that. She let the wind whip her face, glad that she'd freed her hair and didn't have to worry about her short natural staying put.

They lurched into the tiny parking lot where a Mexican valet greeted Griffin by name. They walked into what looked like an English cottage. The foyer was filled with blue and yellow wildflowers, begonias, and irises. The room opened up onto the edge of a cliff that overlooked the ocean. There was one table on the balcony, and it was reserved for them.

It was sunset and the orange glow made both of them appear beautiful.

"I brought you here for the lighting. This is as good as I could ever look," Griffin joked, attempting to put Abra at ease.

The wine, a Graves he always drank, was brought to the table and served.

"So how're you liking the movie business?"

"Um, it's different," Abra said.

Griffin smiled and nodded. "Yeah. What'd you do before?"

"I worked as an accountant, at a firm."

"Big Five?"

"Yeah . . . Anderson."

"Impressive. And you and Natasha went to business school together?"

"Well, yeah, but we actually knew each other when we were children."

"Childhood friends. And where was that?"

"In New Jersey, Newark."

"Mmm, I thought she was from Chicago."

"She is, her family moved there when she was in high school."

"I see." Griffin sipped the wine, held up his glass, and nodded toward her.

"So tell me why I should back *The Yarn*?"

Abra knew that Natasha had had several meetings, answering just this question from Griffin. She knew this meeting was important and tried to quiet the flies in her stomach. She took two gulps of wine before she answered him.

"Well, this is a woman's film, it's a talkie, and it'll cross over agewise, from college-age women to the middle-age set, and racewise. Women choose the Saturday night movie and I know it's a no-lose. We're asking for a bantam budget, we've got Love committed to starring . . ."

"Tell me something I don't know . . . ," he said, looking at the ocean.

"We're going to see a phenomenal turnout on opening weekend."

Griffin turned his attention from the movie talk back to Abra, looking at her as if he'd just noticed something about her.

"So tell me about yourself," he said.

"Well, I ran our New York production office . . ."

"Why aren't you married?" Griffin asked, getting right to what he wanted to know.

"Technically I am."

"Oh, I didn't realize . . . ," Griffin said after a brief silence.

"So, how long have you been married?" she asked.

Griffin looked at her and looked away, as if the answer were somewhere in the Pacific.

"Um, let's see, I've been married since I was twenty-seven and I'm almost fifty-five."

"You have kids?"

"Yep, three. Boys. One about your age. He lives here, the other two are back East."

"And your wife, what does she do?"

Abra was more comfortable asking the questions. She also figured she could buy herself some time to let the wine help her relax.

"Um, she spends most of her time in Taos. She paints and works in a gallery there."

"So you're separated?"

"Well, not technically, but we rarely see each other. I mean she hates L.A. and I have no desire to live in New Mexico, so this arrangement just kind of works. She's on a spiritual path."

Abra tried to imagine the situation he was describing. "What do you mean?"

"Well, me, my life is empty in my wife's eyes, meaningless. And while she doesn't want a divorce, she doesn't really want me. I no longer interest her."

Yeah, Abra thought, my husband no longer wants me either. She wanted to toast to being dumped, but resisted.

"So, what happened to yours?" Griffin said.

Abra looked down at her hands, fighting back the well that was rising. "My husband is living with a model. He left me for her."

"Oh, damn, that stinks. I'm sorry."

"No need."

"Marriage is very difficult." Griffin could tell that Abra was in pain, and he searched his mind trying to find some solace for her. "You're very attractive, you're smart. You could have anything you want. You know that, don't you?" he said.

Abra wanted to say, "I want you to back our damn movie," but didn't. She finished her second glass of wine.

"I like you," he said, emptying his goblet. "I'm fifty-five, my skirt-chasing days are over."

"So, what is it that you're doing?"

Griffin looked at her for a while and said, "I don't know." His honesty warmed her.

After practically two bottles of wine, Abra told him about her childhood in Newark, how being broke and going to college with all those privileged kids was bad, but nothing compared to growing up without a dad.

"Sounds like one of your characters."

"Yeah, the film is quite personal," she said.

He told her about his genteel poverty in Connecticut. His family had a proper last name, but he had to go to Yale on a family-endowed scholarship, because they were broke.

"All I can say is your husband was a damn fool."

"Thanks, I appreciate that."

"I'm not saying it to be nice, it's true."

"You'd better stop. You'll give me a big head."

They shared an easy laugh.

"Can we do this again? Have dinner and just talk?" he said.

"Sure, I'd like that."

chapter 23

CULLEN SAT at the outdoor café in the August heat, inhaling New York bus fumes, sipping iced coffee, waiting for Cynthia to show up. He looked up from his glass and stared at an ad for designer sports gear that featured Cynthia and two other models on the side of the bus. He felt a rage rise from some heretofore unknown place. He replayed the scene at lunch with Bill in his head for the thousandth time.

"What we've decided is to give it a little more time, maybe another year."

Cullen heard his boss, but after "give it more time," his ears stopped working, and he just saw the man's mouth moving. They were dissing him, nicely, at an expensive restaurant, but still dissing. Another year before making partner. How the hell was he supposed to keep working under some vague shit for a year, and keep Cynthia a secret for that much longer?

"We know this is a blow, but with two other senior people coming in from BCC, there's just no room for another partner right now. In a year, after Jesse's retired, things will look better," Bill had said.

Cullen felt heat rising from his mouth. Soon his entire face was burning, just as it had a few days ago when he'd been given the news. He wanted to grab old Bill by his Windsor knot and squeeze it till his red face burst. Instead, he just sat there like a chump and took the dick he was getting. It was what all the schooling had been for. It was to teach him how to take it and shut the hell up about it. He had simply nodded as the senior man continued talking about the firm's entrance into the new millennium, *blah, blah, blah*. Cullen had needed the support of the walls when he got back to his office. He'd stopped at Margo's desk and managed to compliment her outfit. She'd smiled at him and asked if he was okay. He'd sat at his desk and tapped the Plexiglas top with his thumbs. What to do, what to do now? He needed to talk to someone who could help, but who? He needed somebody who was in business, somebody who understood the game, at least some of it. He couldn't talk to Cynthia about it then or now. Natasha and Abra had always been his main advisors, sounding boards, but he couldn't call either of them. They'd just have a good laugh at his sorry ass.

What we've decided is to give it a little more time, maybe another year. He heard the words over and over.

This was what his mother had predicted would happen. His parents had encouraged him to start his own business, anything, a taxi business, a parking lot, anything to be his own boss like Norwood, and not have to rely on anybody, especially "crackers," as his mother would call White people. He couldn't call his parents now. He hadn't even told them about his and Abra's breakup. They'd freak if they knew about his not making partner, too. His brother's drug problem had confirmed Cullen as the star of the family, the one everyone's hopes were pinned on, although both of his sisters were more heroic in his eyes. They were the ones who went to college at night, held down secretarial jobs during the day, and took care of children virtually on their own.

He'd been supportive of Cynthia's career, anything involving her—opening a restaurant, he didn't want to, but she did. Cynthia knew that her fee of two thousand dollars a show wouldn't last long, two years, tops. She wanted to put her money into something, not just a fab lifestyle.

Cynthia's cab pulled up and he relished watching her exit it. She was wearing a simple white-linen dress, sandals, and large, round black sunglasses.

"Hi, sweetheart," she said, and kissed her fingers and touched them to his sweaty forehead.

"Hi," he grumbled.

"What's the matter with you?"

Cullen paused, checking himself. He was glad to see her, always, but he just felt like one of her minions waiting for her. "Nothing . . . I'm just . . . hungry. Let's order."

"Are you sure that's all?"

"Cynthia, what do you think is wrong?"

"I haven't a clue, that's why I'm asking. If you say it's hunger, fine."

Cullen couldn't share with her so instead he said nothing. While Cynthia hadn't pressed him to leave Abra, he always wanted her to seem a little grateful for all that he had given up for her. She never did.

"I have to go to St. Thomas tomorrow," Cynthia said, nonchalantly looking over the menu.

"St. Thomas? For what?" he said, trying to sound calm.

"My father's birthday."

Cynthia was pathologically private and never talked about her family. All Cullen knew was that she was an only child, her mother was dead, and her father had been in the Foreign Service.

"Cynthia . . . ," Cullen said pleadingly.

"It's my father's fiftieth birthday. I didn't think you'd want to go."

"You didn't think I'd be interested in meeting your father and stepmother?" Cullen was furious and was discomforted at the notion of showing it.

"I didn't really think about it. I just got the invitation and booked a flight. It's no big deal. I'll be back in two days."

Cullen knew that Cynthia was unconventional, that things like anniversaries and family and tradition meant little to her. She wasn't unfeeling, he told himself, just indifferent. He knew he wouldn't be able to push her to do anything and the best way to handle it was to let it go.

"Fine, I'll look forward to you coming home."

Cynthia reached across the table and squeezed his hand. "You're a love."

Cullen smiled weakly and picked up his iced coffee.

Cynthia didn't consider her father's birthday or anything having to do with him a big deal. It was merely an obligation. He didn't ask her for much, didn't demand to see her much, didn't intrude on her life. His new wife, a young Filipino woman, was nice enough. Both Cynthia and her father were so numbed by her mother's abandonment—not death, as she told people—that they'd never fully recovered. They were both seemingly incapable of deep feelings for others, since the person they each loved most in the world had so suddenly, inexplicably left.

■

CYNTHIA CAME BACK from St. Thomas and found Cullen dressed in a robe and many days of razor stubble. Several empty Scotch bottles were strewn about the apartment like so many pairs of dirty socks. The place had a quiet, putrid smell, and she realized that he hadn't even bothered to take the garbage to the chute. He was asleep on the couch when she entered their apartment. After two days with her emotionally absent father and too-eager-to-please stepmother, she was in no mood to deal with Cullen and his self-pity. At the moment she saw him, curled up in his terrycloth robe, snoring with his ashy feet tucked halfway under him, she wanted to be rid of him.

She looked around the living room and saw that he'd framed her half-dozen magazine covers and hung them around the room. His enthusiasm for her work would've warmed most people, but Cynthia wasn't like most people. His devotion and his slovenliness made her sick.

She put down her bag and went in to the bedroom to check her messages. There were several, all from her agent about work: three magazine spreads. She was as hot as mink in May, and none of it really mattered to Cynthia. She just wanted the money and most of that she saved. She sat on the edge of the bed and considered how to tell Cullen she wanted out. After a few days with her father, she came home and knew, more clearly, that she was incapable of forming lasting ties. It was her mother's legacy to her, and there was no use fighting it. It's who she was.

Cullen rolled over and saw Cynthia's bag sitting upright near the door. He called out her name.

She didn't answer at first, annoyed that he was now awake. "I'm in here," she said, a bite in her voice.

Cullen gathered himself off the sofa, wiping saliva from his mouth with the back of his hand. He stood forlornly in the doorway to their bedroom and looked at her sitting on the bed.

"Babe, you're back. Why didn't you wake me up?" he said, and walked toward her to kiss her. She turned away from his needy lips and said curtly that she hadn't wanted to wake him.

"So, how was your trip?" he said, sitting down next to her, oblivious to her slight.

"It was fine."

Cullen rubbed her back, feeling her smooth skin through the thin nylon T-shirt she wore.

"It smells in here," she said.

"Oh, yeah, I'm sorry. I didn't take the garbage out—"

"I can see that. Have you left the apartment at all?"

Cullen sat silently for a moment, trying to decide which answer would put him in the most favorable light. "I haven't been feeling well . . ."

Cynthia looked away from him and at the wall. "Cullen, this isn't working out."

"What do you mean?" he said urgently.

"This relationship."

Cullen stopped rubbing her and felt a queasiness in his stomach. "What did you say?"

"I have to leave you," Cynthia said, this time trying to be a little more gingerly.

"What are you talking about? 'Cause I didn't take out the trash, you're leaving?"

"Cullen," Cynthia said, now facing him, their knees touching. "Things have gotten stale between us, and I'm just not in love with you anymore. Your presence irritates me, so before it turns into something very ugly, I think it would be best to just break up."

"Cynthia, I want to marry you."

She looked at him, her pupils and irises blending, giving her stare a frightful edge. He looked into her eyes and was struck by how icy they were, how much she reminded him of Bill and the others at Croft Ventures who made unrelenting decisions about people's lives every day, without an ounce of compassion. At the moment, he felt a fear of her and a loathing of himself for having been so blind to who this young woman really was. The reason she never asked him to leave his wife was because she could carry on an affair without any feeling. She had loved him the only way she knew how, unrequitedly. When he loved back, she didn't want him. He wanted to scream at her, but more at himself for what a fool he'd been. Now he understood that this was his karmic payback for the callous way he'd left Abra. This was what you get for asking for the moon.

Cynthia put her hand on Cullen's knee.

"I'll send you your deposit for the restaurant in a few days. I'll be out by the end of the week."

With that, Cynthia got up, grabbed her keys, and left Cullen sitting on the edge of the bed, immolated.

True to her word, she'd sent movers and the apartment looked as if she'd never been there. Alone for the first time in more than a decade, Cullen had finally faced the fallout from his decisions. What he saw made him reach for the balm of Jim Beam. In a drunken, yet thoughtful, phase, he forced himself, for the first time, to look at what he'd done to Abra. The reality of their breakup hit him the way the smell of garbage must have whacked Cynthia. While he was feeling destroyed by what Cynthia had just told him, he couldn't stop feeling that he'd earned it, and that somehow made him feel better, or not as bad. He looked around the two-bedroom with good light and wondered what he'd do with it. He wasn't particular about staying in the city, although he'd just accepted an offer on his and Abra's old house, which was just as well, since the suburbs were made for twos.

Cullen scuffed back into the living room, flopped down on the sofa, which faced the coffee table where the Jim Beam lived, and poured himself another. He silently toasted himself: *the complete failure.*

chapter 24

Abra sat at her desk, sorting invitations and subdividing what her secretary had already gone through—the personal and business-related. Two for baby showers, both from single women. One adopted, the other artificially inseminated. Abra admired them, but their decisions made her sad. It seemed an admission of defeat that they'd never find a man they wanted to marry and have children with. Was it just the reality of the times and of those damn statistics everyone seems to know so well—ten women for every decent man, or some such? She never bothered learning exactly what they were. She hadn't needed to know. But now it seemed to her, the important part was finding someone who spoke to your soul, and maybe that's what these women, former classmates, were responding to. She knew intimately that fervid desire to have a child, hers hadn't dissipated. She'd simply had to pack it away, along with her wedding album. But unlike her former classmates, she knew what raising a child solo could do. She'd seen it close up and wouldn't emulate what her mom had done, even if that meant never becoming a mother. She now knew the hole inside her was because her dad wasn't around, she didn't want to pass that on to a child. She made a note to send both new mothers presents.

Griffin was proving to be a valuable tutor for Abra. He was teaching her how to take meetings, do lunch and business. She had a closet full of hip, subtle clothes from costly places he'd turned her on to. She leased the appropriate Mercedes two-seater convertible, thanks to the *On the Verge* syndication deal, and did business everywhere, including the hair salon where she got her hair trimmed and her monthly facials. She'd moved into a small house with an ocean view, which in rare moments she got to enjoy. Griffin was teaching her how to be a player.

The phone rang and Abra put down her mail to get it.

"What are you doing there?" Natasha began.

"I'm just going through the mail."

"Abra, it's Sunday. Go to the beach, go home, read the paper."

"I thought you were in New York."

"I am. Miles is out running or at the gym or something. You'll never guess where we went to dinner last night . . ."

"Cynthia's new restaurant."

"How'd you guess?" Natasha shrieked.

"I just knew, that's all. How was it? What's it called again, something French?"

"Délivrance. How's that for pretension?" Natasha said sarcastically.

"And symbolism."

"Oh, don't go gettin' all deep on me. I think she's just a freak, that's what the release thing means."

Abra was silent for longer than she intended. "So was she there?" Abra asked.

"Yeah. I saw Miss Thing. So, let's see," Natasha said, not waiting for Abra's questions. "She's tall, but you knew that, thin, of course; very chocolate, short natural. You know, those model bones. Her face looked like someone sculpted—"

"So, she's really beautiful in person?"

Natasha, trying to be kind, but wanting to be descriptive, held back her true impression that Cynthia was perhaps the most gorgeous thing she'd ever seen, and simply responded with "yes." "But she was wearing this crazy dress, all the boobies hanging out. I don't know where Thing got it . . . and she was there with some Euro-trashy thing."

"So she and Cullen broke up?"

"Guess so."

Abra let the idea register. "So how was the restaurant?"

"You know, a bunch of ingredients nobody's ever heard of. Miles and Cynthia were checking each other out."

"Well, you'd better be careful, we know what she's capable of," Abra said.

"Yeah," Natasha said, trying to sound casual, but knowing she couldn't fake it with Abra.

"So when're you coming home?" Abra said gently.

"I'm taking the red-eye back. I have a breakfast," Natasha said. "Listen, I hear Miles coming in. I'll see you tomorrow."

Abra hung up, concerned about the Miles-Cynthia contact. She knew Natasha was in deep with Miles even though she tried to pretend not to be. More than that, she wondered about Cullen, if he and Cynthia had actually broken up.

Impulsively, she picked up the phone, dialed New York information and then called Cullen.

"Hi," her familiar voice rang through.

"Hi," a happy-sounding Cullen replied. "What's up? How you been?"

"Oh, fine, just fine. We're still trying to get this film produced, you know living the L.A. life."

"Yeah, life in La-La land. You sound good."

Abra reflected momentarily, mentally taking stock of her life and deciding she was doing well. "I am good. I don't know when I've been better," Abra said, stretching it just a little, realizing after hearing his voice how much she still missed him. "And how are you doing?"

"I'm good, too. I'm still at Croft. I'd considered leaving, that partnership thing was put off."

"Oh, I'm—"

"No, it's cool. I think it'll happen next year."

"So Natasha went to the new restaurant, she met . . ."

"Cynthia?" Cullen told her that they'd broken up.

"I guess I'm supposed to say I'm sorry."

"No, no, of course not," Cullen said. "How's it going? You happy?"

"Yes, I'm learning a lot about the business and about myself actually."

"Are you seeing anyone . . . ?"

"No, not really."

Cullen knew that didn't mean no. He figured in all the time since they split, she'd be seeing somebody. It bothered him, but he knew he didn't have a leg to stand on. Cullen sat back on the sofa and looked up at the ceiling, and wondered if she still wanted him.

"Well, I'm at the office, . . ." Abra said.

"It's good to hear your voice."

"Yeah, you take care."

MILES CAME IN and found Natasha on the floor reading the paper, dressed in clothes identical to his, blue sweatpants and a white T-shirt.

"I got bagels," Miles said.

"Oh goody, from Sonny's?"

"The joint."

"Are they still warm?"

"Just for you, baby."

Natasha popped up to greet Miles, who was still damp from his workout. She gave him a big wet, openmouthed kiss.

"Mmm, that's good," Miles said, licking his lips.

He pulled plates from the cabinet and Natasha got butter, cream cheese, tomatoes, and onions from the refrigerator. Miles pulled wrapped salmon and a jar of capers from the white deli bag. She set the kitchen table and they sat down. Just like a real couple, on any Sunday afternoon. Their thing had clearly grown deeper, but was getting to the point where they had to do something. Relationships have to move, and there were only two directions: closer together or farther apart. Miles and Natasha were happy with each other, their temperaments complementary, their sexual attraction intensely mutual.

Natasha was playing the game like the master she'd become, with cool detachment. She was just a little unavailable. She juiced Miles, but not too much. Miles knew Natasha had come as close as any, except maybe the one who'd gotten away. She was fine, successful, smart, down to earth, his four main criteria. But the one thing that turned him on most about her also bugged him the most. She was too flashy and he hated the weave. She could probably tone it down for his client dinners, corporate affairs, of which there were many, but in a way, he didn't want to ask her to do that. It was what he loved about her, that she was nonconformist. It was a quandary Miles found himself facing as he looked toward his fortieth birthday. He understood that a man who wasn't married much past forty was looked at askance—he was either gay or an irredeemable dog. He could picture Natasha being the one, but he wasn't sure that he was ready to hang up his dog-pound membership.

While they ate, Natasha watched Miles from across the table. A picture of beautiful Cynthia flashed in her head.

"So, I talked to Abra . . ."

"Couldn't wait to tell her, huh?" Miles said, piling onions and salmon onto his bagel.

"Well, yeah. So what'd you think of the place?"

"It was an okay, chronically hip place to eat. Manhattan really needs another one."

"What'd you think about Cynthia?" Natasha said, straining to sound casual.

Miles paused, chewing a mouthful of smoked salmon, bagel, and onion. "I thought she was fly," he said with his trademark honesty.

What Natasha wanted to know, but was something she'd never ask was, "Did you get her number, and will you pursue her when I'm on the West Coast?" At one point in the evening, when Natasha came back from the ladies room to find Cynthia lingering at their table, talking with Miles, she felt something in the air. Miles had a history with fashion models, but there was something more to Cynthia than a pretty face. Natasha knew that, based on how Cullen had carried on. It rocked her confidence and she hated feeling insecure.

chapter 25

O H, Ms. LEWIS, nice to see you again," Griffin's secretary said in greeting.

"Thanks. Is he in?"

"Sure is. Go on in."

Abra had a weird feeling. They were being too nice. Please, please let him have good news. She said a silent prayer as she walked to his office. She found Griffin staring out of his window.

"Abra, how are you? You look wonderful."

"Thank you. I'm fine, how're you?" she said.

"Excellent. I just saw some fantastic dailies. Have you had lunch yet? It's a little late, but Jen could order something for us."

"I could eat."

He joined her on the other side of his desk and sat down in the chair next to her, pulling it closer to hers. "You know, you remind me of a girl I knew in high school, Sabrina Daniels. Had the biggest crush on her . . ."

"What happened?" Abra asked, even though she knew

the answer, that he'd lusted after the brown girl in private, but would never have the guts to be seen in public with, as they liked to say, a "minority."

"Oh, who knows? We were young. She went to Berkeley, joined the Peace Corps . . ."

"Mmm. So you never did anything about your crush?"

"Oh, no, it was just a kid thing."

Abra knew she was beginning to sound captious and had to play it nice, since she did want something from him.

"We've been spending a fair amount of time together, but you seem to be holding back," he said.

Abra looked at him as if he were speaking Hindi.

"What I'm trying to say here is that I find you extremely attractive, and I'd like to get closer. Is that possible?"

She continued looking at him as if he were the poet Tulsīdās reincarnated.

Abra didn't view herself in the context of attractive. She knew that objectively speaking, she was pretty, pretty enough, but men didn't make comments like Griffin's to her. She always knew she had the kind of looks that crept up on people. She had no idea how to respond to this. *Where was Natasha when you really needed her? She'd know just what to do. She was the one everybody was always hitting on.*

"Well, Griffin . . . I . . . um . . . don't quite know what to say . . ."

"You don't have to say anything. If you're wondering what this has to do with the film, they are totally separate. I want to do the film, with some changes, of course, whether we get closer or not. That's why I called you to come down today. To tell you that."

"You mean we have a deal?"

"Yep, we have a deal."

"So what kinds of changes?"

"Oh, nothing major, but I think it should be lighter, not so heavy."

"A comedy?"

"No, no. Look, we can talk about this later. So, what do you wanna eat?"

"Just let me call Natasha first. We should set up a meeting to talk about these changes. Is that all right?"

"Sure. I'll give you some privacy."

Natasha convinced Abra that a few changes were no big deal and to relax. Abra wanted to, but there was something that made her feel uneasy about it. Griffin came back into the room, and Abra noticed that Griffin could be considered fine. He had thick, wavy dirty-blond hair and a darker, coarser beard. He was medium height and build and looked ten years younger than he was. Even though he'd been in L.A. in the movie business for twenty years, he still had a kind of Yankee way about him. Abra was attracted to him, flattered by the attention and was lonely. She figured he was just what she needed now, someone to help her deal with the pain, but whom she wouldn't have to worry about getting too attached to: He was White and married, someone to practice on.

Once they began seeing each other regularly, she liked having him in her life. She wasn't committed to L.A., but it seemed to work for now. On the weekends, she stayed with Griffin at his place in Carmel, where they talked, listened to the ocean, and read. He cooked epicurean meals for her, massaged her back, painted her toenails. She indulged his love of chess and read film treatments to him. On her birthday, Griffin invited Natasha and Miles out for a weekend, and he boiled lobsters and corn-on-the-cob.

"So this sounds like it's getting kind of deep, don't you think?" Natasha said to Miles during their drive.

Miles, in the passenger seat, changed the Gap Band CD. "Do you like anything that doesn't have a bass beat?" Miles asked, looking through Natasha's stack of CDs.

"What about what I just said?"

Miles pulled a vintage Sting from the pile and put it in.

"Natasha, baby, I don't have any thoughts about Abra's love life."

"Oh, come on Miles. They're a bit of an odd pair, don't you think?"

"I think your girl seems happy. Maybe she's using him till the film gets made."

Natasha looked at Miles and shook her head. "Not her style. She's got way too much integrity for that."

"Yeah, I guess that's more like something you'd do." Miles chuckled.

Natasha laughed but his words stung. Could he really think that of me? she wondered. They drove up a winding path, in silence, before pulling up to a yellow clapboard Colonial with the wraparound porch and bougainvillea sprouting from window boxes.

"I just don't want her to get hurt again, that's all. He is a mogul, after all," Natasha said, trying to forget Miles' callous comment.

"I'm sure Abra is capable of taking care of herself."

"She really isn't, Miles. She only had like one other boy-friend before Cullen."

"Well, then this is what she needs, experience."

Natasha let out an exasperated sound before pulling up the brake.

"Wow, look at this place. It's so cute," Natasha said,

parked in the circular drive. Calling the house "cute" was like calling a Harley-Davidson a scooter.

Abra heard the gravel crunch and walked out of the screendoor and waved from the porch, which was outfitted with wicker rockers and tables.

"Hey," Natasha said, waving back.

Abra and Griffin trotted over to greet their guests.

Abra kissed Miles on the cheek and hugged Natasha, who handed her a large brown- and white-striped shopping bag.

"A little something for the birthday broad," Natasha said, and kissed Abra on the cheek.

Miles handed Griffin a Cuban cigar and a bottle of Cristal.

"Good to see ya, buddy," Griffin said to Miles, holding up the cigar in appreciation.

Natasha unwrapped the zebra-print scarf that she wore on her head for convertible driving.

"You look so good," Natasha said to Abra, who was dressed simply in a white, sleeveless linen shirt, black leggings, and leopard-print mules.

"Really?" Abra said, genuinely surprised.

They paired off by sex and walked into the house.

"Um, Miss Thing, I'm scared. What is going on here?" Natasha said, the last part in a whisper. "Look at all this." Natasha was observing all the balloons and streamers Griffin had put up.

The women hung back while the men walked through the house and onto the deck, which overlooked the ocean.

"He's gone all out."

"Yeah," Abra said, smiling and looking around. "He's so nice."

Just then, Natasha noticed the sparkles coming from Abra's neck. "Stop!" Natasha shouted, momentarily forgetting herself. She reached out to Abra's neck and grabbed the necklace of diamonds that surrounded it. The piece was a strand of individual diamonds in a platinum-bezel necklace.

"Griffin *gave* you this?" Natasha said, still examining it.

Abra held her head up so that her friend could get a good look.

"Ohmigod! Cadabra man, what are you gonna do with him? I mean, if he's giving you . . . he's serious."

Abra looked calmly at Natasha. "We're just friends. I wasn't going to accept this, it seemed way too expensive—"

"Seemed?" Natasha interrupted, still looking at the necklace. "We're talking many carats. Eight, nine grand."

"I told him I wouldn't accept it, but he kept saying it's just a token of our friendship."

Natasha let go of the necklace, allowing it to lie flat on Abra's chest.

"I don't want him to get the wrong impression," Abra said.

"So?" Natasha said.

"So, I told him that I'm not interested in anything serious."

"Mm-hmm. So, nothing to worry about. You'll be disappointed with my gift."

They laughed and slapped a high five.

"We should join them," Abra said, leading her friend through the house that was comfortably decorated in English country. Griffin and Miles sat at a long wooden table that was covered with a blue-willow cloth, with chilled champagne flutes on top.

"So how're things, Natasha?" Griffin said, pouring two more glasses.

"Good, Griffin, things are good. You know we're out there shopping locations, auditioning actors . . ."

"How're the script changes coming?"

"Oh, fine. You'll have a revise Monday or Tuesday."

"Good. I keep telling Abra this is the fun part. Wait till you start trying to stay within the budget."

"Now, now. We'll do it," Abra said.

Natasha looked at the White man's face, classic aviator sunglasses, faded-blue polo shirt, eyebrows turned white-blond by the sun. He had the arrogant ease of someone who had had a lifetime membership in the ruling class. He could have any blond starlet he wanted. What did he want with Abra? Natasha wondered as she looked at Griffin, who was now talking about the stock market with Miles. Natasha thought Abra seemed in control, but wondered if she wasn't in over her head. He was, after all, a big-time player, big-time slick.

As the day wore on, Griffin put Natasha somewhat at ease when he toasted Abra, saying she was the best student he'd ever had and looked forward to *The Yarn* becoming a colossal hit. They all clinked glasses and the housekeeper brought out a chocolate cake covered with multicolored confection flowers.

chapter 26

*T*HE YARN, under Griffin, had become a yawn. All the depth from the original script had been filled in with feel-good themes. The fatherless theme was dropped completely because, well, don't all Black people grow up that way? He added White characters whose purpose it was to improve the lives of the Black mother characters. Same old story. After several early screenings, Abra saw the project getting further away from what was intended. She complained to Griffin, who told her that she was too close to it. She told him that he wasn't hearing her. She was just learning to hear herself. He was more concerned about having a White actress with some box office draw in the film, even though they had Mona Love, who was a big *Black* name and proven crossover. Abra thought she and Natasha should take their names off the film. Natasha's view was uncharacteristically practical—let's just get it made. Abra agreed to push through, get it made, and put it behind her. They wrapped the shooting in their scheduled six weeks, working well into the night, up early the following day to do it all over again. Too busy to notice that they were barely speaking to each other.

NATASHA AND ABRA sat side by side on the sofa in their office as Carlton, the movie's costume designer, pulled clothes from garment bags. He had pieces for their publicity tour.

"This one would look brilliant on you, Abra," Carlton said, handing a cobalt-blue sheath and jacket to her.

She just took it, not even looking at it, and put it on.

"So, you're all set for the premiere?" Carlton said to Natasha, who was flipping through his copy of *Vogue*.

"No, but thanks for contacting Pischa for me. He's making something. I haven't had time for a fitting yet."

"I'm sure it's brilliant."

Abra came out frowning. "I hate this."

"It looks great," Natasha said. Carlton nodded in agreement.

"I don't like the color, plus Natasha's the front person, not me. It doesn't matter what I wear," Abra said, looking down at the dress. Abra looked through the other long dresses, poufs, minis, and slinky pantsuits that Carlton had laid out on the sofa. "How about this for the premiere?" Abra said, holding up a patent-leather mini and a long silky jacket.

Carlton and Natasha looked at each other and then at her.

"Gone, Miss Two," Carlton said.

THEY HAD TO GO to the East Coast—New York, Philadelphia, D.C., Atlanta—for a week's worth of interviews, chat shows, newspapers, and radio. Abra left the TV stuff to Natasha, who was great at talking in sound bites and looked fabulous. In New York, rather than wait in the green room, Abra went outside to take a walk. She liked being back in New York and just walked without any real direction in mind. Heading down Sixty-ninth, on her way back to the studio, she saw a cute little restaurant tucked in from the street, with two tables in the discreet window. She noticed a beautiful woman with short natural hair. It was the hair she noticed first because it was like her own. She looked at the man who was with the woman and realized it was Miles. Her heart began pumping hard, and she felt her breath shortening. Her first reaction was to cross the street, to run before they noticed her. Her second mind said, *"Fuck* that." She shored herself up, finding her resolve, and walked into the café. Miles looked up and casually said, "Hey Abra." Cynthia looked as if she'd swallowed glass.

"Hey Miles. I was just out taking a walk."

"Oh yeah. You guys are here for the publicity tour. You got time? You wanna join us?"

Abra looked at Cynthia as if she were a pedophile, turned to Miles, and declined his offer.

"Natasha's probably finished now. I'm going to meet her."

"Well, hold up. I'll go with you." Miles held a finger up for the waiter, paid the check. He thanked Cynthia for joining him for lunch. Walking back to the station, Abra was fuming. Miles tried to quell her flame and her suspicions.

"So, she's looking for investors," he said, referring to Cynthia.

"Mmm."

"Yeah, her concept is good, but I'm not interested in the restaurant business."

"Oh."

"Listen, I'm sorry. I'm sure that was uncomfortable for you."

Abra paused, thinking about how she'd felt a moment ago. "You know, I just wanted to deck her."

"Maybe you should have," Miles said.

When they got to the studio, Natasha was waiting. She broke into a smile that filled her face when she saw Miles.

"Hi sweetie, what are you doing here?"

They hugged and kissed and hugged again.

"I just ran into Abra. I was having lunch up the street . . . and she . . ."

"Yeah, I just saw Miles, isn't that funny?" Abra said.

"Well, we've got another one of these downtown," Natasha said to Miles. "You wanna share our car?"

When Abra didn't tell Natasha who Miles was having lunch with, Miles breathed an uneasy sigh. He figured Abra didn't say anything because she wouldn't want to hurt Natasha. He was right, on one score.

"So," Abra said, "when I saw Miles guess who he was having lunch with?"

Miles and Natasha stopped cooing and looked at Abra. Natasha looked at Miles as if to say, who?

"Um, yeah," Miles said. Clearing his throat, "I was having a meeting with Cynthia. She's looking for investors for her restaurant."

Natasha was quiet for a second. "Hmm. And she just called you out of the blue?" she said finally.

"Well, you know, we met her at the opening, at Délivrance. Remember?"

"Yeah, I remember."

"Sweetie, it wasn't like that. There's nothing going on," Miles said.

Natasha looked at him, nodded, and told him she believed him. Abra wasn't so satisfied.

chapter 27

ABRA LISTENED to Odessa humming in the guest bedroom and was glad that her mother was so happy, but the
idea of having to go to the premiere and pretend to be proud
of a film she hated made Abra sick to her stomach. Having
her mom as her date made her feel even more like a loser.
Odessa had been thrilled, and Myrna and Sylvia had gone
into overdrive trying to find "just the right outfit for O."
Abra had considered going with Griffin, but was tired of
trying to explain herself and the film's characters to him.
Natasha had offered not to bring Miles, but Abra knew that
her friend really wanted him there.

"Honey, I'm so proud of you," Odessa said, coming into
Abra's room, dressed.

Abra looked at her mother who was wearing a pale-
yellow belted chiffon dress.

"You look so pretty, Ma."

"Thank you, dear. Why aren't you dressed?"

Abra sat on her bed, in her bathrobe, her hair and
makeup done, feeling like a runner at the end of a marathon.

What should have been a sense of accomplishment was more Pyrrhic victory than anything. They'd made a film, but it wasn't the one they'd set out to make. Mona Love turned out to be as egomaniacal as Griffin and between the two—one White male incapable of seeing Black humanity and one Black woman who couldn't let go of her ego for the sake of the film—it was a disaster.

"You know there's something I want to tell you that I never did."

"What's that, baby?" Odessa said, patting Abra's natural hair and sitting down next to her.

"I know you hate it," Abra said.

Odessa continued touching Abra's hair, but said nothing.

"I never told you that I knew how hard it was for you and the whole thing with Daddy." She paused.

Again, Odessa was uncharacteristically silent.

Abra went on. "I saw you. I watched you just sag, deflate, after he stopped coming around."

"I don't know what to say," Odessa said.

Abra knew she meant it. "I just wanted to tell you that I don't blame you."

"You sometimes had to just raise yourself. Is that how you feel?"

"Yeah, I did, but not anymore; it's okay now."

Odessa stood up, the tears were going to stain her dress. She looked at her only child sitting on the edge of the bed and hugged Abra's head to her belly. "I'm just starting to realize how much I messed up. I'm so sorry."

Mother and daughter held each other for a while, crying, purging. Abra was the first to break away. Odessa reached down, patted her soft, spongy hair. "You know, it's growing on me." Abra looked at her mother and smiled. She pulled on her skirt, slipped on some pumps, fastened her jacket, and looked in the mirror. The muted brown of the jacket looked good against her ruddy skin.

"Watch out, Tina," Odessa said, referring to Abra's stallionesque legs. "You got my looks and my legs." Abra mockingly rolled her eyes at her mother's recurring reference to their great legs.

"Cullen would die if he could see you now," Odessa said, giving her daughter another hug.

"Oh, Ma."

They both got teary as they held on to each other as though for life.

"We'd better get going," Odessa said, wiping a tear away.

EVERY BLACK PERSON remotely connected to the movie business in L.A. was at the premiere and so was every kind of ensemble and hairstyle. Speciousness, however, was the disposition uniformly worn. Natasha, dressed in a tiny, silvery, white-beaded slip dress with angel-hair straps, and Miles, in his classic tux, looked like a Hollywood golden couple. They held hands as they walked into the theater, while mobs of fans, held behind velvet ropes, yelled at passing stars. Natasha actually did a queen's wave as she passed.

Inside the theater, Abra and Natasha sat next to each other; Miles and Odessa on the outside. The old friends whispered gossip to each other, but kept a sangfroid face for their public. Celebs of various levels came over to kiss their rings. Natasha was loving it, Abra felt queasy.

A premiere audience is always kind, since it's composed

of friends, cast, and friends and relatives of cast and staff. Natasha and Abra floated out of the theater, into the party on their kudos. Natasha, Miles, Abra, and Odessa sat together at a reserved table in a cordoned-off, slightly elevated section. More people came over to put in a bid, persiflage, or just genuflect.

"I could get used to this," Natasha said, overlooking the party as if it were her kingdom.

"Tomorrow, it's back to busting your butts, Cinderella," Odessa said.

Miles smiled and shook his head. "Here comes Griffin," he said.

"Hey folks, you all havin' a good time?" Griffin said.

"Hey Griffin," Natasha said, "thanks for the party."

Griffin pulled up a chair next to Abra and looked over at her mother. "So, this must be Mrs. Lewis," he said.

"Odessa," she corrected.

Natasha looked at Miles. Abra smiled and introduced her mother.

"Did you enjoy the film, Odessa?" he asked.

"Well, of course my baby—"

"Ma," Abra said, cutting off her mother.

"Abra, would you like to dance?" Griffin said.

Odessa looked at Natasha and Miles, eyebrows raised. "Sure."

Griffin broke out in a sort of slow step, fists going as if he were playing air drums. Abra, who hadn't danced since the flood, did a version of the Rock.

"Now there's a sight," Natasha said.

"What's goin' on? How'd he know me?" Odessa said to no one in particular.

Abra and Griffin danced a few more fast songs and then did a refined grind through a slow one.

"Where'd they go? You see them?" Odessa said, craning her neck, having lost sight of Abra and Griffin.

Miles asked Natasha to dance.

"Odessa, they probably just went to get some air. You want a drink or something?" Natasha said.

"I'm fine, honey. You go on, don't worry 'bout me."

Griffin led Abra outside to the parking lot where they sat on top of his convertible and looked up at the stars. "So, how's it feel to be a movie producer?" he asked.

Abra thought for a minute, looking around the parking lot.

"I think I like it. I'd like it even more if it was a film I felt good about."

"Abra, we couldn't have made it the way it was. Love wasn't even going for it."

"Listen, you have the power to make 'Mickey Goes to the Moon' and to ensure that it's a success if you want. Please don't—" Abra said.

Griffin held up his arms, as if surrendering. "You're right. I didn't have the guts to make that movie. I went for the sure thing. I'm sorry. So, now what? Are you gonna stay in L.A.?"

"For a little while. I'm not sure what I'm going to do. We've pretty much shut down our New York office 'cause we couldn't handle all those expenses."

"Well, that's not gonna be a big problem now. Do you want to go back?"

"I don't know. I love this weather, but it doesn't feel like home."

"I know. That's why I have a place in New York."

"I should probably get back. My mom . . ."

"So do I get to keep seeing you? We no longer have the movie as our ruse."

Abra inhaled, and considered Griffin. She knew he wasn't talking about just the occasional dinner or lunch. He was a grown-up man who was looking for something more than just someone to hang out with. She liked Griffin, in spite of the cowardly way he'd handled their project. He'd let her see underneath some of that Yankee Yale-superiority mask, and she'd discovered a gentle, sensitive man who was fumbling with relationships, marriage, life, as much as she. He put his hands on the sides of her head, pulled her to him, put his lips on hers, and opened his mouth. She followed, and their tongues gracefully, if tentatively, palpated. Griffin moved his hands to cup her face. Abra closed her mouth and pulled away.

"What's wrong?"

"It's just . . ."

"What?"

"I'm just not sure."

Griffin took his arms away and held up his hands. "No pressure."

chapter 28

*T*HE *YARN* earned out opening weekend, which means it made the money it cost to make. No jumping up to the ceiling, but no hiding one's face, either.

"So are we talking?" Natasha said as she entered their office.

Abra looked up from the *Journal* and looked back down.

"Guess not," Natasha said.

"Natasha, I'm not *not* talking to you."

"But you think I'm a sellout."

Abra didn't respond.

"You know, you're probably right. I went kind of crazy once Griffin said he'd do it."

"Listen, it's behind us now."

"Are you staying?"

"I don't know."

"So, Griffin's still on your case, huh?" she said, trying to change the topic.

Abra had avoided talking to anyone about Griffin, since she hadn't yet figured out what to do about him. "He calls."

"Oh, so you gonna go vague on me, huh? What's up?"

"I don't know, um, he likes me."

"Why can't you just hang out, have fun with it?"

As soon as the words were out of her mouth, Natasha knew she was wasting her time. Abra looked at her friend, took off her reading glasses, and looked away. "Natasha, I pray every night that I could learn to be more like you, where nothing is too serious, but it's just not who I am. I don't do things just for the hell of it. If I'm not learning something or fulfilling my spirit, it's just a waste of time, and the older I get, the more I realize that that's who I am, and it's okay."

The phone rang and Natasha was thankful for the interruption.

"Hey sweetie," she cooed.

"What you up to?"

"Oh, just sitting here, chatting with Abra. So, how's China?"

"Japan. Same thing."

They laughed, and Natasha signaled two fingers to Abra, who gathered some papers and left Natasha alone in the office.

"So how many dreams have you had of me?" Natasha said.

"At least five and I just got here. Why don't you come meet me?"

"To Japan? Miles, I gotta work, can't rest on my laurels, you know that."

Miles sighed a knowing sigh that assured Natasha that he understood. "I'll be there in a few days, a week tops," he said.

"I'll be waiting."

"No you won't, that's what I like about you. I'll see you later."

Miles blew a kiss and hung up. Natasha sat for a moment, letting herself get dewy thinking about Miles. She was in love with him, but they never discussed it, and Natasha understood that that was the only way to handle Miles.

Abra came back into the office. "So, how's Mr. Wonderful?" she asked.

"He's wonderful," Natasha said, hamming it up.

"So, what's up with you two? This is going on what, a year?"

"More."

"So?"

"So, what? Are we getting married? No."

"So, where's it going?"

"Don't know, we don't talk in those terms."

"Mmm, that's probably smart, but you want to, don't you?"

"I want Miles. That's about all I know."

chapter 29

CULLEN FLIPPED THROUGH the business section while sipping coffee and returning calls. After several months of meeting with classmates, weighing their schemes for private enterprises, he had decided to stay at Croft. Having Farah committed to him was a chit he could use to get the partnership. Farah's stores were doing well enough for her to force their hands. He still dreamed of Cynthia, but had given up trying to contact her. She'd moved on, running her restaurant, and dating a Turkish photographer. Seeing her new boyfriend in the party pages of the *Times,* with his long curly hair held back with a scarf, helped Cullen understand that he had merely been an experiment for Cynthia. Cullen was dating various Barbie-type Black women who had predictable careers, but no one who interested him. He was living in the apartment he had shared with Cynthia. He occasionally called Abra, made a half-hearted attempt at reconnecting, and while he didn't regret his decision to separate, he always rethought it. What-ifs were the food of the anxiety-ridden and not Cullen's style. He knew that he hadn't made the right choice to leave his wife for Cynthia, but leaving, he felt certain, had been necessary. He still missed Abra.

DÉLIVRANCE WAS LOCATED in a still-industrial section of Tribeca. It was set up in a former warehouse on a corner, and canvas umbrellas dotted tables set out on what used to be a loading dock. Cynthia was sitting at a table, writing in a ledger, when Miles walked up.

"How you doin'?" Miles drawled.

Cynthia slowly looked up from her work and nodded to Miles. He sat down, and she summoned a waiter, who set down a blue bottle of water. Lunch was over, and the staff was preparing for dinner, still a few hours away.

"You want a drink?" she said to Miles.

"Naw, baby, I'm workin', but you go ahead."

In Spanish, she instructed the busboy to bring her an espresso. "So, what brings you here in the middle of the day?" Cynthia asked.

"Just on my way back to the office, looked up, saw your place, thought I'd take a chance and drop by."

"Mmm."

"So how's bitness?"

Cynthia looked at him with disdain. She hated vernacular and hated it even more from someone who knew better.

"Things are good," she said, locking her jaw, just slightly. "So does your girlfriend know you're here?"

Miles smiled his broadest, shit-eating smile and said that was doubtful. "My girlfriend," he said, emphasizing the noun, "has a very busy life and is incapable of, and probably not particularly interested in, knowing my whereabouts at most points during a day."

His curtness made him more appealing to Cynthia, who

was used to being the one to spit invectives. She checked out his expensive hand-tailored suit, his hand-sewn leather loafers, his Fogal socks. She liked his cockiness and his southern accent. He was clearly comfortable in his skin, and that turned Cynthia on, more than the infusion of caffeine.

"So, you work around here?"

"A few blocks away."

"So, you should come for dinner after work sometime."

Miles looked at his watch, took a gulp of water, and stood up. "Yeah, maybe I'll do that. You take care of yourself." With that, he walked away, leaving Cynthia, once again, dazed by his indifference.

As Miles headed back to work he thought about the effulgence that seemed to emanate from Cynthia. *I could understand homeboy leavin' home for dat.* However, while it was clear that she was no bubbleheaded model, he dismissed any ideas that he had entertained about a dalliance with her.

chapter 30

NATASHA FORCED HERSELF to abandon any thoughts of Cynthia and Miles as she considered what to do for his fortieth. She thought about taking him away, but he'd been everywhere—Italy, India, West Africa, all over Japan, and lots of China. She had no desire to see Australia. France was appealing to her, but he'd done that, too. She couldn't think of a thing he wanted that he didn't own. A party, she could give a small thing at one of his favorite restaurants, like Canastel's. She'd met a handful of his office friends and didn't really feel comfortable giving him a surprise.

"What do you think I ought to do for Miles' fortieth?"

Abra was at her desk, looking over a treatment.

"Natasha, I hadn't given it a thought."

"Oh come on, Cadabra, help me think of something."

Abra put down the document and looked at her friend. "Okay, what does he like?"

"Um, clothes, he likes to travel, he likes, um, women."

Abra smiled at her friend's attempt to joke about the

man she was in love with. "So take him someplace. I was just reading about this fabulous spa in Bali."

"Mmm, Bali, that could be kinda happenin'," Natasha said, "but I was thinking about a small party. What do you think?"

"A party? Are you talking about a surprise?"

"No, no. I'd tell him about it."

"Why don't you ask him what he wants?"

Abra's voice of reason won out.

EARLENE BROWNING came to New York only when her son summoned. That wasn't often. Natasha and Miles decided to have a party for his birthday, and he wanted his mama to be among the few select guests. She was in her bedroom, packing her Samsonite, when she heard the mailman slam the screendoor—his way of letting her know the mail had arrived. She finished folding her good blue-silk blouse and went to look at the mail. A letter for Miles arrived with a *Please Forward* at the bottom of the envelope. She recognized the handwriting even though it was a shakier version of the one she knew. Manns Johnson, Miles' daddy. The weight of it felt like a card. Manns, who hadn't seen Miles since he graduated from college, and prior to that, hadn't seen him more than a dozen times, was sending a birthday card to his only son.

Manns and Earlene hadn't married and hadn't been in love. They'd been two kids in heat in Memphis, who got carried away one night and made Miles. Manns had dreams of big-city life and fancied himself a player. Father and husband didn't fit in with that image, even though Earlene had once been a fine thing. He never did settle down, although age and regret had slowed him. He lived alone, in a neat house on the east side of Detroit, on his General Motors pension. A regular reader of the business sections, he'd actually seen his son's name in the papers a few times. He clipped each one and showed it to his poker buddies, none of them having the heart to laugh in his face, but did so behind his back for what they thought he must've been walking around with—egg on his face for leaving a boy who had gone on and made something big out of his life.

Earlene looked at the card that she held in her hands and tried to decide what to do with it. She sat down on the plastic sectional and felt herself flush with memories of forty years ago, when she lost her virginity and her freedom in one night. She didn't want to ruin Miles' party by giving the card to him there, but she didn't think it was right to not mention it at all. Miles never talked about his father, had stopped asking for him since he was in junior high school, when he figured out that his family consisted of just Earlene and himself.

She went back into her bedroom and completed packing. She called Miles at his office. He was traveling, but his secretary told her she'd have him call her back before the end of the day, which he did.

"Mama, you all right?"

"Oh, hi baby. I'm just fine. How you? I told that gal not to bother you."

Miles was distracted. He was calling from his hotel in San Francisco. "I figured somethin' was up since you never call me at work."

Earlene paused, not wanting to make a big deal out of the card, but wanting her son to help her figure out what to do. "Your father," she paused, letting the word sink in before she went any further, "um, your father sent you somethin' here, a card or letter or somethin' and I . . ."

"Mama, is that all?" Miles said, impatiently.

"Well, um . . ."

"What's it say? You can open it."

Earlene looked down at the pale-yellow envelope and carefully unsealed it with her pointer. She saw a drugstore birthday card with a picture of a cardinal perched on the vine of an orange-and-blue flower, with words in blue script that read simply, *Happy Birthday, Son.* There was a letter written on green steno paper inside, the tops of the pages ragged from being torn from a notebook. Earlene asked Miles if he wanted her to read the letter.

"Mama, I'm not all broken up to hear from him. It means nothing, okay? You can read it if it's short enough, otherwise just bring it when you come, or throw it out. I really don't give a hoot."

Earlene wanted to know what Manns could possibly say after all this time. She looked at it and saw there was nothing there but platitudes. He wasn't dying, but he had Parkinson's and was moving into a nursing home. She told him the abbreviated version.

"I really need to get a little more work done before the day ends here. Thanks for letting me know, Mama."

"You sure you all right?"

"Mama, I'm fine. I'll see you this weekend, okay?"

Miles hung up and went back to work. Earlene reread the letter, looking in vain for some purpose, some explanation.

NATASHA APPROACHED throwing Miles a party the way she did everything—with a vengeance. She brought in friends— a saxophonist, a pianist, and a drummer to provide jazz; a DJ for dancing. She hired a party consultant who hired a florist who hired the baker. The cake was a foot-long sheet, covered with a garden of rose buds. A mixture of Miles' friends from Soldman, college, and grad school, plus a couple of good ole boys from high school mingled and drank champagne as Natasha flitted about like the hostess she was. His friends who hadn't met her whispered compliments to Miles, each one making him more ill at ease. Even though he'd authorized Natasha giving the party, he felt a little uncomfortable at the idea that their relationship was so public. His best girl pal, Brenda, was there with her girlfriend and their new baby, who was strapped to her body in a sling. She was probably the most critical of all of Miles' friends, and even she okayed Natasha.

Abra and Griffin were seated at a table with Miles and Natasha, as well as Brenda, her girlfriend, and their baby. Abra couldn't stop staring at the baby, and at one point Brenda asked Abra if she wanted to hold her.

"Can I?" Abra said, leaping at the opportunity like a child being offered ice cream for dinner.

"Sure," Brenda said, unlatching the sling from her chest.

Abra played with the baby and seemed oblivious to everyone else at the table.

Griffin looked at her and smiled.

"So do you guys have kids?" Brenda's partner, a narrow-faced, biracial woman-child, asked Griffin.

"Um, no . . ."

Natasha jumped in and asked the baby's name.

"Benin, like the former African kingdom," Brenda said.

A collective "ahh" came from those at the table.

Natasha stood up and hit her glass with a fork to get people's attention. "I'd like to make a toast, if you'd all stand please . . ."

Brenda reached for the baby and Abra reluctantly gave her back. Miles stood next to Natasha, his arm around her waist, praying that whatever she said was like her dress, short yet not too revealing.

She kept it simple.

"Many of you have known the man of the hour for many years. I've had the pleasure for almost two, and I'd just like to say 'Happy Fortieth' to a fabulous human being." The crowd clinked glasses and hear-heared. Miles unconsciously loosened his tie and kissed Natasha lightly on her lips.

Turning toward the guests, he said, "I just wanna say 'thanks' to all y'all for comin', for bein' my friends, and . . . what else? Thank you, Natasha, for this wonderful celebration as I officially enter middle age. I just hope my next forty will be as eventful and as productive as the first. I'd also like to especially thank my mama, Earlene Browning, for everything she's done in gettin' me here. You're just the best, and I love you very, very much. Now y'all eat, get drunk, and have a good time."

It was lost on no one that Miles had done the safe thank you to Natasha, but gushed freely about his mama. While Brenda and a handful of other close friends knew that Miles was a mama's boy, everyone was surprised at this public display of it. He'd gotten downright misty when talking about Earlene. Natasha, who was kind of thick sometimes, missed most of it, except the formality of his acknowledgment of her. She was crazy about him and felt pretty sure he felt the same way. She also recognized that the same thing that made him so appealing—his background, how far he'd gone in life, given where he started—had also made him perhaps unable to form any bond other than with his mama.

She looked over at Abra and Griffin, dancing cheek to cheek, and fought back feeling like a fool.

As people ate, danced, and got drunk, Miles, Earlene, and Brenda huddled at a corner table for a visit. Brenda, who had left New York and moved back to her native Chicago, began grilling Miles about where Natasha was from, trying to place her.

"You don't know her," Miles said, laughing, trying to get Brenda to back off.

"Well, where'd she go to high school? Did you say she was from the West Side?"

"I don't know where she went to high school, who gives a fuck, s'cuse me Mama, where she went to high school?"

"Brenda, that baby is just gorgeous," Earlene said.

"Thank you, she is just the light of my life."

"Yeah, you've definitely chilled out since you had her," Miles said.

"You should try it," Brenda said.

Miles lifted his glass in a mock toast to Brenda and drank. "Maybe I will," he said, defiantly.

"I sure wish I had me some grandbabies," Earlene said, looking down and smoothing out her pleated red skirt.

"That Natasha sure is nice, ain't she Brenda?" Earlene said, ignoring Miles' presence.

"Oh, yeah. She's great, but Earlene, I wouldn't go getting too attached, if I were you," Brenda said. "You know our love 'em and leave 'em Miles."

"Damn, why y'all gon' do me like that?"

"Well, am I wrong?" Brenda said.

"I really, really like this one."

"I've heard it all before, Miles," Brenda said, munching on a cheese stick.

"This one could be different," Miles said.

"I sure do hope so, she's the nicest thing," Earlene said.

Miles had stopped introducing women to his mother long ago, so her mental inventory wasn't nearly as long as Brenda's. Brenda had met practically every woman Miles had gone out with in the last twenty years. There had been only one whom he seemed as interested in as he was in Natasha.

"So, you think you gonna do the right thing with this one, huh?" Brenda said.

"I might. She could be the winner, we'll see."

"She said you've been together almost two years, is that right?" Brenda asked.

"Um, I guess, I haven't really been paying attention, you know time flies when . . ."

"Mmm-hmm."

"Look, just because you all hooked up now, don't be . . . ," Miles said.

"Miles, you're forty, don't you think it's time?" Brenda said.

"I got all the time I want," Miles said with an arrogance that irritated the hell out of Brenda, mostly because she knew it was true.

"You guys . . . ," Brenda said.

Earlene looked at the two friends amiably sparring and shook her head. "Seems to me y'all just take a whole lot longer to grow up than in my time. Shoot, in my day, forty was old. Now, seems like you just gettin' started."

They both looked at Earlene, who was smiling and clearly having the time of her life, and laughed.

Brenda took Earlene's comment as closure on the subject of Miles and marriage. "So what's up with Natasha's girl?"

"Abra?" Miles said, closing his eyes to take another swig. "She's cool. She's Natasha's business partner."

"She's cute. She's into babies, huh?" Brenda said.

"Um, I guess so."

"Is the White boy her man?"

"Um, you could say that," Miles hedged.

"He kinda old for her, ain't he?" Earlene added.

"I guess Griffin's in his fifties," Miles said.

"What she doin' with him?" Brenda said.

Natasha joined their table. "There you are. Are you having a good time?" Natasha said to Miles.

"Oh yeah, baby, the party is slammin'. We just over here talkin' 'bout folks. Have a seat," Miles said.

"So, Brenda, it's really good to finally meet you in person. Miles talks about you all the time, and Benin is so cute."

Miles quickly began to feel claustrophobic with the three most important women in his life all together, at one table. He grabbed Natasha's hand and asked her to dance, leaving Earlene and Brenda alone to freely talk.

"So, you really like her?" Brenda started.

"Uh-huh. She just as cute as she can be, and she got some big job, in the movies."

Brenda nodded and watched the couple dance a modified two-step. "They look good together. She could be good for him, seems to give him a lot of room," Brenda said.

"Yeah, but I don't know if that's what he need," Earlene said.

"Whaddo you mean?" Brenda asked.

"You know Miles is all city slick and everything, but deep down he just a country boy, and he really want somebody who's gonna be there right with him. You know what I mean?"

Brenda looked at Earlene, nodded, and waited for her to continue.

"You know, he's just real homey. He's gotta know the woman he's wit ain't gon' leave him," Earlene said.

"You think he's looking for somebody like you?" Brenda asked.

"Well, ain't gon' be like me, but yeah, like somebody who's gonna love him like his mama do."

Brenda sat back and took it all in. She watched Natasha in her chartreuse shift and matching slings, her wild hair and pumped-up arms, as she tickled the nape of Miles' neck, the two of them laughing in each other's face. They looked happy. Brenda wondered if it was possible that Miles would ever settle with one woman.

ABRA WATCHED Natasha talk to a group of Miles' friends from Memphis, charming them, laughing at their jokes. This was the price of close friendship she didn't want to pay. The knowing before your friend does that something they hold dear isn't right, won't work out the way they want it. She felt bad for Natasha, for Miles' toast. While it was obvious that they cared deeply for each other, it also had been glaringly apparent that they wouldn't be able to move beyond the dating stage. Miles had too much baggage, and Natasha was from such a different place, she wasn't equipped to even recognize that, much less help him sort it out. She felt weird being in the city—where she had lived as a married person —with another man and a White man at that. L.A. was much less visibly race-conscious. Surely it had its same obsessions, but it managed somehow not to be so obvious about them. New York was subtle about nothing, including race. As nice as the people were at the restaurant, she felt conscious of being Black and of being with Griffin. It confirmed her feelings about being involved with him.

Griffin came back from taking a call and stood for a moment at the entranceway, just watching. He was struck by all the attractive, well-dressed, well-educated Black people and felt a stab in his chest. This was the audience for the original *Yarn*, the audience he hadn't thought existed—and since he hadn't believed in them, he'd turned a brilliant script into a mediocre movie. He hadn't known any better. He did know better than to comment to Abra about the crowd, as if the sighting were equivalent to seeing some rare cockatoo. His world, as much as he would deny it to Abra, and even to himself, was completely without color. He got to see how Abra experienced the world most of the time. Here he was the "minority." He knew he was a cultural stereotype to them: middle-aged Hollywood-player White guy without a clue about anything that didn't involve him or box-office returns. It was true, but at least he occasionally thought about other things. Most of his peers, his friends, didn't even think about other races. To his friends, *others*, particularly Black people, existed in a mysterious nonparallel universe in which they had no interest. Abra with her keen mind, her sensitivity, was still judged first by her race, which in their minds made her inferior; second by her gender, which only subtracted from the respect due her, and these two aspects were factored as her total being. When they did somehow get closer, they were forced to deal with her, her uniquely American sensibility, her class, which was more elevated than that of most Whites. It made them uncomfortable because she didn't confirm their notions of who she was. The same could be said for every Black person at the party: The larger world either didn't see them at all or viewed them as some kind of backdrop, treating them with either benign hostility or total indifference. This was the thing that bonded these people, not just those at the party, but most Black people who had become successful. It was what Abra had tried to explain to Griffin, during their many talks that ran long into the night. Until now, he had never gotten it.

Griffin joined Abra, who had been sitting alone. All night she'd alternately gulped champagne and pinot noir. She was fighting to keep her head from meeting the table. "Abra, why don't we go for a walk?" Griffin said, pulling her chair out, trying to exit before anyone noticed her. She stood up, took a deep breath, and went with him outside. It was fall, and the chill in the air felt good on her arms, which were covered only in a sheer shawl.

"Good thinking, Griffin. I was about to break down," she said as they walked aimlessly.

"Are you okay? I mean is it . . ."

"I'm not okay."

"Too much to drink?"

"Probably, but the whole Miles and Natasha thing is worrying me. Then I just started missing Cullen, and I don't know . . ."

Griffin took her hand and stopped walking. She stopped and looked at him. "What can I do? I want to help," Griffin said.

"You've been really nice, but there's nothing you can do."

"I can make it easier," Griffin said.

Abra looked into his eyes. "But I've already tried easier."

Griffin reached out to hug her and held her tight as she cried. He dried her face and eyes with his shirt cuff. When they walked back to the party, it had thinned. Miles and Natasha were sitting in a corner with his mother.

"You never told me that Brenda was gay," Natasha said to Miles, "not that it's a big deal, but I was a little surprised to meet her girlfriend."

"I think Brenda's finally happy. She tried for a long time to push it down," Miles said.

"I think it's kinda cool that you have a lesbian friend," Natasha said.

"Natasha, I don't do things 'cause they're cool," Miles snapped.

Abra tapped Natasha on the shoulder and handed her Griffin's number. "We're going," she said. "Great party."

"Did you have fun?" Natasha said to Griffin.

"We had a blast," he answered for the two of them.

chapter 31

MILES, NATASHA, AND EARLENE got into the back of the dark sedan that had waited outside the restaurant. They dropped Earlene off at the hotel—she loved to stay where the doormen dressed in jockey uniforms. After Miles was sure she was okay, he got back in the car and found that Natasha had dozed off and was snoring. He smiled, and didn't wake her until they got to his place. She rubbed her face and got out. It was a few hours before dawn. Inside, Natasha headed straight for the bedroom and flopped on the bed, still dressed, and pulled up the comforter.

"You beat, baby?" Miles said, undressing in front of his mirrored armoire.

"Totally," Natasha mumbled. "Can you help me take my dress off?" He unzipped her dress and handed her a flannel nightshirt to put on.

They both slept soundlessly until Miles woke up on hearing the newspaper dropped at his front door. He got up and dressed in jeans and a gray cashmere turtleneck. He skimmed the paltry Saturday business section and brewed some Sumatra. He thought about the party, the genuine smile on Brenda's face when she met Natasha. He recalled his mother beaming as he toasted her. He even read the card his mother had slipped into his hand, the one from his father. He studied the combination print and cursive handwriting, so similar to his own. He wondered for a moment what his father looked like now in his old age. He considered calling, but pushed that thought away, not so much for his own sake, but for his mother's. He couldn't honor a man who had been so dishonorable to his mama. He sipped his java black, letting its jolt work against the vague hangover that was hatching.

He examined his life. He had certainly become a success in terms of things—he had so much, so many possessions. He couldn't even think of anything that he wanted that he didn't or couldn't have. It was both satisfying and alarming, particularly for someone who had grown up as he had, someone for whom peanut butter and jelly sandwiches with a glass of milk were the occasional indulgence. Even though he worked hard, was smart, he sometimes felt as though he was living someone else's life, as if one day he would be discovered and all his things would be taken away. He needed to know that the person in his life, the woman he chose or who chose him, would not be swayed by a change, a disruption, a downsizing. How could one ever be sure?

He had been sure about the others; he knew that they were in it with him just for the ride, as long as it was in a Porsche. Those women had been as transparent as they had been abundantly available. But what about Natasha? She shared his love of things ghetto, both the superficial, like barbecue potato chips, and the serious, like the wisdom of Miss Mary down the street, Miss Mary, who wore cinnamon stockings. Natasha liked who she was. She, like he, didn't feel her Blackness made her inferior as so many of their contemporaries did. She reveled in it, figured out how to make it work for her, and so far, had done so with her business. That alone made her a worthy companion.

Whenever something scared him, Miles had trained himself not to turn away, but to face it. Commitment scared him more than anything he could think of, and for that very reason, he decided today was the day. He went into his bedroom, where Natasha was lying on her back, hand draped over her forehead, deep asleep. Miles reached under the covers and wiggled her big toe, which made her giggle and groan. He sat down next to her body and gently shook her.

"I have an idea," he said.

Still with her eyes closed she whispered, "What?"

"How 'bout we go jewelry shopping?"

Natasha opened one eye and looked at him with a raised eyebrow as if to say, "Did you say jewelry?"

Miles laughed and nodded.

"Well, what kind of jewelry are we talking about?" Natasha said, now moving toward sitting up in bed.

"I ain't buying you no earrings."

Natasha thought she knew what Miles was talking about, but didn't want to presume that he meant a diamond ring. "Okay, so where are we going?" she asked, now moving out of bed.

"I figure we can hit Tiffany, maybe make an appointment at Harry Winston . . ."

She reached over to hug Miles, who by now couldn't stop grinning. "I'll be dressed in twenty minutes," Natasha said, and headed to the bathroom. Miles lay back on his sleigh bed, looked up at the ceiling, and started to whistle.

They saw a dozen different stones and about half as many settings. They'd agreed on a round stone, in a channel setting. It would be ready in a couple of days. They headed south on Fifth Avenue—looking like two people who'd just gotten engaged—toward the hotel where Earlene was staying to have lunch with her before she flew back to Memphis. Natasha talked fast about picking a date, finding a bigger place in L.A., telling her mother, and how jealous her perfect pediatrician sister was going to be when she saw her ring.

"Oh shoot," she said, stopping midstride, "I forgot to call Abra." Pulling her phone from her backpack, she pushed at numbers. "I'll just be a minute," she said to Miles, who was looking impatient.

"I don't think she'll want to hear about it," Miles said.

"What are you talking about? Of course, she will. I'll just tell her to meet me later, like tomorrow." Which she did. They went and had lunch with Earlene who was waiting in the lobby.

"Whew, that was some party last night," Earlene said, looking down at the menu. "My head is killin' me."

Natasha looked through her bag, fished out some Tylenol, and offered it to Earlene.

"Naw, baby. I took me some Excedrin, it'll get to workin' afterwhile."

After she had drunk a pot of coffee, and her headache had subsided, Earlene noticed that the two of them had been holding hands since they sat down. "What you two so giddy about?"

They looked at each other, and Miles looked down at his western omelet. "Natasha and I are getting engaged," he heard himself say evenly, as if he'd just told his mother that her cab was waiting.

Earlene looked at her son and then at a beaming Natasha. She put her hands on her full cheeks, her attenuated red acrylic nails almost poking her eyes.

"Oh, Miles," she blubbered, "I'm so happy." She reached across the table and squeezed Natasha's hands and then gently brushed the back of her hand on her son's face. "I was hopin', but I had no idea you were plannin' this," Earlene said.

"I wasn't," he said, looking at Natasha. "I just woke up this morning and it felt right."

"So when is it? How about a place? You think you'll do it in New York?"

"Whoa, slow down, Mama. We haven't even talked about those things yet."

Earlene looked at her son and then at Natasha, trying her best to read what wasn't being said.

"That's right, Earlene, we've just picked out the ring," Natasha said.

"Oh, I see, okay . . . ," Earlene said, slightly crestfallen. She looked at her watch, and said that she'd better be getting to the airport.

"Don't be sad. We're gonna let you know everything, as soon as we figure it all out," Miles said.

Her smile returned, and outside, waiting for a cab, Miles hugged her and then included Natasha in the embrace.

Natasha and Miles went back to his place and took a bath. After making love on the bathroom floor, they wrapped themselves in his bathrobes. "So, you think this is a good idea?" Miles said, sitting opposite Natasha on the sofa.

Natasha closed her eyes and silently thanked God, Buddha, and Allah, making sure to cover all her bases, for this day. "It's a brilliant idea. We're made for each other," she said. She looked at Miles as if to say, "That's settled," reached for her reading glasses, and began reading from a pile of ever-present scripts. He smiled at her and felt an uneasy peace.

The next morning, after her run on his treadmill, Natasha was out the door to meet Abra for brunch. When she got to the restaurant that specialized in popovers, Abra was sitting at a booth reading the *Times* and sipping coffee. Natasha waved at her friend through the window. Abra waved back and pointed to her watch.

"I don't know why you can't be on time," Abra said, as Natasha slid into the booth.

"I really tried today, but I couldn't get a damn cab. You know down there where I came from? Cabbies have a choice between me and some White person with a riding crop, they're driving all on top of me."

Abra listened to her friend and laughed.

"So how's Griffin's place?" Natasha said, looking at the menu.

"Great. Huge, sunny, old. You know, the perfect co-op that neither of us would get because we'd never get past the board."

"Yeah. So what'd you guys do yesterday?" Natasha asked.

"I hung out with Sherry. You know the one who's married to David Warren? You and Cullen went to Howard with him?"

"Yeah, yeah."

"We went to the Guggenheim, down in Soho. Just walked around, talked. It feels weird being in New York. I keep thinking that I see Cullen." Abra stopped talking when she noticed Natasha seemed to be levitating. "So what's up with you? What'd you guys do yesterday?" she asked.

"Miles proposed," Natasha said, ready to burst.

"What? You're lying! Get outta here!"

Natasha sat looking at her friend, smiling and nodding.

"Oh, my God! Natasha! When? I can't believe this," Abra said, as if the breath had been taken from her.

"I know, honey, I was shocked. But he said, 'Let's go jewelry shopping and I ain't buying you no earrings.' "

"That's how he asked?"

"Uh-huh."

"Well, damn. Congratulations! I don't know what to say."

"Say you're thrilled, 'cause I am."

"I know you are."

Abra got up to sit next to Natasha and they hugged.

"I am happy for you," Abra said.

"Thanks," Natasha said, reaching for napkins for her full-fledged weep.

The waitress came balancing their orders of eggs Benedict and whole-wheat pancakes. "Was it something I did?" she cracked. The three women laughed and Abra shared the news.

"Oh fabulous!" the waitress said. "I'll be right back."

She brought back two flutes of mimosas and Natasha and Abra toasted.

"Is it gonna be weird helping me plan this thing?" Natasha asked.

Abra thought for a minute, chewed her eggs, and said probably. But not for the reason Natasha assumed. "I wouldn't not do it. I know you really love him."

"I do. It's so strange that this is happening to me. I'd completely given up . . ."

"I know, but that's when it happens. So, I already know the answer to this, but are you gonna do a big thing?"

Natasha tilted her chin down and looked at Abra as if to say, "Bigger than you've ever seen."

chapter 32

WORD OF Miles and Natasha's engagement spread through the BUP community like chicken pox in a nursery school. Even people who didn't know them were talking about the whopper from Tiffany.

Men and women, especially on The Street, speculated about Natasha like miners during the gold rush.

"Well, I heard the boobs aren't hers, and you know about the hair."

"I heard she went through Howard on her back."

"She's a bunny with an M.B.A."

"Is she pregnant? She must be pregnant."

"Miles is getting married? I'll believe it when I see it."

"I know he got her to sign a pre-nup."

"You know her daddy's rich. Owns rib joints."

"So, he's signing the pre-nup."

"Did that movie of hers make any money?"

"Of course, he'd marry some Hollywood person. Doesn't it just fit?"

"I heard he's gonna move out there."

Cullen had heard the news when he ran into Jackie Jones at a cocktail party. When Abra had called Jackie to background-check Miles, she had no idea that she knew the woman in question. And given Miles' steady stream of women, there was no need in bothering with who she was, because whoever it was, it wouldn't last long. Jackie had been wrong, and she and every other woman who had dated him or who just knew him was rethinking their assessment of old Miles, many of them privately wondering what this Natasha had.

Cullen stood off in a corner, chatting with some guys, holding a highball of Scotch and slyly surveying the crowd, checking out the women whom he didn't know. Jackie made her way over to him, and at first he didn't recognize her. He was about to go into his rap.

"Hi Cullen," she said brightly.

"Hey, hey. How you doin'?" he said, searching his mind for her name.

She held her hand out to shake, "Jackie Jones, from business school."

"Jackie, of course. How you doin'? How've you been?"

"I'm good."

"You still at Holoman?"

"Soldman."

"Right, right . . . right. So how's it goin'?"

"Fine, and you, what're you up to these days?"

"I made partner at Croft . . ."

"Well, that's great, and what's Abra up to?"

Cullen paused, trying to calculate what she might know. "Um, Abra's good. You know she and Natasha are in business together?"

"Yes, I did know that, and I hear that Natasha and Miles Browning are getting married."

Cullen asked her to repeat what she'd just said. One of his best friends in life was engaged, and here he was hearing it from practically a stranger. Finally the reality of his and Abra's separation hit him. He didn't just lose a wife when he left her, he had lost his net, his center, his community. Natasha had been like a sister, and now she belonged solely to Abra. His girl was getting married, and she didn't even pick up the phone to tell him herself.

"So, you know this guy? This Miles?" Cullen asked, trying to sound casual.

"Yeah, he a managing director at Soldman."

"Oh, I see. So is he a nice guy?"

"Um, I suppose. Don't you know him?" Jackie said.

Clearly, she didn't know about their separation. Cullen began to deflate. He looked down into his drink. As he went through several more Scotches, he revealed his whole story, the affair, the end of the marriage, his partnership nightmare. He figured accurately that she knew most of it anyway, the circle being so tiny that news traveled at the speed of light.

What had begun as a perfectly fun evening of success bonding, ended with a Lean Cuisine and a repeat of Seinfeld. He and Jackie had promised to get together again. He got home and thought about calling Natasha, yelling at her for her insensitivity, but what would that do? He knew why she hadn't called him. He'd fucked up his marriage. Why would someone just starting out want to talk to him? Plus the obvious that he'd fucked over her best friend. He sat on his sofa, holding the remote, flipping the channels during the commercials. He thought about Miles, then he thought about Cynthia. He thought about Natasha. He hoped that she'd found that elusive thing that he had thought he'd had with Cynthia.

ABRA WAS SITTING in her office, looking at the mound of scripts that sat before her. She didn't love the script part as Natasha did. Her strength was putting all the pieces together. For her, this career was business, not passion. She looked at the congratulatory dendrobium that sat on the desk for Natasha. How wrong had Abra been about Miles' toast and his commitment to her friend? I used to have good judgment, she thought. What she had picked up from Miles was a reluctance to announce to the world that he and Natasha were a couple in love, and she knew that there was something in the air when she'd stumbled on him having lunch with Cynthia.

Two things had happened to Miles that Abra would know nothing about: his father and his old girlfriend—the one who had married someone else, the one he had been in love with. Miles had missed out on her because he just was too afraid to commit. He made up excuses—his career wasn't where he wanted it to be yet; the timing was bad. While he did love Natasha, she also came along at the right time. People don't always marry the person they love the most, simply the one with the most advantageous arrival. Most important, though, was the card from his father. It reminded him of all that he didn't want to become—a pathetic, lonely old man. It was that simple. Once your player days were over, and that day does arrive, what happens to you? You get sick and die and no one really gives a damn. Miles believed he wanted a family and that he wanted to be there for his children, to teach them to love themselves, to succeed and to be true to themselves, all the things his father didn't teach him. His father taught him how he didn't want to be. How not to live. Manns Johnson had reached out to Miles because he had to move out of his neat little house on the east side of Detroit into a nursing home. Parkinson's disease had made it impossible for him to take care of himself. He wanted to send Miles his old Army uniform, things he didn't have any room to store and things he thought his only child might like to have. All Miles felt was pity for the old man for wanting to pass down things to someone who was a stranger.

NATASHA SAT in the wide first-class seat, holding her hand up so that the sun coming under the shade reflected glimmers of light off her new ring. The seat next to her being empty allowed her such behavior. She looked at the ring from the left, from the right, twisting her hand all the way to one side, then the other. She smiled at the recollection of how Miles had given it to her—in the bathroom, when she was brushing her teeth and he was on his way to work. She didn't care about the lack of ceremony, the gem more than compensated. He'd knocked before he came into the bathroom, where she stood in front of the mirror in a chenille robe and a short nightgown.

"I, um, picked this up yesterday," Miles said, pulling the small light-blue box from his suit pocket.

Natasha stopped brushing, quickly rinsed her mouth with water, and patted it dry with a hand towel. She looked at him expectantly, knowing what he was talking about. She had stayed on in New York a few extra days so she could wear it back to L.A. She took the box from his hand, carefully untying the silky white ribbon. She took out the small velvet box and opened it. She put her arms around his neck. "Thank you, it's just beautiful." She kissed him on the ear then on the mouth.

"So, I take it that you like it?"

"I love it," she said, slipping it on her finger.

"Good," he said, elongating his Os. "I gotta go now. Call me when you can, have a good flight." He left and she sat down on the toilet, staring at the ring. A call that came from car service saying that they would be there in twenty minutes was the only thing that got her out of her mesmerized state and into the shower and dressed.

On the flight, she leafed through phone-book size copies of *Brides* and *Modern Bride,* ripping out pages of bouquets, tuxedos, mother-of-the-bride and bridesmaid dresses. Experts say it takes a year to plan a formal wedding, she figured she could do it in six months. She knew she'd have to fight with her parents about not getting married in Chicago, but really L.A. was home for her. Her dad would surely see her side, as he always did, and persuade her mother that Natasha should have whatever Natasha wanted.

By the time her flight had touched down, Natasha had checked in with Abra, making sure there were no fires that needed to be put out, and made appointments to look at a few possible places to hold the wedding, like the Nikko and the Hotel Bel-Air.

"Between the rock and those huge magazines, I'm surprised they let you on the flight," Abra said, smiling at Natasha when she walked into their office. "Okay, let's see," she said, holding her hand out for Natasha to show the ring. "It's spectacular," she said, holding the tips of her friend's fingers. "I think it's the most beautiful ring I've ever seen."

Natasha nodded and looked down at it, for the billionth time that day.

"It's certainly the biggest," Abra said.

"Isn't it? Whaddya think it's worth?"

Abra laughed at her friend, who was only half-joking. "Whatever it is I'm sure Miles has it insured up the wazoo."

"Probably had it appraised at twice its cost, knowing my Miles," Natasha said.

"So," Abra said, looking at the magazines tucked under Natasha's arm, "you're planning?"

"Oh yeah, let me show you this amazing dress," Natasha said, flipping through the torn-out pages that made up her newly created wedding folder.

"Look," she said, holding up a picture of a woman in a white satin gown with a simple fitted bodice, a fabric tie belt, and a voluminous skirt. "Isn't it perfect?"

Abra looked at the picture and nodded.

"And look at this one," Natasha said, digging through some more pages and then holding up one of a silk taffeta coat over a silk crepe-satin gown. "This would be perfect for evening."

"You could do both," Abra said sarcastically.

Natasha ignored her friend and continued on to show pictures of flowers.

"What color do you think for the bridesmaids?" Natasha asked.

Abra shrugged her shoulders, meaning she didn't know.

"How about a really pale lavender?"

Abra nodded.

"What about orange?" Natasha continued, becoming more and more like a hyperactive five-year-old.

"That might be a bit much. How many bridesmaids are you having?"

Natasha crinkled her forehead and her mouth and said, "I don't know."

"Well, who are your close friends?"

"Other than you? Well, it used to be Cullen, and I guess I'll ask my sister. I don't have any other friends."

"Well, so it's me and Natalie. Have you told Cullen yet?"

"Nah. I haven't talked to him in a while."

"Natasha, you should call him. You were really close."

"Yeah, but . . ."

"You need to forgive him. I have."

"You have?"

"I had to, it's more for me, than him, believe me. I couldn't hold on to all that bitterness," Abra said, examining the wedding-dress pictures. "I mean I can't figure out my life if I'm holding on to what Cullen did to me. Maybe walking out of our marriage was the best thing that could've happened. It was surely what he needed to do for himself."

Natasha looked at her friend and smiled, although she was a little confused.

"You know, I'm discovering all kinds of things about me that I never would have if I were still married to Cullen."

"Really? Like what?"

"Like what I'm capable of. Like this business. I would've never moved out here and—"

"And figured out how to work it," Natasha finished.

"It's like, for the first time, I finally feel like I can do whatever I want. I realize how strong I am and that my value is about what's going on inside."

Natasha reached out to hug her friend.

"You need to tell your family, too," Abra said, getting back to her laptop.

"Yeah, I know. My dad's gonna be pissed that Miles didn't ask him . . . but shit, I'm a grown woman."

"Damn near middle-aged, but still his baby," Abra joked.

chapter 33

THE PHONE RANG several times before a distracted female voice answered.

"Um, hi, is Cullen there?"

The voice cleared itself, rebounded, clearly contrite for the initial greeting. "No, I'm sorry he isn't, he just stepped out, but he'll be back in a few minutes, um . . ."

"Okay, um, this is Natasha Coleman. Would you ask him to call me back? I'm at work for another half hour, till about eleven-thirty, East Coast time."

"Natasha? . . . Sure . . . I'll have him call you."

Natasha hung up, wondering who the woman was who seemed to recognize her name. She went back to work and a few minutes later the phone rang.

"I thought you'd forgotten all about me," Cullen said.

"Well, I tried, but your Windsong stays on my mind. How the hell are you?"

"I'm good. Working too hard again, but what else is new? And you? I hear congratulations are in order."

"Yeah, I finally snagged one."

"So, are you happy?"

"I'm stupid, I'm so happy."

Cullen closed his eyes and smiled. He could picture his old friend's face and feel her joy. Her tone convinced him that she'd found what he had thought he had with Cynthia. He was glad for her and told her so.

"So, you're dating again, I see," Natasha said, wanting to get to who was answering his phone.

"Um, yeah."

"So . . . who is she? Anybody?"

"Um, Jackie Jones. She went to business school with you and Abra."

Natasha had a horrible memory for names. She tried to search her memory bank, but was coming up blank. "Who? What'd she look like?"

"It's not serious."

"Uh-huh. What does she look like?"

"She was in your section, kinda short, big legs, uh, glasses . . ."

"Cullen, that tells me nothing. What does she look like? What's her hair like, what color is she, is she cute?"

"Oh, um, yeah, of course she's cute. She had long hair in school, and she's kinda light-brown."

"What's light-brown? Like Abra?"

"No, no, little bit lighter than you. In school she always wore skirts, loafers and . . ."

"Oh, yeah, I know who you're talking about. She was kinda heavy, very serious, from California, San Fran someplace . . ."

"Oakland. She's not heavy anymore."

"I remember her, Abra called her, she checked Miles with her. So, how's it going?"

"Fine. She's funny, easy to be with, but it's not serious."

"Yeah, right. You said that already."

"So, you and Miles, when's the big day?"

"Um, we haven't set the date yet, but I'll send you an invitation."

"I can come?" Cullen's voice brightened.

"Yeah, but you can leave Miss Jackie at home."

"Did you check with Abra?"

"Of course."

"Good, I'm glad, how's she doing?"

"She's great."

"Still seeing that same guy?"

"Um, yeah."

"He's a White boy. Seems to me if she wants a family, which I know she does, she should find someone who's viable."

Natasha felt a heat rise up in her but let Cullen finish his thought before lighting in to him. She knew he had no idea what it was like for women, especially accomplished Black women. He could just move from one woman to another and never have to think the words *dearth* and *women* in the same thought. She bit her tongue.

"Plus, Tasha, he's married."

"Abra's just trying to enjoy her life," Natasha said, straining to keep the anger out of her voice.

"I just meant . . . ," Cullen said.

"I know, you ain't got a clue, as usual. Abra's seeing somebody who's White, and he has a wife whom he never sees. They like each other and that's that. I don't think you're in any position to talk about her choices."

Cullen was momentarily silent. "You're right. I know I put her through hell and she should be applauded for going on the way she has."

"And for forgiving you," Natasha added.

"And for that."

"Look, I don't want to go over all that stuff. I was calling to invite you to the engagement party my parents are having."

"In Chicago?"

"Of course."

"Yeah, I'll be there. Wouldn't miss it."

Natasha hung up the phone, still pissed at Cullen. She went back to her list of people to call.

ABRA LISTENED to the relaxed, refined voices from the public radio station on her drive back to L.A. from San Diego, where she had attended a conference of television executives. She savored the solitude and the chance to let her face muscles relax. She'd smiled endlessly during the panel discussions and dreadful network sessions and was glad to finally be free to be with herself. She thought about how happy Natasha was, she even moved differently. Abra wished that she could be totally happy for her friend, but she couldn't stop wondering what had pushed Miles to propose marriage. She wanted to talk to Natasha, felt that she had to, but what would she say? *Be careful, I have a funny feeling.* She couldn't do that, not unless Natasha asked. *Maybe she'll ask. No she won't, Natasha is now in never-never land. She's not herself—somewhere with the cow, over the moon.*

Abra thought about her recent time in New York, how much more like herself she felt there. After the museum, she and Sherry went to one of her favorite bistros and spent the evening talking. Sherry had become more resolute in her decision to be married to David, especially after Cullen and Abra had broken up. She'd begun to view her marriage as a natural progression from her own parents' passionless but functional marriage. "We always live out their stuff," Sherry had said. That rang in Abra's head, *We always live out their stuff*. What did that mean for her? She was determined not to live out her mother's legacy to her and have a child on her own. So what are you left with if you choose not to live a legacy? You have to feel your way. And the path is dark, unpaved, and scary.

She got back to L.A. and found several messages from Griffin. He wanted to have dinner, check out a screening. He used a shorthand, the way people familiar with each other do. She wanted to forget about what happened to their film and just let herself be with Griffin, but she couldn't. The fact that he was White did bother her. She liked being with someone who experienced life the same way, who liked the same music, who had the same history. She liked people, especially men, who had worked for what they had and who didn't take things for granted. An arrogant, spineless man had to be the worst thing she could imagine, and while Griffin was better than the White guys she had known in school, in many ways, he was still one of them with their private eating clubs and secret societies. She fingered the diamond necklace that he'd given her. It *was* too much. As much as she liked Sherry, Abra didn't want to ever again feel like her and settle for the easiest deal offered.

chapter 34

MILES LEANED BACK in his swivel chair, looking at a framed picture of Natasha taken at his birthday party that sat on his desk. She looked rhapsodic. He looked like a fox at the commencement of a hunt. It was how he felt now. He touched the Cohiba in his breast pocket and looked at his watch, knowing that he should've already been on a flight to Chicago. Meeting Natasha's father, mother, and all their friends in one night was not something he was looking forward to. He looked at the photograph, at her face. She was pretty, not beautiful. She wasn't what he thought he'd end up with. She was smart, but not cerebral, like his first love. She was flashier than anybody he'd ever been serious about and probably the most successful in terms of owning her own thing. She was cheerful, that was a plus. They would be bicoastal, another appeal. Marriage terrified him, but he strained to push that aside in favor of doing something real with his life, something more than merely making money. If it didn't work out then at least he could say that he'd made the attempt, that he wasn't a chump, that he'd stepped up to the plate.

On the flight out, Miles nursed a glass of brandy and thought hard about what he was about to do. Natasha was a wonderful person, of that he was sure. She was honest and hardworking and would probably be a good mother. She would be there for him. He reclined his seat and turned off the lamp. Why, then, knowing all that to be true, did the serenity he craved elude him? He always had a gnawing sense inside him that his life was not all that he'd wanted. He figured that that itch was to be something more than a person who just makes a lot of money. He'd always assumed that once he made a commitment to someone, the gnawing would go away and he'd relax into a Zen-like calm. Instead, ever since he'd given Natasha the ring, the gnawing had just gotten worse. He knew that he wanted to be with one woman, to come home at night and eat dinner in the kitchen and go to his kids' school plays. Perhaps it was the one thing he wouldn't be able to have. Perhaps as much as he thought he wanted it, deep down, he liked his life just the way it was.

Miles made the long walk down the O'Hare terminal out to a taxi stand, his legs feeling like his pants were cuffed with ballast. The Colemans had rented the once grand and now grand again South Shore Country Club and invited a thousand of their closest friends. The immediate family and bridal party would gather first for an intimate dinner at the Pump Room, which judging by his lateness, he'd missed most of.

When he arrived at the restaurant, he stood at the maître d's podium, the gnawing even more intense. He spotted Natasha who was dressed in an animal-print jacket with a mink collar and a short velvet skirt. All that hair was piled high and her makeup was the work of a professional. Norwood sat at the head of the table telling stories, his robust voice ricocheting off the walls. No one dared to complain, because he was, after all, the Rib King. Abra noticed Miles first, checked his tentative expression, and worried that her first instinct about his diffidence had been right. She nudged Natasha, who jumped up to go and greet him. She hugged him gently and rubbed his midsection.

"How you doing sweetie," she cooed in baby talk. "Was your flight okay?"

Miles kissed Natasha on the cheek and told her she looked beautiful. "We need to talk," he said, trying to get her to meet his eyes.

"In a minute, honey. Everybody's waiting."

She walked him up the few steps leading into the restaurant and toward the table where her mother, father, sister, Earlene, and Abra were seated.

Once they were within a few feet of the table, Norwood turned his seat slightly, looking at Miles from shoes to shave, before meeting his eyes.

"So this is Miles," Norwood said, gathering his considerable physique out of the chair. He was full-bodied, not fat.

Natasha and her father were tuned in to each other the way compatible souls were. She always knew when he liked something and when he didn't. She understood what a shift in his chair meant or when he held a smile a little too long. He was always gracious and many people mistook that for approval. Natasha knew better. She studied every one of Norwood's moves, silently pleading for his benediction.

He got up, shook Miles' hand. "Miles. It's good to meet you."

Norwood's six-four dwarfed Miles' average height.

"Hello sir," Miles said in a voice reserved for his most

esteemed associates. He apologized for being late, explaining that something had come up.

"Sir, I like that," Norwood said to the guests at the table who all—especially Natasha—seemed to be holding their breath, as they watched the men's encounter.

"It's good to finally put a face with the name," Norwood said, heartily shaking Miles' hand and slapping his back.

"It's an honor to meet you. I'm really sorry I was late—"

"Nonsense boy, you a bizness man, got to take care of your bizness first. We went ahead and ate though. There'll be plenty of food at the party. You can eat there."

Before Miles sat down across from Natasha, between Abra and Norwood, he kissed his mother on the cheek and Natasha's mother's hand. Natalie, Natasha's sister, had a distant air about her like so many women Miles had known, and she wore an expression as if she smelled something unpleasant. He shook her hand.

Marge, Natasha's mother, whispered to Natasha that he was a "fox." They giggled like girls. On the other side of Marge sat Earlene, beaming. Marge began the conversation with pleasantries about their town, who was going to be at the party—the mayor was expected to stick his head in, and *Jet* and the *Sun-Times* would be covering the event. A bottle of Cristal sat at each end of the table.

"We did wait till you got here to open the champagne," Norwood said, summoning the waiter.

As the waiter filled their glasses, Norwood looked at Earlene as he spoke.

"It's been a real pleasure meetin' your mama, Miles. She's some woman," Norwood said as Earlene blushed.

"She's family already," Marge added, holding Earlene's hand.

Once everyone had a glass, Norwood held his up.

"Natasha, you're my baby girl, always will be. You know your mother and I only want the best for you. Today marks the beginning of two families becoming one. Here's to you."

It was a runaway train.

The Colemans' twin S600's waited outside the restaurant to take the group to the party. It was supposed to be the parents and Natalie in one car and Abra, Natasha, and Miles in another. Outside, under the brightly lit awning, Miles pulled Natasha aside and told her he needed to be alone with her. He asked Abra to ride with the parents.

Natasha, head full of cotton candy dreams and happy endings, thought Miles simply wanted a private moment with her. She cooed and carried on until they got into the back of the car. Miles told the driver to take the long way to the South Side.

"We're staying he-er . . . ," Natasha sing-songed, referring to the five-star hotel they were pulling away from.

"Baby, we've gotta talk." They sat in the cavernous back seat and he put his hands over hers.

"You know that I'm crazy about you, don't you?" Miles began.

"Of course."

"And I hope you know that I'd do anything to keep from hurting you. You know that, right?"

"Miles, what are you getting at. What is it?"

They passed the Hyde Park Hilton. Natasha looked out the window and said they were almost there. "Do you want him to keep driving?"

Miles inhaled deeply, trying to figure out the best place to tell Natasha what he knew was going to devastate her.

Right now, he'd do anything, almost anything, to keep from having to say what he was about to tell her.

They rode for a few more blocks. Natasha pointed out areas where Norwood had stores, many more since Miles had been an undergraduate in this town. He'd always liked Chicago. It was like a big country city. The people were friendly, like southerners, yet wary of outsiders.

"You can tell me anything, Miles, it won't change the way I feel."

The driver announced that they were a block away. Fine, Miles said, we'll get out there. The Colemans' other Mercedes, along with a few limousines, was parked in the semicircle in front.

Miles looked up as they walked inside and noticed a balcony. They walked inside the limestone structure into a large marble foyer that had a stone circular staircase. Inside the main room, gold, silver, and black balloons and streamers dangled from the ceiling and mural walls. A band played Duke Ellington, and Coleman family and friends were on the floor dancing the Lindy hop. Guests who spotted Natasha squealed in delight, young women grabbed her hand for a look at the ring, older women checked out Miles. They hugged her, kissed her, patted her. She was comfortable in her role as Rib Princess. She greeted her subjects with kindness and care, oftentimes shuttling Miles to the side. When she did introduce him to one of the throng, no one's name stuck. After what seemed like hours to Miles, but in fact had been only a few moments, he firmly seized Natasha's arm, jolting her out of her reverie.

"Miles, what is it?"

"Please, Natasha, come with me."

She excused herself from the person who had been congratulating her and followed Miles up the stairs. "Miles. What is wrong with you!"

He opened the French doors that led onto the balcony. They stepped outside, Natasha hastily rubbing her hands against her arms. It was fall, but fall in Chicago was a non-event.

"You cold? You want my jacket?"

"No, no, I'm fine. The air feels good."

Miles took the cigar from his breast pocket, running the length of it under his nose to better experience the aroma. "Peter gave it to me today, at work."

"Oh," Natasha said, not knowing how to respond.

He put his finger up to his mouth, as if telegraphing his brain to guide him carefully. "Natasha, this is probably the hardest thing I've ever done."

Her stomach sank.

"I want you to know that I believe I love you and I know you're a wonderful person."

As Natasha watched him, tears flooded her eyes.

"But I can't give you what you want. I really thought that I wanted the same things, the kids, the Range Rover, the whole nine, but I don't. I knew this relationship stuff was not easy for me but I thought I could do it. I thought I could make myself do it, will it, like I've done everything else in my life. But I can't. And knowing how much I'm hurting you right now makes me wanna hurt myself. I'd take the pain, baby, if I could."

Natasha's moist eyes took it all in; her head bobbed slightly as she looked at him and tried to sniffle back the tears. The softness in her eyes let him know it was okay to open his arms. She fell into his chest and he closed his eyes and held her tight as her body jerked in syncopation with her sobs. They stood, him holding her firmly and wondering what the hell to do next, wishing he could say something to make her stop. He opened his eyes and walked her over to a cement bench where they sat down together. He reached inside his jacket and handed her a cotton handkerchief. He always carried a handkerchief. It had been one of the first things she decided she liked about him. He carried one, just like her dad always had. When Natasha was growing up, whenever she needed one, whether it was when she cried all the way home because someone at school had hurt her feelings or when she'd cry with her parents at the airport, on her way back to Howard but already homesick, Norwood would offer his handkerchief for her to blow her nose, dry her face. When she became a woman the thought of how her daddy would take the used handkerchief back, fold it up, and put it in his pocket melted her heart.

Natasha stopped crying and sat, just staring out at the dark outline of the trees before them, feeling Miles' shoulder against hers. She thought back to the beginning of the evening, when Norwood first glimpsed Miles. The body shift in his chair told her what her dad would've been pressed to say – that he didn't approve, that there was something not quite right about this match. She inhaled deeply through her nose, trying to recover her demeanor although her head felt like a short-circuited toy.

ABRA WALKED AROUND the party, casually looking for Natasha and saying hello to a number of graduate-school classmates who were living in Chicago. Most of them were coupled off, living in the 'burbs, living the life she used to have. Some of them greeted her warmly, complimented her new short hair, her outfit—a long wine-colored jacket and

slim pants. Some of them, the severely coupled, acknowledged her with pitying looks and body language that said
don't get too close, for fear of catching her social disease of
divorce. Abra laughed to herself; a year ago their rebuffs
would've hurt her, but now she felt pity for them, for she
knew that their carefully constructed facades, the cocoons
they'd built, were as sturdy as the blanket tents she used to
make as a kid. They'd opted, as she once had, for a perfect
patina of a life, one torn from the pages of a magazine, where
the models have spent hours under lights and made up to
grant them a look to want but impossible to get, where kitch-
ens never have spilled milk, and living rooms were free of
dust. In buying the patina, they'd become freeze-dried, growing no more, missing out on the imperfections that make life
rich.

Standing on the outer rim of the dance floor, twirling
the base of his champagne flute, Cullen appeared in her line
of vision. It was the first time in almost two years that she'd
actually seen him. Her first reaction was a small, startled flip
in her stomach, but just as quickly it was gone. His hair had
grown out a little and he'd gained a bit of weight—both
changes for the better—otherwise he looked exactly the
same, his glasses still slightly jacked, the skin on his face still
a little ashy. A few seconds, it was as if he'd felt the heat
from her gaze. He turned and looked at her, smiled. His smile
was returned. He walked to her and gently kissed her cheek,
repeating what the others had said, that she looked fantastic.

"So do you," Abra said. "You needed a few more
pounds."

"Yeah, you think so?"

She nodded, a tender look on her face. Her expression
made Cullen uncomfortable. *Why'd she have to be so nice?*

I was such an asshole and she's giving me the Mother Teresa treatment.

He quickly changed the subject, reached for something neutral. "So," he said, looking around, "this is some party, huh? Of course, I don't know why I'd expect anything less. I haven't seen Natasha yet. Do you know where she is?"

Abra told him that she'd seen her earlier but hadn't seen her at the party either. "I was sort of looking for her when I saw you."

"I haven't even met the man yet, Miles."

"I don't see him either. I guess they're together."

MILES AND NATASHA sat on the bench until their butts were numb. They hatched a plan to tell the parents that it was Natasha's decision to break it off. Their absence from the festivities had surely alerted the family that something was up.

"So, what do you want me to do?" Miles asked.

Natasha, who was still in mild shock, understood that they had to face their families. She wanted to find a name for what she was feeling. She didn't hate Miles; not only did she still love him but she liked him even more. She respected his honesty. She looked down at her ring and smiled at the memory of how happy she'd been when they went shopping for it.

"I want you to keep it," Miles said, looking sideways at her.

She looked at him and said, "I didn't intend to give it back."

They shared a genuine laugh.

"So, what will you do now? I mean you almost gave it all up," Natasha said, feeling some of herself return.

Miles too understood that she was recovering. He felt relieved. "I don't know. I guess I'll just go back to my empty ways."

"And all those other women?"

"I still love you. I don't expect that's gonna go away, just because we didn't go all the way."

Natasha put her hand on his and leaned her head on his shoulder. "Why does it have to be so hard?"

"I think it's called life, baby."

"I guess we should go tell everybody."

They walked back down the wide circular stairway, holding hands, Miles holding on to his cigar. The music was still going, but now a DJ had taken over. Natasha and Miles saw their mothers on the dance floor, which was filled with folks doing the Electric Slide. They found Norwood talking with an alderman. He stopped when he saw them.

"There you are. We been lookin' for you half the night," Norwood said, looking at Miles' damp, crinkled shirt, knowing that Natasha had been crying. Norwood excused himself from the politician. "You want me to get your mother?"

Natasha looked over at her mom, happy, dancing, in her element. "No. I'll talk to her later."

She and Miles stuck to their story. Norwood listened and nodded. He knew they weren't telling the truth, but he let that pass because the more important thing was that they'd sensibly averted disaster.

Miles shook Norwood's hand and Natasha kissed her dad on his razor-bumped cheek. She slipped her hand into Miles' and they walked toward the door.

"I can handle it from here," she said. "You can take one of Daddy's cars to the airport."

They stood in the entranceway and looked at each other.

"You sure you're okay?" he asked, misty-eyed.

"No, but I will be. If you leave now, you can still get a flight back to New York." He kissed her forehead and thanked her for being a class act.

Natasha stood in the breezeway and watched Miles walk away. She watched him reach into his pocket, take out a cigar cutter and nip off its edge. He got into the backseat, leaned back, and lit up. Her pain was almost unbearable, as was his, but she knew she would survive.

ABRA AND CULLEN looked around, obviously avoiding looking too much at each other.

"So you must be seeing lots of old friends," Abra said.

"Yeah. It's like this is my life . . . all these folks."

"I'm sure. Are your parents here?"

"Just my dad. You know my mom can't deal with all this society stuff."

They continued about everything exterior—the Bulls, the weather, how huge Natasha's wedding would surely be. Not once did Abra feel like saying anything more meaningful. It was over. She'd known it for a while, but seeing him confirmed that the end was authentic.

"So did you bring a date? That guy?"

"Um, no. I don't see him anymore."

"Oh," he looked down, "I'm sorry."

"No need. It wasn't what I wanted."

Cullen brightened at the knowledge that the breakup was her doing.

"So I heard you're seeing Jackie Jones."

He looked at her, surprised to see that she was smiling. All he could manage was a "yeah."

"She's nice," Abra said.

"Well, it's not serious."

"Mm-hmm. Well, listen, I see Natasha. It was nice seeing you and I'll see you at the wedding."

With that, she walked away. No lingering, no attempt at flirting over a drink, or promises to stay in touch. While Cullen had convinced himself that he didn't want to get back with Abra, he still wanted her to want him. He was amazed at the change in her. He watched her walk away, shoulders back, head erect, and it was as if she were a different person. And she was. Their breakup had forced her to confront herself, the self she'd ignored, tucked away, tried to silence. It made her examine herself, invite her demons in for coffee, look at all those interiors she thought would be ghastly and discovering they're not. Coming out on the other side of her pain, she was finally able to feel joy. The process isn't easy, but the longer you put it off, the harder it is. She knew Natasha would be okay, but she pitied her smug classmates, knowing what they had in store for them, thinking the way she used to, doing easy. Sometimes, it's the easy way that's hard. The truth is that you either pay now or you pay later, but everyone has to find and listen to the self at some point. It's the only road out. What Cullen now saw in Abra was a woman fulfilled and not because of a man doing life for her, or a job that she could hide behind, or a stock portfolio giving her false comfort. She'd identified her itch, scratched underneath, saw the hole, and began to heal.

acknowledgments

Thank you to my family, Clifford and Baldwin, for giving me love, faith, and a safe space; to Faith, for being extraordinary; to Dominick for keeping the bar high and Ana for helping both of us. Thank you Christine for spreading the word and taking care of me on the road. To my birth family—Mom, Daddy, Marc, and Duane, thanks for always having my back. To my friends, I continue to be grateful for you.